SECOND TRY, DIFFERENT RULES

MARIELLA STARR

Published by Blushing Books
An Imprint of
ABCD Graphics and Design, Inc.
A Virginia Corporation
977 Seminole Trail #233
Charlottesville, VA 22901

Second Try, Different Rules
By
Mariella Starr

eBook ISBN: 978-1-63954-474-5
Print ISBN: 978-1-63954-475-2

Cover Art by ABCD Graphics & Design

Chapter 1

OCTOBER 1914, *Philadelphia*

Standing before a large window, Kara Douglas didn't see the marble balcony beyond the bedroom. The dispelling darkness of the night would have displayed dead flower gardens and trees that had lost their foliage. The fall season had arrived early with freezing temperatures.

"Why so gloomy, darling?" Matthew Douglas asked, sliding his arm around his wife's stiff shoulders.

"You promised we would only be here a month," Kara said. "We've been here four months. You promised."

"I know, darling, but I didn't expect my father's business to be in such a bad state. It won't be much longer," Matthew said, trying to soothe her worries.

"I can't stay here any longer," Kara said. Her voice broke, and she was trying to hold back the tears. "Your mother hates me, and I shouldn't have to put up with her insults. Something is wrong with her. I'm beginning to fear for my safety."

"Don't be silly," Matthew said dismissively. "My mother is high-strung, but she doesn't mean any harm."

"You're not here when she threatens me, and you always take her side," Kara said, shrugging off his hand and stepping away from her husband's embrace. "Your mother hates me. She's dominating every second of our lives! She won't even call me by my given name!"

"Kara is an unusual name, darling. She thinks Vivian is more dignified."

"It's my name, and it's none of her business!" Kara snapped.

"It's just a name," Matthew said. "It's easier to give Mother what she wants than get into an argument. We won't be here much longer, I promise. Calm down and be fair. You're letting your insecurities get the best of you. I've been told some women become irrational during their pregnancies."

"Undoubtedly by your mother!" Kara said angrily. "It's not irrational to want to be called by my own name or to pick a name for our child! She is constantly barging in on us! Constantly sticking her nose in our business! I will not dress in a manner more appropriate for a woman her age, regardless of what she says!"

"Viv... I mean, Kara, we'll have to discuss this later. I'm running late," Matthew said firmly. "I know it's a lot to ask, but you must try to get along with Mother. It won't be for much longer. She only wants what is best for us."

"She does not want what is best for us, and you have repeatedly made that promise to me and broken it every time!"

"I promised, and I will keep my word," Matthew said.

"You said that months ago, and it was a lie!"

Matthew felt his wife stiffen, and she jerked away from his touch. He backed off and glanced at the clock. He needed to get dressed for work and went to the closet. When he returned, his wife didn't answer when he said goodbye. She stood stiff and angry where he'd left her.

Frustrated at being caught between his mother and wife, Matthew left his parents' house. He had to prepare for an important meeting. The bank was threatening foreclosure on his father's business. At the bottom of the staircase, he retrieved his briefcase from a side table where he'd left it. His mother appeared before he could make his exit.

"Matthew, darling, you can't go to the office without breakfast," Blanche scolded.

"I don't have time, Mother, and I can't be late. Father's business affairs are not in order," Matthew said, pulling on a coat and opening the front door. He was keeping a lot from his mother, but she had never shown any interest in his father's business affairs.

Blanche Van Heusen-Douglas, watched her son leave and stamped her foot in a childlike manner. Her chest heaved with temper. Her son wasn't willing to spend time with her because of that horrible, trashy girl he'd married. That Branbridge girl had put her son under a spell. She was a witch. Otherwise, why was he distancing himself from his own mother? Her daughter-in-law was just like the obscene, harebrained aunt who had raised her.

Blanche had only met Selina Branbridge once, and the woman had dared to look down her aristocratic nose at the Van Heusen-Douglas family!

Kara closed her eyes as the bedroom door closed behind her husband. They'd had a perfect marriage until her husband received a telegram informing him of his father's death. At fifty-eight, Wilber Douglas died by his own hand. He'd hung himself in the attic and had been found swinging from the rafters. It gave Kara the chills to walk by the attic door.

Everyone assumed her father-in-law hung himself because his business was failing. Kara's personal opinion was that Wilber Douglas had chosen death over having to continue living with his dominating wife! She couldn't voice that opinion to her husband, but it was true. Blanche's constant disapproval made it impossible to be in her presence. Kara wanted to get on a train and return to her home in New York City. The idea of continuing to live under her mother-in-law's domination made Kara daydream of running away. Facing Blanche Douglas daily made her cringe, but she had to endure it for the sake of her husband.

Matthew didn't see his mother as others did. Her husband knew she hated living in his mother's home, but Blanche refused to allow them to live elsewhere. Matthew had gone from promising Kara they were there only temporarily to ignoring her pleas to leave and return to their New York City apartment. Matthew had no real attachment to his parents' home or Philadelphia. If the truth was known, he didn't have a strong attachment to his parents. He'd been sent to a boarding school in New York State at the tender age of eight.

Blanche was ecstatic about the return of her son. She'd been less excited when her son had arrived with a wife she'd known about but had only met once. A wife who had announced she was carrying her son's child soon after they had arrived. Blanche knew how to play the game, though. She was all sweetness and cooing smiles around her son. She was determined to run that silly girl out of her son's life.

Matthew waved at the second-story window as he slid into the chauffeur-driven vehicle his mother insisted he use every morning.

Kara watched from the window, but she didn't wave back. She knew Blanche Van Heusen-Douglas would revert to her true personality the second Matthew was gone. Her mother-in-law was an annoying, overbearing snob.

Kara had been raised in upper-class wealth in a chic neighborhood in New York City. She vaguely remembered her mother and father. Her parents died in a boating accident when she was only five years old. She'd been well provided for financially by her parents and left in the care of her only living relative, her father's sister Selina Branbridge.

Selina wasn't a fussy old aunt. She was a socialite, an avant-garde free spirit in a very elite sphere of wealth. Selina loved her niece but wouldn't abandon her lifestyle because she was responsible for a child. Her niece's care had been delegated to nannies and servants. She turned the child over to nannies and the nuns at Sacred Heart School for Girls while she continued a decadent lifestyle of opulence and freedom.

At one of her aunt's flamboyant parties, eighteen-year-old Kara met the young man who had stolen her heart. Matthew was a young attorney quickly gaining a name and reputation. He'd recently won a corruption case against a crooked politician and received a promotion in the law firm where he worked.

Matthew Douglas had swept Kara into a whirlwind courtship, and they had married four months later, against her aunt's wishes. Selina Branbridge considered the institution of marriage unnecessary and *démodé* (old-fashioned). She believed life was to be lived freely with abandonment and no constraints. Aunt Selina traveled and enjoyed her freedom, as only the *nouveau riche* could, and was involved with many married and unmarried suitors.

Feeling the baby move inside her, Kara smiled and gently touched her abdomen. She was only four months along and thought she was feeling the quickening of the unborn. Because she was small and thin, she was barely showing.

Mother-in-law, Blanche, had been harassing her daily about dressing appropriately for a woman 'in the family way.' She'd even gone so far as to tell Kara she must not go out in public because it was unseemly. Kara's pregnancy had given her mother-in-law something to constantly harp and nag about.

When Kara left her room, she had already missed breakfast served precisely at seven a.m. each morning. Charlotte Newsome, who everyone called Cook, wouldn't complain about fixing Kara something to eat later. Blanche would, but not Charlotte. Kara was on good terms with all the servants because she treated them as friends. Cook would provide a late breakfast when Kara was ready to eat. The early days of her pregnancy hadn't allowed her to keep food down in the early mornings.

At the top of the stairs, Kara looked down. Even if she wasn't happy living in the Van Heusen-Douglas domicile, she did admit it was a beautiful home. The staircase was elaborate, with two landings and ornate banisters. The view from the first landing over the beautiful marble floors of the foyer was lovely. Kara stepped to the edge of the landing. She heard a noise behind her, but before she could turn, she was shoved. She screamed, tumbled down the steps, and struck her head on the newel post. Her world turned black, and excruciating pain ripped through her abdomen.

Alice Anders, the head maid, came running. "Oh, my God!" She knelt beside the young Mister's wife as Diane, a young maid in training, came running.

"Ring the hospital," Alice ordered. "Tell them to send an ambulance!" She glanced to the stairwell landing and saw a large dark shadow moving up the stairs, not down.

Diane came running back. "I called! They'll be here in a few minutes."

"Go upstairs and tell Mrs. Van Heusen-Douglas there's

been an accident," Alice ordered. The young maid looked frightened, but Alice snapped, "Go!"

A few minutes later, Diane came running down the stairs. "She said she is getting dressed."

"As if," Alice mumbled. "It's after eight o'clock, and she hasn't been late for a seven o'clock breakfast in the two years I've worked here."

"What are you saying?" Diane whispered.

"I'm not saying anything untrue," Alice hissed. "There is something evil about that woman."

There was a loud knock on the door, and Alice ran to open it. Two hospital attendants carried in a stretcher and gently lifted the young Mrs. Douglas onto it. They carried her out to the ambulance.

"Is anyone coming with her to the hospital?" one of the attendants asked.

Alice looked to the stairs. "The mistress of the house has a driver."

The attendants tipped their hats and left.

"Alice!" the sharp voice of Mrs. Van Heusen-Douglas was heard from the first stairway landing.

"Yes, ma'am?"

"Tell the staff to take the rest of the day off. I want everyone out of the house except Jacob. Tell him to go to the servant's dining room and wait for my instructions," Blanche ordered."

"Yes, ma'am," Alice said. "What about the young Mistress? The ambulance has taken her to the hospital."

"How dare you question me! Tell Cook she is to leave the house too!" Blanche ordered. Then she pointed a finger at the youngest of the maids. "You will stay here!"

Diane's eyes widened, and she looked frightened.

"Should Mr. Douglas be called?" Alice asked.

"Mind your own business, and clean that mess off the

floor before you go," Blanche ordered, pointing to the blood on the marble floors.

"Yes, ma'am," Alice repeated.

Diane scurried close to her mentor. "What was that all about?"

"I don't know," Alice whispered. "But I'm not staying here another minute! If you're smart, you'll leave too!"

"What about the young Mistress?" Diane whispered.

"I'll go by the hospital to look after her," Alice said. "Leave with the rest of the staff, and go straight to the employment office on Calvert Street. There are always jobs for maids."

Kara awakened to a throbbing headache. "Lie still," a nurse instructed quietly.

"What happened?"

"You had a bad fall," the nurse said.

A doctor entered the room. He looked into her eyes and checked the stitches at her temple. "How are you feeling, ma'am?"

"Woozy and tired," Kara whispered. "I fell... no! I was pushed!" She jerked awake and tried to raise her hands to touch her abdomen, but her arms were wrapped tightly under the blankets. "Is my baby okay?"

The doctor held a gas mask over her face. His patient struggled for a few seconds and then closed her eyes. Turning to the nurse, he issued orders. "Keep her sedated. We can delay telling her of the miscarriage until she's a bit stronger. By then, her family should have arrived."

Matthew escorted the latest of his father's creditors out of his father's office, assuring the man he would be paid as soon as possible. He was surprised to see Jacob, the chauffeur sitting in a chair in the secretary's office.

"What's wrong? Is Kara sick?" Matthew demanded.

"Not that I know of, sir," Jacob said. "I was told to fetch you by your mother. I saw Dr. Hillsboro coming and going but was told to wait in the servant's room. After he left, your mother told me to bring you home."

Matthew dashed into his father's office and dialed his mother's number. The phone rang repeatedly, but no one answered. He hurried back into the secretary's office. "I'm leaving for the day, Mildred."

Matthew burst into his family home and yelled for his mother, but there was no answer. He ran through the rooms, looking for the servants, but they weren't responding because they weren't there. Even Cook was gone, and she rarely left the house. She was a live-in.

"Jacob, where is everyone?" Matthew demanded of the older man standing by waiting for his next order.

"I don't know, sir," Jacob said.

Matthew hurried up the stairs and burst into the bedroom he and Kara had been sharing. She wasn't there. He ran down the hall, knocked, and called out for his mother. There was a weak answer he could barely hear, and he opened the door.

"What's wrong?" he demanded.

"I've fallen ill, son," Blanche whispered.

"Where is Kara? Where are the servants?"

"I don't know where Vivian went. She's never around when I need her. I had the doctor come around. He says it might be a while before I'm on my feet again. Vivian said she wasn't going to tend me and left. I don't know where she went, and the servants have ignored my calls. Dr. Hillsboro might have told them to leave. Please don't leave me. I'm frightened."

"What did the doctor say?" Matthew demanded.

"Dr. Hillsboro never tells me what's wrong," Blanche whined. "He's never been able to understand my spells. He said I needed to be nursed, but everyone has abandoned me, including that horrible girl you married. I know Vivian doesn't like me, but I didn't think she would abandon me in my time of need."

"My wife's name is Kara, Mother, and she wouldn't abandon you. She's not that kind of person," Matthew said. "It would help if you'd call her by her given name."

"Kara is a ridiculous name, and it's unsuitable for a Van Heusen-Douglas. She did leave me!" Blanche snapped. Then she began to cough. "Water!" she gasped between coughs and then lay back against the pillows.

"I need to find out what is going on," Matthew said.

"Stay with me, son. I feel so weak, and I'm frightened!"

"I'll stay for a little while," Matthew said as his mother grabbed his hand and closed her eyes.

Every time Matthew tried to leave, his mother had a coughing fit. When the doorbell rang, he disengaged from her clinging hands to answer it, even though she protested. He opened the door to Dr. Hillsboro and demanded, "What's wrong with my mother?"

"Not a damn thing I have ever been able to diagnose," the physician said gruffly. "Your mother is a malingerer. She has been for years. She claims to be ill and often imagines symptoms and illnesses that don't exist.

"I thought I'd stop by and find out why you haven't visited your wife in the hospital. When I was doing my morning rounds, I saw her there. She's going through a perilous time and needs your support!"

"What? Kara is in the hospital? What happened?"

"She fell down the stairs, and she has a concussion. I'm afraid she lost the baby," Dr. Hillsboro said matter-of-factly. "When she was told, she went into hysterics. She screamed and claimed your mother pushed her down the stairs and murdered her child. She's been under sedation for hours, but someone from this household should have the decency to show her some respect and support!"

"I didn't know. I wasn't told," Matthew admitted, his voice breaking. "Dear God!"

Dr. Hillsboro gave the young man in front of him an assessing appraisal. "Mr. Douglas, your mother has pretended to be ill many times over the years. She has screaming outbursts, lashes out at others, and claims she will harm herself but never does.

"My recommendation to your father has been the same for years. She needs to be examined by a psychiatrist. If you don't know, that's a doctor who specializes in mental issues. Your father refused to accept my diagnosis.

"Severely disturbed individuals should be confined for their safety so they don't harm those around them. I have always believed your mother fits into that category. You should question your long-term staff, Mr. Douglas. The house help generally have a good idea of what goes on in their places of employment.

"When your wife was brought in this morning, the stretcher carriers were told she fell. Your wife is telling a different story. Frankly, I wouldn't be surprised if she is telling the truth. She is understandably upset. Whether your wife fell or was pushed, as she claims, she needs support to accept the loss of her unborn child. The only good news I can give you is that she is young and should, in all likelihood, be able to bear more children."

"Yes, sir," Matthew said. "Thank you for coming by, Dr. Hillsboro. Do you wish to see my mother?"

"No, I don't," Dr. Hillsboro said frankly. My time is valuable young man. I doubt I will find anything different now from what I have observed many other times. I have actual patients that need my time and attention."

Matthew closed the door and leaned against it. He'd always known his mother was a high-strung woman. She demanded attention, and her needs and desires were the highest priority when he was a child. Nothing was more important to her than forcing everyone to bend to her will.

As he grew older, he understood why his father sent him away to boarding school. His mother's behavior was why his father had encouraged him to take holidays and summer vacations with the families of his school friends. Matthew had preferred to bunk in with his friends or stay at school rather than endure his mother's smothering when he visited. The same applied during his years at law school. He reluctantly climbed the stairs to face his mother.

"Who was it, dear?" Blanche asked, sounding weak and fake to him now.

Matthew walked over to his mother's bedside. He picked up a pitcher of water and dashed it over her.

"What!" Blanche screamed, sitting up instantly and trying to scramble from the soaked bed.

"That was Dr. Hillsboro, and he said nothing is wrong with you," Matthew said furiously. "Meanwhile, my wife was seriously hurt early this morning, hospitalized, and you didn't bother to contact me!"

"I'm ill," Blanche moaned.

"My wife is in the hospital, Mother. We have lost our child!" Matthew said furiously. "The fall caused her to have a miscarriage."

"I didn't know," Blanche said in a weak voice. Then a strange look appeared on her face. Her eyes were flickering around the room rapidly. "My sweet boy, do you know what this means? She has no hold on you now. You can divorce her. We can move away, and no one will ever know you were married."

Matthew stared at his mother in disbelief, shocked by her words. "What kind of a woman are you? I love my wife, and I loved my unborn child! She said you pushed her."

"I didn't," Blanche denied. "She lost her footing!"

"And you didn't think I should be told while you are pretending to be sick?" Matthew demanded. He stepped away from the bed. He was seeing his mother as others had seen her for years. Blanche Van Heusen-Douglas was a spoiled, heartless woman beyond redemption. Turning from her, Matthew walked away.

"Don't leave me, darling," Blanche pleaded. "I love you!"

"You don't know what the word means," Matthew spat in disgust. "I've always known you were selfish, but this goes beyond belief. Have you no decency?" He went downstairs, where Jacob sat in the hall, waiting to be released from his duties. "I'm sorry to keep you waiting, Jacob. You may go. I'll drive myself to the hospital."

"Yes, sir."

"Wait," Matthew said. "Jacob, you've been with my family for a long time."

Jacob nodded and smiled. "Since you were in short pants, Mr. Douglas."

"Tell me the truth, Jacob," Matthew asked, thinking of the doctor's words. "Has my mother always been mentally incompetent?"

The chauffeur looked uncomfortable at the question. He looked to the floor and then raised his eyes to the young man.

"Please, I need your honest opinion," Matthew said.

"This might get me fired, Sir, but I reckon your mother has been tetched in the head for a long time, young sir. Your papa sent you to that boarding school to get you away from her lunacy. You didn't come home often, and he encouraged you to take that job in New York City after you graduated from law school. I always knew your papa was behind you not coming back. He wanted you to be your own man. Bless his soul, but the Mister couldn't stand up against your mother. He was the one who suffered the most from her fits.

"Staff ain't supposed to notice what is going on, Sir, but your papa had a hard time dealing with the missus. She had screaming tantrums, would throw and break things, and fired anyone that dared to challenge her. Whatever she damaged was blamed on someone else. There's always been a high staff turnover because no one wants to be screamed at and accused of something they didn't do. Cook and me are the only ones who have stuck around. Your papa paid us well to put up with her shenanigans and tell him the truth."

"What happened to the rest of the staff today?"

"I don't rightly know, sir. I was in the carriage house. I heard Alice tell Cook and the others to leave the house. I reckon it wasn't extended to me."

"I'm going to ask something strange of you, Jacob. I'd like you to watch over my mother," Matthew said. "Don't let her know you are here, and if she tries to leave the house, refuse to drive her. You've been loyal to my family for a long time, and I'll make sure you are paid a full retirement. You have my word, although I don't have time to discuss it now."

"Thank you, Mr. Douglas. My son has started a fleet of cabs, and he's been after me to drive for his company part-time," Jacob said.

"Thank you. My father's business has been lost, and I don't know yet if I'll be able to keep the house out of foreclosure. Whatever happens, I will reward you for your years of service" Matthew promised, offering his hand to shake. "I remember Fred. We played together as children. I'm glad to hear that he's done well for himself. I'll be back as soon as I can."

"I'll keep an eye on things, sir," Jacob responded.

"Thank you," Matthew said. He went upstairs and deliberately removed and hid his mother's purse and barricaded the two doors leading into his parents' bedrooms. Jacob took a seat on a chair between the doors.

When Matthew arrived at the hospital, he asked for directions to his wife's room. Walking down the hallway, he saw the maid Alice sitting in the hallway on a bench. She stood when he came closer. "How is she?"

"I've only been allowed in for a few minutes at a time, sir. When she's awake, she's taking the loss of the baby hard."

"Thank you for staying with her. I just found out!"

Matthew entered the room to find Kara huddled under a blanket, sobbing. "Sweetheart, I'm so sorry. I just found out what happened. I'm so sorry." He leaned over to kiss her, but she cringed from his touch and turned away. There was a bandage on her head, and the left side of her face was blackened with bruises.

"Go away," Kara whispered. "You let her murder my baby!"

"Honey, you need to tell me what happened."

"Go away," Kara repeated hoarsely. "Go away!"

"I need to know what happened," Matthew said. He touched her shoulder, but she jerked away from him.

"That bitch you call a mother killed my baby! She pushed me down the stairs! *GET OUT! GET OUT! GET OUT!*" she screamed and dissolved into sobs.

"Sir." A nurse appeared. "You must not upset the patient!"

"I need..."

"Sir, she needs rest," the nurse exclaimed. "I can't allow you to be here if she is going to be this upset."

"Viv..."

"Don't you ever call me that again! Get out!" Kara sobbed. "You wouldn't listen, and you let her murder our baby!"

Matthew backed away, hurt by her accusation, although he knew she was reacting to the trauma of losing their child."

"Please, sir," the nurse repeated.

Matthew nodded, although he was near tears himself. He left the room and stood outside the door. He gradually became aware that Alice, the maid, was still sitting on the bench. "What happened, Alice? Did my mother push Kara down the stairs?"

"I didn't see Mrs. Douglas fall, sir, but I did see your mother's shadow on the landing wall. Your mother was the only one upstairs when it happened. She didn't come downstairs to help. I was cleaning the foyer when I heard the scream. I was too far away to stop her from falling. The young Missus was lying on the steps, bleeding from a cut on her head. We called for an ambulance, and I had Diane tell your mother that the ambulance men were there. She didn't come downstairs until after they left. When she did come downstairs, she told us to leave the house except for Jacob and Diane. I wasn't going to take the blame for the accident, and I wasn't going to let your mother blame it on Diane either. I've worked for your parents long enough that I know what Mrs. Douglas is capable of doing."

"Why are you here?" Matthew asked.

"I came to see if the Missus was okay. She's always been nice to me," Alice said. "When I found out she'd lost the baby and no one was here, I stayed. She needs someone to be here for her, sir."

Soft-spoken and sincere, the words sliced through Matthew as sharp as a knife. "Thank you. I wasn't told my wife was here," Matthew said. He raised tear-filled eyes to the ceiling. "How can she forgive me for not being with her?"

"The doctors wouldn't have let you in when it was happening," Alice said kindly. "Men aren't allowed in during childbirth or... I am sorry, sir."

"Thank you, Alice. Thank you for being here for my wife."

"Mr. Douglas, there is a phone call for you at the desk," a nurse said.

Matthew went to the nurse's station. "Hello?"

"You'd best get home, sir," Jacob exclaimed over the phone. "Your mother tried to set the house on fire! I only left the hallway to go to the john, and she snuck out and set fire to your wife's clothing in your room. I put the fire out, and I've got her locked in a closet. She's gone plumb crazy, sir. What do you want me to do?"

"Don't let her out, and call Dr. Hillsboro and have him come to the house. He'll know what to do. I'll be there as soon as I can," Matthew promised.

He turned to the nurse on duty. "My wife is understandably upset, but I'm dealing with another emergency at home. I'll be back as soon as possible."

Alice watched the son of her employer rush from the hospital. She'd never liked Mrs. Van Heusen-Douglas. The woman was rude and snobbish, insisting that she be called by her last name in addition to her married name. The staff was paid well to deal with the temper tantrums and the crazy fits, although there was a constant staff turnover. Alice had only stayed because the job allowed her to live elsewhere, and it paid enough that she could afford rent and the cost of night-class schooling. After Mr. Douglas hung himself, his wife had been even harder to deal with.

Alice watched the nurse go into a wardroom, and she slipped into the private room. The young Missus had been kind and pleasant from the moment they'd been introduced. Kara had treated Alice more like a friend than a servant. She took the young woman's hand and squeezed it. "Please calm down, ma'am. You'll just make yourself more ill."

"Alice, help me get away," Kara whispered desperately. "His mother tried to kill me and has murdered my child. I can't go back there. I can't. Please help me!"

"What can I do, ma'am?"

"Help me get out of here," Kara said.

"The doctors won't let you out so soon," Alice said.

"The worst is over," Kara said in a voice void of emotion. "Find my clothing, please, and take me to where you live."

"Ma'am, it's not fittin'. I live in a tiny room in the basement of a tenement building," Alice whispered.

"It will do until I can get on my feet," Kara said. "Please help me, Alice, please. Once I'm stronger, we can decide what to do next."

"What about your husband?" Alice asked.

"I can't go back there," Kara whispered. "He made his choice, me and our unborn child or his mother. He chose his mother. I won't go back to that. I won't."

Alice nodded slowly. "I'll help you, ma'am. I'll do the best I can." She went to the door, looked out, and returned to the bed. "I worked here as part of the cleaning staff before I went to work at your house.

"It's getting late, and soon the nurses will be busy giving the patients medicine for the night. They'll treat the patients in private rooms before they go to the wards. Pretend to be asleep when the nurse makes her rounds. I'll hide over there behind the privacy screen. They won't want to wake you. We'll get you dressed and leave while they are in the ward rooms. I live about ten blocks away."

Matthew had a terrible evening. The fire damage to the

room was severe, and he didn't know how Jacob had put it out before it spread through the entire house. Dr. Hillsboro had restrained Blanche to her bed with leather straps and forced medicine down her throat that would make her sleep. He'd called for a nurse and a male attendant to stay in her room and watch over her until morning.

Blanche Van Heusen-Douglas was obviously a danger to herself and others. Matthew was being advised by Dr. Hillsboro, and he was given very few choices. He wanted to get back to the hospital. Calling the nurse's station several times, he was assured that Kara was asleep for the night. He was asked to stop disrupting the nurse's duties. Visiting hours began at nine o'clock in the morning.

Kara was safe. His mother was a danger to herself and everyone around her. Long after midnight, he fell asleep in a chair guarding the door outside the room where his mother lay restrained and sedated. In the morning, Dr. Hillsboro would admit his mother to the Northside Sanatorium for evaluation.

Alice whispered in Kara's ear and promised that she would return. She ran to her room blocks away and grabbed a long cloak, a wool hat, and a blanket. Returning to the hospital, Alice entered through a side door used by the night workers. Silently she went into Kara's room and hid behind the dressing screen. She knew the schedules of the nurses.

Kara pretended to be asleep while her temperature was checked. The nurse couldn't awaken her to take the medicine, so a notation was put on her medical chart before leaving the room. The nurse left a bottle of medication on a side table by the door.

When the door closed, Alice came out of hiding and helped the Missus get dressed. When they were ready, Alice slid the medicine bottle into her pocket before looking out to ensure the nurse wasn't at her station.

With Alice's help, the two women quietly left the hospital. Once outside, Kara was wrapped in the blanket and hat. There was no street or pedestrian traffic at that time of night. They limped along the sidewalk, occasionally stopping for Kara to rest on a brick stoop.

When Alice unlocked her door, she supported a weak Kara inside and helped her into the single bed.

Matthew and Dr. Hillsboro were going to check Blanche into the Northside Sanatorium for a mental evaluation by expert physicians. His mother was locked in a windowless room and would remain there until the medical assessment was completed. He'd been told the doctors would take a week or more to determine her mental health. Matthew hated doing this to his mother, but Dr. Hillsboro insisted it was the proper course of action.

The next morning he followed an ambulance to the sanatorium. Although he could still hear his mother's screams, pleading, and swearing, Matthew signed the commitment papers. Then he drove Dr. Hillsboro back to his practice and went straight to the hospital.

Matthew was praying that his wife would be calmer and they could talk. He'd turned a deaf ear to Kara's complaints because he already had too much to deal with. Dealing with his father's financial problems and complaints from creditors had consumed his time.

Charlotte Newsome, the cook, had returned to the house early that morning and given him an earful of his mother's mistreatment of his wife, father, and servants. It wasn't the first time Matthew had heard the complaints.

He was ashamed to admit that when Kara had made the same complaints, he had ignored most of what she said as exaggerations. He knew Kara didn't like his mother, didn't like living in Philadelphia, and wanted to return to New York City. His father had always dismissed the complaints from the staff, claiming they were inept or too lazy to do their jobs properly. Now, he knew that wasn't the case.

Matthew had been called home to deal with Wilber Douglas' suicide. His mourning had been cut short when he realized that his father's factory was on the verge of bankruptcy. He was dealing with angry workers, suppliers, and banks. All were owed money.

Every evening when he returned home, he faced complaints from his mother and wife. Matthew hadn't realized the extent of harassment his mother spewed or how badly his mother had treated Kara when he wasn't present. Now, he was getting the truth and he felt like he was drowning from guilt.

Returning to the hospital, Matthew was silently berating himself. He was beginning to realize how much he had ignored in the name of tranquility. He had to explain and apologize to his wife and hope she would forgive him.

Matthew swore when he couldn't find a place to park his automobile near the hospital. Parking was becoming a problem on the streets of Philadelphia, as it was in every major city. So many people were buying automobiles and not using public transportation. Most men and even women were learning to drive, although the newspapers and public officials discouraged women from doing so. He finally found a place to park and walked several blocks to the hospital. Matthew knew something was wrong when he approached the nurse's desk.

The nurse rose from her chair, but he panicked, ignored her, and ran down the hall. He opened the door to an empty room, already cleaned and prepared for the next patient.

"Where is my wife? Is she okay?" he demanded, addressing the nurse who followed him.

"We don't know, sir," the nurse said. "We assumed you

had taken her home. That happens when people don't want to pay the bills."

"My wife was in no condition to leave the hospital!" Matthew shouted.

"Sir," a doctor said, approaching. "Your wife went missing during the last rounds of medication last night. No one saw her leave."

"How could you allow that to happen?" Matthew demanded.

"Sir, we have other patients who need our care. We can't be held responsible for decisions made without our advice or permission. We hoped she had gone home, but we didn't have any information since she was unconscious when she arrived. We were going to ask you to fill out her admittance forms, but you left before we could get that information."

Matthew felt a wave of emptiness sweep over him. His wife was missing. He needed to find her and beg for forgiveness.

Chapter 2

MAY 1919, *New York City*

Kara and Alice walked down the gangplank of the magnificent steamship appropriately named *The Majestic*. Hundreds of people were on the docks with signs or searching the crowds for someone they recognized. There would be no one to greet them on their return to America. Kara had no one to contact. Alice did, but she hadn't wanted to disappoint anyone if the voyage was delayed.

They had left New York City five years earlier when transatlantic travel had still been considered safe, although most of Europe was being invaded by German troops. That was before the truth of the European troubles was reported accurately in the U.S. newspapers.

Kara and Alice had departed, excited to experience a new life in Paris. Little had they known how a world war would change those plans.

They had planned to live in Paris with Kara's Aunt Selina Branbridge, but those plans had been changed only weeks after their arrival. They had retreated to Selina's flat in London only days before France was invaded by German troops.

Selina Branbridge hadn't survived the war. She hadn't done well in an environment of deprivation. Nearly all goods, including food, were difficult to procure. It wasn't until the previous year that Britain devised a fair rationing system. Food and goods were still being rationed and probably would be for years. Rationing was still better than the starvation of other war-torn countries.

As a woman of wealth and stature, Selina Branbridge had never understood that she was expected to do her part in a war effort. She didn't believe it was necessary and refused to allow what she called *'the incompetence of men'* to disrupt her privileged lifestyle. The only concession she'd made had been to move from her Paris flat to her apartment in London, taking Kara and Alice with her. Aunt Selina had been killed in one of the many Zeppelin air strikes over London.

"Let's get through customs, and then we'll be able to find a transport for our luggage," Kara said as they entered a large building. Looking upward, she pointed to a sign that read 'Americans' versus several lines designated by labels of non-Americans.

They stood in line and presented their renewed passports.

"Are you traveling together?" a man in a uniform asked.

"Yes," Kara answered.

"Do you have family or somewhere to go?" the official asked.

"We are American citizens, and, yes, we have accommodations. It's all documented in these papers from the American Embassy in London," Kara answered.

"Go through," the officer ordered after scrutinizing the papers and passports. He waved them through a turnstile.

"Why do I feel guilty when I haven't done anything wrong?" Alice whispered.

"I think customs officers are trained to make people feel that way. We've dodged death many times since we left. It takes more than a uniform to scare me. Except for losing Aunt Selina, we've been lucky when there were so many casualties."

"We managed well enough, but I'd like to do what the returning servicemen do," Alice said.

"What's that?"

"I want to bend down and kiss American soil," Alice said honestly.

Kara nodded and gave her friend a weak smile. "I ran from crazy and endangered both of us in an even more bizarre world of war."

"The war wasn't your fault. We have to do what everyone else is doing. We have to put it behind us and move on," Alice said kindly.

"Absolutely," Kara agreed cheerfully. "Let's hail a cab and claim our luggage. It took Mr. Harrison's letter four weeks to reach us in London. As Aunt Selina's attorney here in New York, he has assured us that her suite in the Wolcott Hotel will be waiting for us."

"You," Alice corrected. "Along with your aunt's fortune."

"I never expected the inheritance, but as her only living relative, I should have guessed. She was eccentric. I expected her to leave her fortune to one of her favorite organizations, not to me. She knew I had my parents' inheritance."

"Selina was generous," Alice remembered with a smile. "And brazen. She didn't care what anyone thought of her. Sometimes wish I was that brave, but I'm not. She swore like a longshoreman and was very blatant about her sleeping partners. I don't think she ever stopped shocking me!"

Kara laughed. "When I was a small child, and my

parents visited her, she was a lot of fun. I vaguely remember my father scolding her for wasting her inheritance. She wasn't the mothering type, but she took me in when they passed, cared for me, and loved me in her own way. She hired an au pair to do most of the daily maintenance of a child's needs. She also sent me to good schools.

"I knew we lived in a flat at the Wolcott Hotel, but I was a child. I didn't question it. I didn't know she was a part owner of the hotel until I was informed by her attorney after she died. I asked about the hotel at the embassy, and the lady dug out an old brochure. The hotel is supposed to have three hundred rooms. Can you imagine that? The Wolcott Hotel was described as French neo-Classicism based on an audacious display of Ecole Des Beaux-Arts."

"Translated, that means a School of Fine Arts," Alice said with a grin. "The French language makes everything sound élite."

Kara laughed. "I remember the massive building but not much about the flat's interior. She redecorated her living quarters almost as often as she upgraded her clothing. Who knows what it looks like now! We can only hope Mr. Harrison has aired out the place for our arrival."

The registrar at Hotel Wolcott was expecting Miss Kara Branbridge and her associate, Alice Anders. The hotel's lobby was gilded magnificently in rich gold and burgundy carpets and drapes, with magnificent crystal chandeliers overhead. The bellhops wore red and gold uniforms.

When Kara approached the check-in desk, a clerk informed them that the Branbridge suite had been prepared for their arrival. Mr. Daniels, the concierge, was called, and he assured Kara that all their needs would be addressed. An army of bellhops descended on their luggage, and it was whisked away. Mr. Daniels escorted Kara and Alice to the privately owned suite on the top floor in an elaborately scrolled private elevator.

"Thank you very much," Alice said as the bellhops trooped out the front door, and she tipped each one of them as they clicked their heels together and gave a slight bow. Mr. Daniels repeated that he was there for their convenience and to call anytime. When the door closed, Alice and Kara admired the opulent apartment.

"Wow!" Alice exclaimed. "This sure beats the tiny room we shared in London. It's similar to Selina's apartments in Paris and London before the war, except it's a lot bigger. I will miss all this fancy living when I marry Thomas."

"Not too soon, I hope," Kara said. "I'll be lost without you."

"Not too soon, and you aren't losing me," Alice said with a smile. "Thomas and I met under the circumstances of war. I love him, but we need time to settle into normal lives. I was a maid before I became your companion and friend. Thomas comes from a wealthy family. I'm not sure they will accept me as his wife."

"Nonsense! You are my best friend and co-owner of our line of designs," Kara corrected. "You were my strength until I could pull myself together. I don't think I would have survived without you. You've always been loyal, and I owe you a great deal."

"I owe you too," Alice said. "You never treated me as less and taught me how to sew and design," Alice said. "Thomas and I have been separated for eight months since he was shipped back to the States. He was an architect before the war. He's had to re-establish himself now that he's out of uniform. I'm a little afraid that he might have found someone else."

"If he loves you, eight months won't make a difference," Kara said. "It hasn't changed how you feel for him, has it?"

"No, but a part of me is still scared," Alice admitted. "He knows I came from a poor background."

"Stop that," Kara said. "People are people, and how much money you have doesn't have anything to do with having a work ethic and integrity. You stood by me and are now a partner in our design business. We will launch our clothing line, and women will love it. We planned to do it in Paris or London, but the rebuilding there will take decades. We can only thank God that airplanes can't fly across the Atlantic.

"If Thomas has changed his mind, he isn't the man I thought he was, and I'll kick his butt!"

Alice laughed. "I'd like to see that. Little you, at only five-foot-nothing, taking on a six-foot-four man. People still mistake you for a child!"

"Don't I know it, and don't forget I'm five-foot-one inch," Kara complained with a smile. She turned to go to the bedroom where the bellhops had taken her trunks. She smiled over her shoulder at her friend. "I'm going to unpack. Call Thomas. The phone is there by the radio, and Mr. Daniels said he had it reconnected. Tell Thomas you have arrived! I won't listen when you get all *lovey-dovey* and *kissy-kissy* on the phone."

Thirty minutes later, there was a discrete knock on Kara's bedroom door.

Alice was beaming with happiness. "Thomas will be here in a few minutes. It was wonderful to hear his voice again. Sometimes I regret not marrying when we had the chance. Letters simply can't convey how much I love and miss him."

Kara turned away and stiffened slightly, and Alice went to her and touched her shoulder. "We've talked about this many times. Are you sure you want to go through with a divorce?"

"I'm sure," Kara said stoically and forced a smile. "It's

straightforward. Blanche won. It's time to get on with my life. It's been a long time."

Kara checked her gown one last time in the mirror and was satisfied with her creation. As maid of honor, she wanted to look her best but not so good as to overshadow the bride. Alice was beyond beautiful in her wedding dress. Thomas Markham and Alice were ready to tie the knot, and their reunion had barely been three months in the making.

Thomas and Alice had happily reconnected. Had it been left to Thomas, he would have married Alice the next day. Alice had been more reticent. The newspapers were full of articles about war brides ending their marriages in divorce courts.

When she did accept Thomas' proposal, there had been a scramble to set the date. Kara and Alice were preparing to show their dress designs to buyers of New York City's finest stores and boutiques.

A similar gown to Alice's wedding dress had been presented in their fashion review, along with pre-war Parisian-inspired designs. Couture designs could only be afforded by wealthy patrons.

It had taken them weeks to find a suitable location to launch their design boutique. They were still working hard to reach their goal date for a grand opening.

Having lived the last four years under the harsh conditions of war, Kara and Alice hadn't forgotten the lessons they learned from Coco Chanel, Madeleine Vionnet, and Jean Patou in Paris. Aunt Selina Branbridge hadn't been shy in introducing her niece to well-known couture designers she had supported for decades. Some couture houses had foolishly tried to have runway shows during the dangerous enemy occupation of Paris. Nazi officers, in particular, had no sense of fashion and didn't appreciate being ignored.

All that was behind them now. The 1920 fashion line would be a new era of clothing design. No longer were women bound to undergarments forcing their bodies into unnatural hourglass figures. During the war, women wore modified men's uniforms and trousers depending on their jobs. Clothing had to be practical, and the use of separates instead of one-piece dresses had become necessary and comfortable. The volume of fabric used had to be lessened as clothing factories were refitted to produce wartime necessities for soldiers.

Women had taken on jobs previously held only by men. They had also become more active and assertive in their choices of clothing. Skirts were simple and worn slightly above the ankle. Male-style blouses were tucked into natural waistlines. The simplicity of the drop waist dress, appearing on runways in 1916, was now the rage. The colors of black, gray, and dull greens, so standard for the duration of the war, were replaced with softer, brighter colors and enhanced with adornments of pearls, beads, and fringe. Female fashion was beginning to become an expression of freedom and better times.

"You look beautiful," Kara said with a wide smile.

Alice nodded. "I can't believe the size of the wedding. Thomas' parents insisted. There will be photographs at the church and at the reception."

"This is normal in their world," Kara said. "You are marrying a man with a skyrocketing career. He's making a name for himself at McKim, Mead & White. He works directly under Mr. McKim. You should be proud of him!"

"I am," Alice exclaimed, beaming. "Who knew a flight instructor I met at a canteen would become the love of my life. I'm still surprised he loves me, a girl who came from nothing."

"Listen to you!" Kara protested. "You're a talented designer, and he's promised not to interfere with your work. On top of that, Thomas' parents are wonderful people. His mother is an absolute gem, and so is his father! Are you ready to become Mrs. Thomas Markham?"

Alice took a deep breath and nodded. Her face lit up with a smile she'd been wearing for weeks. "I'm ready."

Matthew Douglas fiddled with his tie and rebuttoned his tuxedo waistcoat. He hadn't worn a tuxedo for quite some time. He'd planned on being a guest at his friend Thomas' wedding. A last-minute phone call had asked him to substitute as best man. Thomas' younger brother, Vincent, was hospitalized with a badly broken leg, hoisted above the bed, and attached to a pulley system.

"Are you sure this will do?" he asked Thomas.

"Very sure," Thomas said. "I'm grateful you agreed on such short notice. My idiot younger brother should have known better! Imagine trying to jump over a water fountain on a bicycle!"

"We all did crazy things in our university days," Matthew said.

"Yes, we did, and if my father hadn't already chewed him out royally, I'd be giving him a thumping myself!" Thomas agreed, sounding both annoyed and amused. He fumbled in his pocket and brought out a ring box. "Whatever you do, don't lose this. It's taken me three years to talk Alice into marrying me. I would have married her while I was in London, but she didn't want to be a war bride. Although, technically, she wouldn't have been since she's American.

"You'll like her," Thomas exclaimed. "She's the sweetest woman alive! Brave too. She and her business partner were trapped in London for the duration. Alice was an ambulance driver for the Red Cross. Her friend was trained as a medic, but she changed course mid-war and became a bomb spotter. With dangerous jobs like that, it's a wonder they survived! I'm sorry things haven't worked out, and you haven't met them yet."

"We've both had deadlines to meet," Matthew said. "How did you meet Alice?"

"I was teaching pilots at a Royal Naval Air Service training depot. We were in the thick of it."

"Why was she living in England?"

"Alice went to France originally to learn fashion. They were living in Paris, studying and working with famous dress designers. Something called *couture*. When France was invaded, they managed to get on one of the last boats crossing the channel. They planned to return to the States, but those plans were scuttled when the bastards began to sink non-military ships. They were stuck in London for the duration, and they pitched in to do their part. I'm not complaining because that's where I met her."

The minister's wife shushed the two men as the music started. Kara was motioned to come forward. As the maid of honor, Kara walked down the aisle next. She looked at Thomas and the man standing beside him.

Startled, Kara almost tripped when she recognized the best man standing beside the groom. She caught herself, plastered on a fake smile, and continued down the aisle.

The bride's big moment was next, and she was escorted by John Markham. Thomas' father had proudly taken Alice's arm as his future daughter-in-law had no living parents.

Alice was gorgeous, and Kara's eyes softened and went from the beaming bride to the stunned groom. She tried not to look at the best man but could feel Matthew Douglas' eyes boring a hole in her with his steady gaze. Kara wanted to scream. She wanted to run, but she wouldn't do either. Alice was her best friend and chosen sister. She had seen Kara through horrific times and continued to stand by her. She would never do anything to spoil her best friend's wedding.

Matthew tried not to stare as Thomas whispered, "That's Kara. She's Alice's business partner and her best friend. She's pretty, but standoffish with men." That was when Matthew realized Alice had been a maid in his mother's home.

Kara hadn't withered or hardened under the conditions of war. If anything, she was more beautiful now than when he married her. His wife had turned twenty-four a few months earlier. Yet, she hadn't aged a day. She was a small woman, appearing fragile, but she wasn't. She'd cut her hair, and the long blonde tresses were now short in what women called a bob. Her eyes were still the aquamarine color that had first caught his eye.

Matthew tried to pay attention but heard very little of the ceremony. He responded when nudged and handed over the wedding bands to his best friend. Sucking in a breath, Matthew glanced at Kara's hand. She wasn't wearing her wedding ring, but he couldn't fault her. He didn't wear his either. The wedding band tended to bring up questions he didn't want to answer.

Thomas and Alice said their final vows, kissed, and faced their friends with glowing faces.

Matthew offered Kara his arm, and she took it with a false smile and turned her head, nodding to the people in the pews. They were followed by Thomas' parents. Alice gasped when she recognized Matthew, causing Thomas to look at his new wife with confusion.

"I'll explain later," Alice whispered to her new husband.

Although she was keenly aware of him, Kara didn't look at Matthew as they formed a receiving line. Most attendees would be at the reception in the ballroom of a well-known hotel a few blocks away. They smiled as the guests walked by and down the church steps. Most of the attendees would walk to the hotel. Kara and Matthew never spoke to one another.

Thomas cast several worried glances at his best friend. He was aware of the tension, but not why. After the guests passed, his parents ushered him and his bride into a limousine, although it was only a four-block walk to the venue.

The best man and maid of honor were seated on each side of the couple at the formal table. Both of them were ignoring the dead elephant in the room.

During the traditional dances with the family members, Matthew danced with Alice. "I didn't know you were friends with Kara," he said.

"I helped her through a tough time," Alice said bluntly. "We've been friends since. I wasn't aware that you knew Thomas."

"We went to boarding school together," Matthew said. "I went into law, and he went into architecture. As it happens, his company uses the services of my law firm."

"I thought you were in the publishing business," Alice said.

"No, that was my father's business," Matthew said. "After he died, I stepped in trying to keep it from going into foreclosure."

"Did you?" Alice asked.

"No," Matthew said, looking over her shoulder at Thomas' father dancing with Kara. "The damage had been done. I sold everything and paid off the creditors as best I could. Have you been with Kara all these years?"

"If you want answers, you will have to speak to her," Alice whispered with a definite chill in her voice.

"My wife walked out on me," Matthew growled, missing a step.

"She fled for her life," Alice hissed. "Your mother tried to kill Kara and did murder her unborn child. You made a choice in her greatest hour of need, Matthew, and it wasn't for your wife. Kara has suffered enough!" Alice turned and left Matthew alone in the middle of the dance floor.

Thomas intercepted his wife and watched his best friend walk off the dance floor. "What's wrong?"

"I don't want to upset the reception, but you must ask Mr. Douglas to leave. He's already given his speech and filled in for your brother. We don't want a scene," Alice whispered.

"Why?"

"Matthew is Kara's husband. Please, Thomas, your parents have been generous and helped plan this beautiful wedding and reception for us. I don't want it ruined."

Thomas nodded. "I'll be back in a few minutes." He danced Alice over to his father and whispered in his ear. John nodded and guided his new daughter-in-law back onto the ballroom floor.

Matthew was on the patio. He stubbed his cigarette out when his friend approached him. "I'm leaving," he growled.

"Alice hasn't told me what happened yet," Thomas said. "I didn't know Kara had any connection with you."

"She's my wife," Matthew said bitterly. "It was a bad time for both of us, and she disappeared rather than face our problems."

"That doesn't sound like the woman I know," Tom said. "She and Alice were doing work primarily handled by men. It wasn't easy for two American girls to fit in. Americans were viewed by a lot of Brits as Johnny Jump-Ups. The Brits had been suffering through the war for years. Then the

Americans showed up late and bragged they would win the war. There was cause for a lot of resentment. The Brits needed our help, but they still resented us."

"Being in uniform and remaining stateside wasn't a picnic either," Matthew growled.

"The war department considered your job vital. You were a decoder," Thomas said. He hated what he was about to say. "I'm sorry, Matthew, but..."

"I'm leaving," Matthew said. "Give my regards to your parents and your bride."

"Matt..."

"Thomas, I made some terrible decisions after my father died," Matthew said. "This won't affect our friendship. Enjoy your honeymoon. You deserve it."

Kara was watching the door and chewing on her thumbnail. Thomas reappeared, but Matthew didn't, and she took a deep breath of relief. She would have to face her husband sometime in the future, but she had hoped it would be through an attorney. She couldn't continue to live a life in limbo. Married but not married was a purgatory of uncertainty. During the war years in London, she'd been nicknamed 'Say no, Sheila.' She'd also been called toplofty. That was English slang for snobby by many of the people she worked with—mostly the men. She wasn't, but she had earned a reputation for rejecting and not being one to entertain men at the pubs and servicemen canteens. She wasn't distributing her favors, and having sex with soldiers.

Sex had become an expected normalcy between soldiers and young women. The legitimacy of the fast relationships didn't matter. There had been a desperation for intimacy before men went into battle and when they were on leave. Women who wouldn't *put out* were harassed by the women who did. Some women claimed they were doing their part for the men in uniform and claimed Kara and Alice were called Stuck-up Sheilas because they didn't.

Kara had avoided all temptation, but she'd known many women who hadn't.

The London Police authorities had hired women to take on the jobs of so many missing men from their forces. The Women Patrols were primarily hired to maintain discipline and monitor women's behaviors because promiscuity was rampant. Women were always blamed for it, not the men. Condoms, although illegal, were easily purchased as black-market items. A simple request with the euphemism *"a little something for the weekend"* at pubs, pharmacies, and barber-shops, made them available to men who bothered to take precautions.

Matthew went to his 1915 Templar Roadster and put the top down. It was a beautiful day, but he was in no mood to enjoy it. Halfway to his downtown apartment, he changed his mind and turned eastward. An empty apartment wasn't going to clear his head. Finally, he decided to head for the familiar territory of Long Beach Island.

When the reception was over, Kara kissed Alice and Thomas goodbye. They were going on a three-week honey-moon to Maine. Kara helped Helen Markham organize the cleanup. The table arrangements were sent home with anyone that wanted them. The leftover arrangements and table favors were gathered in boxes to take to a nearby hospi-tal. If the patients couldn't have them, the nurses would enjoy them. Kara took several boxes of expensive chocolates home with her. She loved sweets and had to force herself not to overindulge in too many now that they were available again.

Having said her goodbyes, she walked several blocks to where she'd parked Aunt Selina's Rolls-Royce. She'd taken it out of storage as the suite at the Wolcott Hotel provided a garage. It was a beautiful car and drew a lot of attention.

The Labourdette Silver Ghost had required maintenance since it had been in storage for years. Aunt Selina had sailed off to France without a worry in the world, even though Europe was about to implode. Kara had to admit she and Alice had done the same.

The Silver Ghost hadn't been maintained during Salina's absence. When Kara had claimed it, the tires had to be replaced. The mechanic Kara hired had fixed other problems she didn't understand. Speaking *car* was a foreign language she hadn't learned yet. The dealership had wanted to purchase the Labourdette, but to Kara, it was a connection to her aunt. She'd driven an ambulance in London and was struggling to get used to driving on the right side of the road. Mr. Daniels had found a driving instructor, and she had learned, although sometimes she still made mistakes. She knew the Silver Ghost was sporty because it drew attention. She was constantly being honked at while driving.

Chapter 3

MATTHEW WAS ABOUT to reach the end of his patience. His wife lived in New York City, but he had no idea where. He had gone to the Wolcott Hotel, where Selina Branbridge, his wife's only relative, had lived. The manager had informed him that Miss Branbridge hadn't survived the war. The manager had claimed no knowledge of her niece.

Thomas and Alice had been gone a week and had two more before they were expected back. Matthew didn't think he was going to last that long. He'd been short-tempered with his subordinates and clients lately. He was about to explode with frustration. The senior Markhams had been no help, as they had only met Kara a few times before the wedding.

Kara had walked out of Matthew's life nearly five years before. He'd regretted her absence every single day. He hadn't known she'd moved to France and then to London. Hadn't known she was in Europe amidst a world war! Had he known, he might have tried harder to be sent to work in the intelligence agencies based in Britain or had her returned to the U.S., where she would have been safe.

Very few of his friends knew he was married. Of those who knew, most had advised him to file for a divorce on the grounds of abandonment. That was easier said than done. It was advice that wouldn't do him any good, even if that was what he wanted. Matthew had never considered it. He knew the New York divorce laws.

Now that he'd seen Kara, he had to find her. His wife hadn't changed at all. She was an uncommonly beautiful young woman, almost fairy-like and delicate. She was more beautiful now than she'd been in her youth. She had lost the child-like look of innocence.

His last memory of her still haunted him. He would never forget the bruises on her face, the stitches at her hair-line, or the accusing eyes. The condemning screams for him to get out had echoed in his consciousness and invaded his nightmares for years. He couldn't forget them. Matthew had lost more than his wife and unborn child that day. His very soul had been ripped away.

While Kara had run, he had committed his mother to a mental sanitarium. Her behavior worsened until she was confined in a jail-like room. She had to be sedated and kept isolated for the safety of the caretakers and other patients. Under the advice of physicians, Blanche Van Heusen-Douglas lived there until her death several months later.

"Sir, Mr. Hamner of the Detective Agency is here to see you," Mildred Morehead, his secretary, announced.

"Thank you, Mildred. Please close the door," Matthew said, motioning the agent to a chair.

"How can I help you, sir?" Mr. Hamner asked, pulling a small black book and a pen from his pocket.

"I need to find someone," Matthew said. "This matter needs to be handled with discretion."

"Of course," Mr. Hamner said, waiting.

Matthew stood up and looked out his window to a Manhattan Skyline. "The person missing is Kara Vivian Branbridge Douglas. She is my wife and has been missing since October 12th, 1914. Apparently, she went to Paris and then London. She continued to live there for the duration of the war until it was safe to travel transatlantic again. She is now living in New York City, but I don't know where."

"How do you know she's in New York, sir?"

"Because I ran into her accidentally," Matthew said.

"And she didn't wish to speak to you?" Mr. Hamner asked.

"The occasion wasn't appropriate without causing a scene," Matthew said.

"Does she have any friends or relatives in New York?"

"Not that I would know about. Our only mutual friends are on their honeymoon somewhere in Maine."

"Relatives?" Mr. Hamner inquired.

"My wife doesn't have any family. Selina Branbridge was living in Paris when my wife and I married. Selina was a world traveler, and I only met her a few times. I was told she was a casualty in a bombing raid in London. Mr. Hamner, my wife has returned to New York City, and I'd like to find her."

"She may not want to be found, sir."

"That's why I'm paying you," Matthew said.

Kara woke up with a start and caught herself before she fell off the chair. She'd fallen asleep at her drawing table again. Stretching, she tried to get the kinks out of her back and legs.

Leaving the workroom, she wandered into the bedroom. The bedroom was five times larger than the small room she'd shared with Alice for many years. Selina's apartment was too large for two people. Now with Alice gone, it felt lonely.

The Wolcott Hotel suite had resulted from an investment her aunt had made with the builders in 1904. The bank advisor had explained that as Selina's inheritor, Kara owned the suite in perpetuity.

Kara hadn't lived alone since the fateful night when Alice had come to her rescue. Alice had become her dearest friend and protector during that horrible time. They had lived in the tiny tenement room in a basement for months while Kara regained her strength.

Alice had nursed and supported her on a maid's salary during those dark months. She had even changed her last name, so she couldn't be found through the employment agencies in Philadelphia. When Kara had been well enough, she and Alice had taken a train to New York City.

Once there, a trip to the bank eased their financial worries. Kara and Alice had lived comfortably in a boarding house living off an inheritance account left by Kara's parents. Ocean crossing letters between Kara and her Aunt had taken a while. Selina offered them her apartment in New York City or advised them to make travel plans to join her in Paris.

Unfortunately, Matthew knew where Selina lived, and Kara hadn't wanted anything to do with him or his mother. She needed to get away and had jumped at the chance to put an ocean between herself, her husband, and her mother-in-law. When she married, the promise of a European honeymoon had been made but was never fulfilled. Matthew had delayed the trip because his mother had claimed to be ill. He vowed to make it up to Kara later but later never came.

Alice had protested the expense more than the move

across the Atlantic and feared it would take too long for her to get a passport. That issue was resolved quickly, as Kara's passport included traveling with a companion or servant. *(Common practice before WWI.)*

A shopping trip had been necessary to fill out their wardrobes to look presentable in first-class onboard the luxury liner. The passage was booked, and Kara felt safe once they passed through the port authorities. Alice would share the stateroom onboard the ocean liner. They traveled together, claiming to be cousins.

Having lived and worked with her friend for over four years, the two women were as close as sisters. Kara knew her friend was going to marry when they returned stateside. She'd been there when Alice and Thomas had met.

She and Alice would continue to work together, but Alice would live on the east side of New York in a townhouse Thomas' parents had owned. His parents had deeded the house to their son when he returned from the war. The Senior Markhams had retired to the Hamptons.

As had happened so often since Alice's wedding, Kara's thoughts drifted to Matthew. She'd avoided what needed to be done for years. She had looked into divorcing her husband while she was living in London. British divorce laws applied to their citizens, not foreigners, even if those foreigners were trapped there during a wartime blockade. She was back in the States now. There was no excuse for not filing for divorce, except bringing up what had broken their marriage was still painful.

Kara took a long shower and dressed for an outing. Looking in the mirror, she represented the working class more than high fashion. That was okay for a drive out of the city and into the countryside. She covered her short, bobbed blonde hair with a newsboy's cap. Wearing boy's knickers, black stockings, and a shirt with billowing sleeves, she looked like a young newspaper hawker, and that was her intention. Binding her chest was uncomfortable but necessary to pull off the disguise. She'd learned to disguise herself as a boy during the war when she'd taken on the night job as an air warden. There was freedom in not being a girl under so many social restrictions. Taking a path of hallways through the Wolcott Hotel, known more by the employees than the guests, she went out a service door and across two alleys to a private garage.

Matthew had arrived at the Wolcott Hotel at dawn and parked in the back among the delivery trucks. He had checked with the hotel periodically for years but had always been told the Branbridge suite was unoccupied.

The private detective Matthew had hired had discovered the truth. His wife was living there. The detective had followed her for several days, noting her comings and goings. Then he delivered a portfolio of information on Kara Branbridge's activities to his client. Matthew now knew she was living quite well in her aunt's suite. He also learned that Kara and Alice were partners in a clothing design boutique being launched in the garment district.

The detective had detailed more crucial personal information. He reported that Kara hadn't been seen in the company of any male companions. She was often seen wearing trousers, as many young women were doing, post-war. She also disguised herself as a boy to escape the city.

Matthew almost missed Kara as she darted out of a side door of the hotel. Had he not recognized her at the last second, he would have assumed she was a boy of about fourteen, not a woman in her mid-twenties. He followed her to a garage, where she unlocked a gate and drove out in a Rolls-Royce Silver Ghost, a vehicle any car enthusiast would covet. She stopped and locked the gate before jumping into the driver's seat.

Running back to his vehicle, Matthew pulled down the brim of his hat and followed his wife several cars behind. He realized very quickly she was a careless driver. No, he corrected himself, she was a terrible driver. Kara didn't seem to understand the concept of traffic signs. She stopped for policemen directing pedestrian traffic, although she often overshot the markings on the pavement.

Matthew held his breath a few times, as her erratic driving was an endangerment to anyone walking on the curbside of the sidewalks. Thank God, it didn't take long before she drove on less congested streets and crossed the Queensboro Bridge into Long Island. He was familiar with Long Island since he'd spent two years at a military facility in North Haven. He knew the road led to the beaches and fishing areas at the far Northern end of the island. He knew it was a deceptively dangerous road with curves, and she was driving too fast. When she barely missed an oncoming truck, Matthew honked his horn in aggravation, but she didn't turn her head to look behind her, and he belatedly realized that wasn't something he wanted her to do. She needed to keep her eyes on the road! Another tight curve caused a close call as the Rolls skidded on the graveled shoulder and came dangerously close to a metal barrier separating the road from the ocean-side cliff.

The more he followed and observed her erratic driving, the angrier Matthew became. Had no one taught Kara the basic rules of driving! He kept his eyes on the vehicle, but there wasn't anything he could do about the way she was driving. She was a menace!

He considered trying to force her off the road but decided it was too dangerous. He was familiar with this area. The government facility where he'd worked as a decoder was at the end of the island. The not-so-secret base was closed now, and the small town had reverted to its previous fishing industry. Going around a curve, Matthew lost a visual on the Silver Ghost. He realized on the next straightaway that Kara's vehicle wasn't ahead of him. Pulling to a stop, Matthew made a U-turn and backtracked. He came across a break in the safety barrier. He parked on the shoulder, jumped out of his roadster, and slid down the sandy embankment upon spotting the car.

His heart jumped into his throat when he saw steam coming from the engine, and he slid down the embankment to the car, searching for his wife.

"What are you doing here?" Kara demanded from behind him.

Matthew turned around furiously. "Following a female driver who doesn't belong behind the wheel of a car! Who in hell told you, you could drive?"

"My instructor," Kara snapped. "And it wasn't my fault the car went off the road. Those are brand new tires, and one of them blew out!"

"Are you hurt?" Matthew demanded.

Kara frowned. "No, and why are you here? Were you following me?"

"We can get into that later," Matthew said. "There's a mercantile with gas pumps about ten miles from here. We'll have to see if they have a tow truck or crane to pull out the Rolls. It's a shame you've ruined it."

"This wasn't my fault," Kara denied. "And I don't want your help. But if you would be nice enough, please stop at the gas station and have them send someone to get me. I would appreciate it."

"I'm not leaving you here alone," Matthew growled. "This isn't New York, where help is a few blocks away. Why the hell are you dressed like a boy?"

"How I dress is none of your business," Kara exclaimed.

"Everything you do is my business," Matthew said, giving

her a shake. "I'm your husband, Kara! Or have you forgotten your vows?"

Kara shoved him away forcefully in anger. "I wasn't the one who forgot them! You were the one who broke your promises! It was your mother who destroyed us!"

"My mother died in an insane asylum."

"Don't expect a pity party from me!" Kara said in a flat voice. "That bitch tried to kill me, and she did kill my baby!" She turned, walking away from him and toward the Rolls.

Suddenly the car's front end burst into flames, and there was a small explosion under the hood. Matthew grabbed her by the arm and forced her up the sandy embankment in front of him. They were almost to road level when there was another explosion. Flattening his body over hers, Matthew protected her from the falling debris. He yelled as something hit him on the upper fleshy part of his left arm. There was a roar from the flames below them and another louder explosion. Then there was a crash of breaking glass as debris fell around them. It was quiet for a few seconds, except for the roar of the flames. He rolled off of Kara, and they both stared at the remains of a beautiful Rolls-Royce classic, still burning.

"Damn," Kara exclaimed.

"Watch your mouth," Matthew said out of habit and grimaced. He twisted around to try to see the damage to his arm. There was a piece of metal embedded in his arm. He was going to pull it out, but Kara stopped him.

"Don't," she ordered. "If you pull that out, you might do more damage." She pulled a small pocketknife from her pocket and cut his shirtsleeve off around the piece of metal. "It's not bleeding badly, so you haven't hit a major blood vessel."

She cut the other sleeve off his shirt and wrapped it loosely around the bleeding wound and the metal fragment.

"Hold that in place, but don't put any pressure on it. Can you make it the rest of the way to the car? You need to be seen by a doctor."

"I can make it, but I'm not going to be able to drive," Matthew complained.

"I can drive."

"I'd almost prefer to bleed to death."

"Fine, I'll leave you here and go for help," she snapped.

They both looked down at the beach below. The fire was burning itself out, and there was nothing around it to continue to feed the flames.

"Crashing that car is almost criminal," Matthew said. He dangled his keys in front of her but snatched them back when she tried to take them. "If you drive over ten miles per hour, you'll be in more trouble than you are already!"

She snatched the keys and walked ahead, but they both stopped and looked at his smashed windshield. The Rolls' steering wheel was embedded in his car's windshield.

Matthew took his keys back, opened the trunk, and tried to pull a leather glove on his right hand but couldn't one-handed.

Kara had followed him. "Don't move your arm!" she ordered, and she helped him get the glove on. She looked at the crate filled with what her husband considered necessities for any car trip. He had constantly exasperated her with his thoroughness and being prepared for anything. In this case, though, she was glad he did. She picked up a small first-aid kid and opened it.

"Sit down on the running board, and let me attend to the injury," she ordered.

"When did you become a doctor?" he demanded.

"I'm not, but I was a certified medic for the Red Cross in London," she corrected him.

"You used to faint at the sight of blood," Matthew said, trying to watch her over his shoulder.

"I got over it after dragging dead bodies out of bombed buildings," Kara snapped. "Do you want me to remove the piece of metal or leave it in until we can get to a doctor? It doesn't look like it's sitting on a major blood vessel."

"God, yes," Matthew exclaimed. He was in a lot of pain but was trying to watch her every move. Kara knew what she was doing, but when she poured alcohol onto the wound, Matthew almost passed out. Gritting his teeth, he didn't want to embarrass himself by fainting. In the past, the woman he'd married would have fainted at the first sight of blood.

When Kara finished wrapping his wound, she took the gloves and shoved her small hands into them. She pulled the steering wheel from the windshield frame and removed the broken glass. Then she used a small whiskbroom from the trunk and swept the glass from the seats and floorboards. When it was safe to sit, Kara opened the driver's side door and held her hand for the keys.

Matthew maneuvered himself into the passenger seat, trying to make himself comfortable, but it wasn't easy. The cut was still bleeding and seeping through the bandages.

"The town of Peconic should be about ten or twelve miles ahead. Maybe we can get help there," Matthew advised.

"I've been through there several times," Kara commented. She did drive slower for several reasons. She didn't want to jar Matt's shoulder because she knew he was in pain. The other reason was the wind was fierce, with no windshield to block it. She would have lost her hat if it wasn't bobby-pinned on.

Kara was keeping an eye on the makeshift bandage. It was soaked with blood already. She'd trained and worked as a Red Cross medic for over three years in London. Then, because a doctor had fancied her and wouldn't take no for an answer, she had retrained as an air warden. It was dangerous work, being on the roofs of buildings during the blitz raids. It was also a job that allowed her to carry a gun to protect herself. She had dressed as a boy for years.

A small group of buildings came into sight, and she guessed it was Peconic. Pulling into a small store with gas pumps, a concerned young man directed them to the nearest doctor's office. While Matthew was in the doctor's office, Kara told the nurse of the accident, and she called a local law officer, who said he would be right over.

The doctor gave Matthew a shot before redressing his wound. The needle helped with the pain, but cleaning the cut was the worst. The injury wasn't as bad as he'd thought. He was given five stitches, a tin of aspirin and advised to see his doctor if the cut site reddened or looked inflamed.

To his relief, Kara was still in the waiting room, although Matthew had taken the car keys from her. He paid the bill for services rendered, and she walked outside ahead of him. She stopped abruptly, and he bumped into the back of her. Looking over her head, Matthew saw a local Constable's vehicle parked beside his car. He stepped around Kara as she pulled her hat down further on her forehead and dropped her chin.

The Constable stepped out of his truck and offered his hand. "I'm Melvin Nichols, the local law around here. Are you the one who called in about the accident out on the highway?"

"Yes, sir," Matthew said.

"Was he the one that caused it?" the Constable demanded, pointing at Kara. "That whippersnapper has been tearing around these parts for the last couple of months. I ain't got no authority to ticket him for reckless driving, but if I did, he'd get a whopping big fine. Is he with you?"

"Yes," Matthew said, realizing that Kara's manner of dress had disguised her identity as a woman. "As a matter of fact, my little *brother* drove me to the doctor."

"Brother?" the Constable snorted. "Well, if you're in charge of that whelp, he needs a good hiding, and that fancy car needs to be taken away from him!"

"I couldn't agree more, and the fancy car is history," Matthew said, turning and giving Kara a nod. "Is there someone local I can hire to tow the wreckage to a junkyard?"

"Roy Dillard. His place is at the far end of town. You can't be driving that car without a windshield," the Constable warned.

"My vehicle was damaged when the *fancy* car exploded. Is there somewhere around here that I can get the windshield replaced?"

"At Roy's place. He runs the auto shop and junkyard, but he ain't around much on the weekends. You'll be lucky to catch him at all. If he's not there, he's on his boat fishing."

Matthew looked around the town. It was little more than a dozen small shacks on each side of the road. "If I remember correctly, there's a motor park further up this road. Is it still in business?"

"Yes, sir. It's past Roy's place. Stop in and see if Roy is there. If he's not, you'll have to wait until Monday morning. Joe Proctor owns the motor park. He ain't had much business since they closed the base."

"Thank you," Matthew said. "Obviously, I must drive the car without a windshield until I can replace it."

"That's understood," Melvin Nichols said. "Joe's place is somewhat isolated, but he's got electricity and refrigerators in some of the cabins. You might want to stop at Sheridan's Store for food supplies to get you through the next few days."

"Thanks for the information," Matthew said, offering his hand.

"You need to be stricter with that boy. It wouldn't hurt my feelings if you'd keep that youngster off the roads. He's a damn nuisance!" the Constable added.

"I'll see what I can do about it," Matthew agreed.

"Come on," Matthew said, motioning for Kara to get in the car after the Constable drove off.

"He's a jerk," Kara said. "I thought I was driving."

"Not now, you're not. It sounds like you've earned a reputation around here."

They found Dillards, but neither the auto repair nor the junkyard was open. A high chain-link fence was padlocked, and several vicious dogs raced to the gate, jumping, snarling, and showing a lot of teeth.

Matthew drove on until he spotted a small sign with an arrow indicating a motorist camp. He turned into the property and followed the signs to the office. The motor park had always been full when the base was operational. Soldiers had taken advantage of a day's pass to meet their wives and girlfriends.

An old man came out of the cabin next to the office. "I ain't busy. Ain't been busy since the base closed. Pick a cabin. The keys are in the locks," the proprietor said. "There's a red tin placard inside. If you take the cabin, stick it in the window so you won't be bothered. The cabins don't got hot water, but there's a propane hot plate, so you can heat it yourself."

"It will do, and we don't want to be disturbed," Matthew said.

The proprietor snorted. "Ain't my business what you do. Just don't bust up the place."

Matthew drove through the campground and finally stopped at a cabin set back from the others.

"Could you get any further from civilization?" Kara demanded, getting out of the car.

"You were the one joyriding, and it doesn't sound like you've made any friends around here," Matthew retorted. He shoved a sack of groceries into her arms.

"I don't know these people," Kara said. "I just drive through town. What's the big deal?"

"Possibly that you're a terrible driver. They probably see you coming and run for their lives," Matthew said, removing the lock and opening the cabin door. He gave her a nudge inside.

Kara looked around and started shaking her head. "I'm not staying here!"

"You don't have a choice," Matthew warned. "We have a few things to settle."

"The only thing to settle between us is a divorce," Kara exclaimed.

Matthew shook his head and looked around the single room. It was simple, but it would do. He'd played a thousand possible scenarios about how this meeting with his wife would go. Now that it was here, he could only see one option.

Kara had already figured out that this Matthew wasn't the same man she had married. This man wasn't the thin, unassured young man of twenty-four she'd married. This Matthew was confident and decisive. He'd grown more masculine and developed into a manly man, with a broad chest and muscles he hadn't displayed before. His hair before had been a reddish brown. Now it was darkened, and there were a few stray gray hairs. He stepped toward her, and she backed away. She'd been concerned because there was only one bed in the cabin. Now she realized that wasn't her biggest worry. Matthew was advancing on her, and she didn't like the look in his eyes.

"What do you want?" she demanded.

"Five years of retribution," Matthew said. "And I've even got the Constable's permission."

Kara backed up against the bed, fell back on it, and scrambled to escape.

"No, you don't," Matthew exclaimed, and he hauled her back and tossed her over his lap. Fighting with her was hurting his arm, but he didn't give a damn. He unhooked the suspenders supporting her knickers and yanked them down, exposing her bare bottom.

"No!" Kara screamed as his hand whacked her across her bottom. His large hand covered nearly both of her buttocks, and he was spanking her hard! She yelped, cried, and tried to fight her way off his lap, but he kept dragging her back over his knees and smacking her bottom even harder.

Kara would have loved to be strong and brave, but every whack burned on her bare skin. Soon she was sobbing, but he ignored her tears and continued to spank every inch of her bottom.

Only when her buttocks were bright red did Matthew consider stopping. Then he stood up, rolling her off his lap and onto the mattress.

Kara curled into a ball of sobbing tears.

"How could you?" she cried.

"How could you?" he returned. "You ran out on me, Kara, and you kept running. The results would have been the same if I had caught up with you sooner. The war might have separated us, but I'm restarting this marriage. I've had years to figure out where I went wrong!"

"You can't force me to live with you!" she cried.

"Don't bet on it," Matthew said firmly.

Chapter 4

MATTHEW LEFT the cabin and went to his car for a pack of cigarettes. He hadn't smoked when he was younger. It was a habit he'd picked up after entering the service. Now he was finding it difficult to stop, and he did want to stop.

After Kara disappeared and his mother died, Matthew didn't know what to do with his life. Angry at the world, he'd joined the war effort, expected to be sent overseas. Instead, he'd been put into a testing environment where the government assessed young men on intelligence. He was commissioned into the Army as a 2nd Lieutenant and rapidly gained rank to 1st Lieutenant. He had been promoted to Captain three weeks before the Allied and German officials signed the armistice that ended the war in November 1918.

Although technically, the U.S. hadn't declared war on Germany until late December 1917, all the U.S. military services had been involved years earlier. Matthew had worked with a mix of the services and civilians. He'd spent part of the war in a secret underground bunker in Maryland, not far from Washington, D.C. Toward the war's end; he'd been stationed at a not-so-secret facility on Long Island.

Although he hadn't seen combat, Matthew had been part of vital code-breaking units. He'd also grown up a lot. The decoders were essential to the military services. Because of their importance, the men in those units couldn't wander far. Matthew had become good friends with two older officers. They had become mentors and father figures. They had also taught him a lot about being a man and a husband.

Matthew faced his family's underlying problems only after his parents were gone. His father hadn't been a model of strength or the head of his family. His mother had ruled his father through intimidation and threats. Only after it was too late did Matthew understand that he'd been dealing with a mentally unstable woman. He'd also realized that he'd been a weak husband going along with anything his young wife wanted to keep the peace.

Colonel Simon Rathforth and Major Harry Warner were his senior officers and role models. Both were married men with solid marriages, with loving wives and children. It had taken him a while and a lot of observation to understand why their marriages worked. It was because there was respect in their households. Even when they were absent, Simon and Harry were the heads of their families.

Both men believed in strict conformance to their principles, and they believed in discipline. Not only discipline for the children but also for their wives. Both of his superiors believed in discipline within the confines of marriage. Only after the two officers had taken Matthew under their wings had they spoken openly about the rules in their marriages. Both men spanked their wives when they thought it necessary. They understood the dynamic of order, and their wives accepted it. Both women loved and respected their husbands more for it.

Matthew listened when his mentors discussed their family issues and even asked questions. Simon and Harry were of similar mindsets. Matthew knew he hadn't been a strong husband or the head of his home. He accepted that he'd failed in his marriage and was at fault for not putting his wife first.

As he watched the success of his mentors' families, he matured. He accepted the principles both men and their families lived by. Matthew began to believe discipline, guidance, and spanking could have helped his marriage. He loved Kara, but she was spoiled and headstrong. It was no wonder, with Selina Branbridge as her role model.

Matthew had also done a lot of self-reflection. Looking back, he'd wavered repeatedly to appease his mother and wife and had failed both. He hadn't recognized his mother's mental problems. Worst of all, Matthew hadn't been there to protect Kara from his mother's insanity. He'd learned a lot by spending time with his mentors. There was truth in their advice. He needed to be strong to counteract five years of absence and independence.

His mentors had provided him with several privately published books advocating their views and principles on marriage. Reading those books solidified Matt's understanding of male and female roles within marriage. He wanted to be a good husband and realized he had to be the head of his house and undo the carnage he'd created by not being a strong husband.

Kara had returned to New York City, and he had found her. Come hell or high water, he would not lose her again. Pure determination was going to guide him to rebuilding their marriage. It might take a while, but he wouldn't let Kara get away from him again.

Kara was cried out and miserable. She finally stumbled from the bed and over to the bathroom, containing only an old chipped sink and a toilet. There was no bathtub or shower. She turned on the water, and it came out rust-colored at first and finally became clear. There were only two stiff white towels, and she washed her face with one and applied the other cold cloth to her still-stinging bottom.

She couldn't believe Matthew had spanked her. Except he had, and she still felt the sting and ache. Peering out the window, she saw him leaning against the car hood, smoking.

Matthew stepped on the cigarette butt, then picked it up and fieldstripped it. Some habits were harder to break than others. Loving Kara was a habit he would never relinquish. He walked purposefully into the cabin. Kara was standing in front of the door he thought was probably the bathroom.

"Are you ready to talk?" Matthew asked.

"What good will it do?" she countered.

"We won't know until we try," he said firmly.

Kara shrugged.

"Why are you dressed like a boy?" he asked.

She shrugged. "I don't like to be bothered by men."

"Are you bothered a lot by men?"

Her chin went up. "Quite a few, actually," she said.

"Why have you bound your breasts?"

"It's hard to pretend to be a boy with bouncing titties," she retorted. "I like to drive on the weekends. I enjoy getting away from the city for a little while."

"According to Constable Nichols, you've been terrorizing this part of the island."

Kara looked up to the ceiling in exasperation. "What do you want, Matthew?"

"An explanation."

"Why?" she demanded. "You wouldn't listen before. How many times did I plead with you to get us out of that hellhole? How many times did I tell you your mother was the devil reincarnated? It didn't do any good, and you wouldn't listen! She tried to kill me, and she..." Kara stumbled over the words, closed her eyes, and spit them out. Brutal words and horrible memories. "Your mother tried to kill me! She murdered our baby! She murdered a part of me! A part of us!"

"My mother was clinically insane. I didn't find out until it was too late. If I could undo what happened, don't you think I would?" Matthew asked. "I didn't realize that I was being manipulated or what my mother was capable of doing. I was young and stupid. Truthfully, I didn't know either of my parents that well.

"My father shipped me off to boarding school at eight years old. It was rare for me to spend more than a few days with my parents over the holidays. During the school breaks, I was encouraged to spend summer vacations with one of my school buddies or sent to summer camps. I didn't realize until later that I probably spent less than twenty days a year with my parents. My mother claimed my father didn't want me around. I realize now that she was trying to turn me against him. Yet, there was truth in her words. According to Jacob, my father did try to keep me away from my mother.

"I heard your words, Kara, but I was torn in too many directions. I'd lost my father and was trying to salvage his business, although it was a lost cause. Every day I was confronted with angry creditors and employees who wanted their debts paid. There wasn't any money to pay them! I had to let the business go bankrupt. I tried to referee between you and my mother and failed miserably.

"That last morning, I should have told you, but you were angry with me, and for whatever reason, I didn't. I'd already found a small furnished apartment for us to live in while we remained in Philadelphia. It was a weekly rental, and I was trying to get you out of that house. I left that morning upset and frustrated, knowing I had to meet with bankers who wanted to foreclose on my father's business before I had time to sell it.

"I went home that evening to an empty house. I wasn't told until that evening what Mother had done. I rushed to the hospital, and you wouldn't even look at me. I know I let you down, but I was hurting too. I lost everything that mattered to me in those few moments. Your words have echoed in my nightmares ever since.

"Even though you were screaming at me, I didn't want to leave. The doctors told me they would give you something to make you sleep. I planned on staying with you, but all hell broke loose again.

"My mother set the house on fire, and I had to admit her to an asylum the next morning. By the time I got that straightened out, you were gone. I searched everywhere and contacted all your friends, with no results. Then there was the war."

"Yes, the war," Kara repeated. "I don't see how this changes anything. It's been a long time, and we are different now."

"We're still married," Matthew said. "We made those vows and owe it to ourselves to try and put the past behind us. Hundreds of thousands of husbands, wives, and families were separated by the war. They're making it work again."

"They have returned to something they believe is worth saving," Kara said. "We don't have that!"

"I disagree. Have you been with other men?" Matthew asked bluntly

"No!" Kara denied loudly, and then she looked at him with accusing eyes. "Have you been with other women?"

"Once," Matthew answered truthfully. He saw the admission hurt her, but he wouldn't lie. "I was at a very low point, and liquor was involved. I am still a man."

"So, it's okay for men but not for women?"

"No, it's not okay for either, and I have no excuse except loneliness and too much alcohol. It's wrong to expect a woman to excuse a man for infidelity. It's a double standard, and it's wrong. I don't drink now, except occasionally having wine at dinner, and that's few and far between," Matthew said. "I pretend to drink with my friends, but I don't." He walked over and raised Kara's chin. "I'm glad you haven't been with anyone else. You're still mine."

"Leave me alone," she exclaimed, jerking away from him.

"I'll give you some time to think. I'm going out for a few minutes and locking you in so you don't attempt to run away again. Running away isn't the answer. I've already checked, and the windows don't open. I won't be gone long," Matthew said.

Kara heard the door lock snap, but she still tried to open it after she heard the engine of the car start. He was right about the windows. They didn't open. She was stuck there unless she wanted to break through the glass windows, and she did consider it for a few minutes.

Her husband's version of what happened so many years ago, rang true. Matthew had never been one to lie. The blame for their break-up rested fully on Blanche Douglas, and she felt no sympathy for the final demise of his mother.

Looking back to her previous self, she'd probably been too young and sheltered to marry. She'd loved Matthew, but she'd been inexperienced and naïve. All she had ever known was kindness and indulgence, not evil. Her husband had been only four years older, and while he might not think it, he had experienced nearly the same lifestyle. Neither of them had been mature enough to handle Blanche's insanity.

Kara went into the bathroom, rewet the towel, and laid it over her stinging bottom. Matthew hadn't said where he was going or when he would return. She might as well try to be as comfortable as possible.

Matthew returned to the small town and stopped at a

sporting goods store. It was the only place to purchase clothing, and he and Kara needed clothes. She'd destroyed her shirt to make a bandage for his arm. The clothes they were wearing were splattered with blood. Since she was dressed as a boy, he had to guess what size of the thick fishermen's trousers would fit her and went with a boy's size. He thought loose trousers would be more comfortable. She was a small woman, but her curves were still there.

The same was true of shirts. The townspeople disapproved of Kara's driving skills but hadn't been close enough to realize the driver was a girl. He wasn't going to tell them any different.

He'd seen her bottom half, still curvy, soft, and attached to slim legs. He'd seen an undergarment that she was wearing that flattened her breasts. He paused because Kara had always had small but full breasts, more so than a person would think, considering her slenderness. He outfitted them with several shirts and extra trousers. The rough clothing would suffice until the windshield could be replaced. Returning to the motor park, Matthew stopped at a tavern. He went inside and asked for fifty cents worth of nickels.

"Big night planned?" the bartender smirked.

"I believe in being prepared."

The tavern was empty, except for two men at the other end of the bar. The bartender looked around and lowered his voice. "There ain't no condom machine in the bathroom. The county made us take it out after they closed the base. I can sell you a full box for two dollars."

"I'll take it," Matthew agreed, sliding two one-dollar bills across the bar.

The bartender went into the back room and returned with a small bag. "There's a box of twenty in there," he said in an undertone. "Good luck."

Matthew stowed the box of condoms under the car seat

and answered the bartender, who was still inside the tavern and wouldn't hear his response. "Thanks, I'm going to need it!"

When Kara heard the engine's roar outside, she pulled up her knickers and waited for Matthew to enter. He came in carrying several bags and dumped them on a side table.

"These will have to do until we can get out of this burg," he said. He laid a box of pencils and a drawing pad on the table. "I found these at a shop and thought you could use them. We'll be twiddling our thumbs until we can replace the windshield."

"Thanks," Kara said honestly. "I always have a drawing pad with me. Always. It went up in flames."

"It could have been worse," Matthew said, wincing as he moved his arm. "It could have been you going up in flames."

"Is your arm still bothering you?" Kara asked. "I should look at it to ensure it's not getting infected."

"Okay. I still have a hard time thinking of you as a medic," Matthew said, unbuttoning his shirt. He wasn't wearing an undershirt. The doctor had removed it and tossed it in the trash bin. He sat in a chair, and she approached him and helped him out of the shirt.

Lifting the bandage and looking at the wound, Kara pressed the bandage back in place. The stitches were intact, and there was no bleeding.

She was standing before him, surprised by the width of his shoulders and the hair on his chest. The Matthew she'd known hadn't had chest hair, and he'd been thinner. Now he had well-defined muscles and definition in his abdominal muscles.

Matthew looked up and into Kara's eyes. He stood, crowding her, pulling her closer to his naked upper body. He searched her eyes before lowering his head to kiss her.

The meeting of their lips was the fourth explosion of the

day. Searing heat rose between them. Kara shivered and found herself responding to his kisses. She felt a need rise that had remained dormant for a very long time. She knew better, but knowing and doing were two different things. She was still angry with him, but it had been years since she'd allowed herself the pleasure of the flesh. As Matthew deepened the kisses, she leaned in to his naked torso and responded.

Matthew pulled back, breathing hard. "Say yes," he demanded.

"Yes!" Kara gasped as her tongue tangled with his again.

Matthew ripped her shirt open, and the buttons flew in every direction. It was tossed on the floor, and he yanked at the cloth that flattened her chest. Releasing those beauties, he lowered his head to suckle her nipples. His hands were everywhere, touching, feeling what he'd been denied for years. They stumbled over awkwardly and fell on the bed together. Shoes were kicked off, and clothing was discarded carelessly.

He released her breast only long enough to attach himself to the other. Matthew groaned as he dragged his mouth back to hers. His hand went between her legs.

"Are you sure you want this!" Matthew growled.

Kara gasped, "Yes!" and groaned as he inserted his manhood into her. She bent her knees and lifted her legs around his waist to make the entry easier. He thrust into her, deep and hard, and she knew he'd grown bigger there too.

The motion as he rocked back and forth made Kara's eyes darken with passion and need. It had been so long since she'd been touched. She arched her lower body and matched his efforts, thrust for thrust. Her breaths came in short gasps as she realized how much she'd missed the simple pleasure of sex. Somewhere in her deepest thoughts, Kara knew what she was doing was wrong, but as a wave of sensual desire swept over her, she ignored her misgivings. She'd denied herself of this pleasure for far too long.

Matt's breath came in gasps. At the very moment when he couldn't contain himself for another second, Kara's body jerked, squeezing and milking his release. He continued to pound into her deeper and more forcefully. Their bodies were locked together in a battle of pure sexual gratification.

Kara moaned, thrashed, and made a gurgling sound as an orgasm rocked her. Matthew followed with his own release, groaning.

Collapsing on top of her, he rolled over to remove his weight. They were both hot and sweaty, and he moved off her only to lie on something wet and cold. He pulled the towel from under him, and Kara took it. She slipped from the bed, and Matthew could still see the results of his handprints on her bottom. She went into the bathroom and returned a minute later, still naked but partially covered with a towel.

"I can't believe we did that," Kara said, sounding shocked.

"We did," Matthew said. He sat up against the headboard and patted the mattress beside him. "Yes, ma'am, we did, and it won't be the last time."

"I can't go through this again," Kara worried. "I hired a lawyer two weeks ago! We've been separated for years!"

"The filing won't be valid," Matthew said. "New York divorce law decrees that the only legal cause for divorce is adultery."

"Then I can file on adultery," Kara exclaimed. "You've admitted it!"

"True, but there were extenuating circumstances. Separation by war is being accepted by most judges. Also, if a wife has sex with her husband after admitting adultery or vice versa, the law believes the adulterer has been forgiven."

"That's a load of crock!" Kara exclaimed. "I'll tell them you forced me!"

"It won't stand in court," Matthew chuckled, and with a tug, his wife was sprawled against him, naked flesh against naked flesh. He kissed her, and she struggled at first but gave up and leaned in to him. "You're my wife again, sweetheart, and I'm not letting go of you this time. Admit it. You enjoyed making love with me again."

"No!" Kara pushed him away and ran into the bathroom, slamming the door shut.

Matthew took a deep breath and sighed. It was time to put his new convictions on marriage and family into practice. He knew it wouldn't be easy, but if he wanted the love of his life back, it would be worth it.

He knocked on the bathroom door. "If you're not out of there in five minutes and ready to behave like an adult, you'll get another spanking. We need to talk, and you need to understand where I stand! Five minutes!"

Kara wasn't wearing a watch. She also wasn't wearing clothes. All the feelings she was experiencing in the aftermath of having sex were jumbling around in her brain. Their love life had always been good, but she didn't remember it being as spectacular as she'd just experienced. Matthew wasn't the same shy and inexperienced young man he'd been when she married him. They had been two kids fumbling around and not knowing what they were doing. Matthew knew what he was doing now, while she was the one who was floundering for many reasons. A jealous voice was in her head, wondering *who* had taught him.

"Kara! Open the door," Matthew ordered firmly.

She opened the door, and he stepped aside to let her pass but caught her arm and smacked her bottom three times.

"Oh!" Kara exclaimed, putting some distance between them. "You can't keep whacking on me!"

"Actually, there's no law saying a man can't spank his wife," Matthew stated. "Beating is something else, but spanking is considered acceptable. I know that because, in the last year, my law firm has made more income from divorce cases than any other kind of lawsuit. I don't specialize in divorce, but if the firm's solicitors get bogged down, sometimes I have to step in and take a few cases. I've studied the laws on cohabitation in the State of New York."

"You can't force me to live with you, have sex with you, and expect me to put up with you spanking me!" Kara exclaimed.

"I didn't force you to have sex! You were a willing partner," Matthew said with a grin. "Besides, as my wife, the law says I have a legal expectation of cohabitation and marital relations. And, yes, ma'am, I have the right to spank you. Recent rulings by judges, one in New Jersey and another in Virginia, have decreed that a husband has the right to spank his wife. According to the court decisions, men and women have finite responsibilities and roles within a marriage."

"And what exactly are a woman's roles?" she demanded.

"Generally, a woman's place is beside her husband," Matthew said. "Kara, I want a marriage based on love and mutual respect. I know you are starting a new business, and I won't stand in your way. I will support you in every way I can. I also want a wife who yields to my lead as the head of our home. It just so happens you are the only one who fits that description because you are still my wife."

"Did you get shot in the head or something?"

Matthew shook his head and laughed. "No. As a matter of fact, I wasn't issued a weapon after basic training. I had a desk job during the war. We had something special, Kara, and we let it go too easily."

"That was a long time ago. We're different people now," she protested.

"Hopefully, we've gained insight as we aged. Both of us have had a long time to consider what went wrong. I want what we had before," Matthew said honestly. "We can't turn back time or pretend what happened didn't. But, before we had the issues with my parents and dealt with the war, we had a beautiful, loving marriage. What happened between us a few minutes ago was extraordinary. I want my wife back in my life. I want sex back in my life, but it has to be different this time."

"In what way?" Kara asked, wrapping a blanket around her naked body.

He walked over and gave a tug to the blanket. "First, you must understand that I am your husband, and I make the rules."

"Oh, sure, that's going to work," she exclaimed dismissively.

"It will work if we want it to work," Matthew said. "It may not seem fair until you understand the principles, but it's how marriages have worked for centuries. As your husband, I need to make you feel loved and secure in all areas of our relationship. I didn't before, and I take full responsibility for it. I will be in charge this time, and don't shake your head because this isn't negotiable. I make the rules, and *we* follow them. I'll try not to be too restrictive, but what I say goes."

"And, if I don't like your rules?"

"Then you will be spanked for not obeying them," Matthew said.

"This isn't the dark ages!" Kara exclaimed.

"No, in a few months, it will be 1920, and I will remind you that it is not illegal for a husband to spank his wife. In fact, it has been encouraged by several judges. Women have had to take on more than their share of work and responsibilities because of the war. Now that their husbands are back, they must become loving, supportive wives again.

Husbands must return to supporting and caring for their wives and families.

"In our case, we will have a different lifestyle than we had before. We'll both have careers, and they are important to us. We will also have social obligations because of our careers. I won't hold you back, Kara, and I'll help in any areas you think I might be helpful. In return, I expect you to extend the same support.

"Our private life is where most of the structure will change. You have never been good at listening or obeying. I'm sure nuns did their best, but your aunt's influence and being spoiled countered their efforts. Selina was, to put it mildly, outrageously decadent. I'm sure you'll learn what is acceptable and what isn't because not complying with my wishes will result in a sore bottom."

"When did you become cruel?"

"It's not cruel," Matthew protested mildly. "Men, as husbands and fathers, have been dominant in relationships and marriages from the beginning of time. If you need a name for what we will be practicing, it's *domestic discipline*. I am asserting myself as your husband to be the leader in our marriage. The rules are simple enough for both of us. We have to be honest and show respect to each other. Not adhering to the new rules means your bottom will pay the price. It's my responsibility to love and guide you.

"I do not want to be spanked!" Kara snapped.

"I'm afraid you will be," Matthew said matter-of-factly. "I didn't think this would be easy, and we have several days to iron out some of the kinks. It will take that long to get the windshield fixed. Meanwhile, we can consider this time our post-war honeymoon."

"You've lost your mind!" Kara said seriously.

Matthew shook his head and walked over to kiss her. "You're my wife, and I have never stopped loving you. I've had long conversations with a woman who wasn't here for years to hear them. I've abstained from becoming involved romantically because there is only one woman for me, and there is no substitution."

Her head shot up at his words, but he silenced her with a kiss. "I've admitted to my mistake. I was lonely, and I'm afraid liquor was a prelude to my infidelity. The woman I was involved with didn't mean anything to me, and I've carried a lot of guilt for breaking our vows. I accept the guilt for what I did. Except for an occasional sip of beer with my buddies, I haven't over-imbibed since. I was wrong, and I've matured. If you haven't, it's time for you to do the same."

Matthew lowered his head and kissed her, and she resisted a little but not much. He'd shocked and confused her with his announcements, but he had a plan. It started with using Kara's weakness against her. His wife had never been able to hide her interest or enthusiasm for sex. She couldn't deny the sexual pull between them. It had always been strong, and he wasn't above using it against her. He had three or four days to convince his wife that staying together and rebuilding their relationship was not a mistake. He intended to make her enjoy every second of their lovemaking.

Chapter 5

KARA SAT on the bed wearing only a shirt and flipping through a magazine. They had been in the motor park for four days, and she hadn't left the cabin. Matthew had left a few times. He'd returned with food, magazines, newspapers, and a timeline for replacing the windshield. The auto mechanic and junkyard owner, Dillard, had sent someone to another garage to get a new windshield.

Matthew had called his office and told them he was taking the week off because of a family emergency.

The only emergency Kara had dealt with was a flaming red and tender bottom. Talking with Matthew had led to arguments and disagreements, shouting and swearing on her side, and spanking on his. Protesting his new ideas and rules had led to her being tossed over his lap and adding more tenderness to an already sore backside.

Matthew spent a lot of time explaining his responsibilities as a husband. He reinforced those ideas with her sprawled over his lap, smacking her bottom when he didn't think she was paying attention. He called those spankings 'warnings,' which meant he was reminding Kara who was in charge. It was hard to pay attention when your butt was being set on fire.

"Spanking should be necessary for newlyweds," Matthew informed his wife. He stroked her beautiful buttocks. He had always admired a sexy butt, and Kara's was perfect. Perfect for spanking and other sexual activities he intended to enjoy in their new relationship.

"A husband should take a dominant role in the relationship from the beginning. Part of being in a domestic discipline marriage is a husband giving his wife maintenance spankings. Those spankings reinforce the idea that he is in charge. It's the husband's decision to decide the why, when, and the severity of the discipline. Scheduled spankings reinforce rules that may not be adhered to properly," Matthew explained, quoting almost verbatim from a book he'd read on the subject.

"That's ridiculous!" Kara disagreed, which only earned her several stinging spanks.

"No, it's not," Matthew stated firmly. "If you like sitting comfortably, you will learn and pay attention. We will be keeping a spanking calendar. That's so I can determine if you are behaving or not. If you're not, measures must be taken to ensure you make more effort."

"Your plan is to beat me into submission?" Kara exclaimed.

"Never," Matthew corrected her with a hard spank. "It's to love you into submission. I don't expect an overnight change in your attitude. I do expect you to behave like a lady. There will be no more escapades of behaving like a hoyden," Matthew said, rubbing his hand across her bottom. "Is this making any sense to you?"

"Not particularly. I've never been spanked before, and I don't like you doing it now! No woman wants her ass set on fire."

"Exactly. That's why knowing a spanking is the punishment for bad behavior will keep you from misbehaving. Swearing is not ladylike behavior."

Kara yelped as she received another hard spank. "This isn't fair!"

"Maybe not," Matthew said. "But, I'm unwilling to throw away what we had before. We loved each other, and we were happy. I believe we can have that kind of relationship again. This time there will be rules that we must abide by. Otherwise, you will not be happy with the consequences. You are a young woman who needs rules and boundaries. You're spoiled, and even though you've had a few rough years, you have also taken on some very unbecoming mannerisms. These are new behaviors, and it's up to me as your husband to determine what is acceptable and what isn't."

"I can't believe this!" Kara exclaimed. "I'm not a child, and I'll hate you!"

"Stop behaving like a child, and no, you won't. Once you realize I'm doing this because I love you, you will adjust," Matthew promised.

Matthew was serious about the spanking rules. He spanked every inch of her beautiful bottom, turning it bright pink several times while living in the cabin. An organized man, Matthew had been working on the rules in his head for a long time. He did believe Kara needed boundaries and consequences. Delivering spanks to his errant wife made her pay attention, making him feel more in control. He had stated his position and wasn't going to change his mind.

Kara was very aware of her husband's new role and her role in their marriage. He was no longer the sweet young man who could be talked into anything simply because it was easier to go along than argue. Kara hated Matt's so-called rules and limits. She also hated that she hadn't been able to sit comfortably for several days. The first spanking had been painful, and others had followed! She didn't know this new Matthew. He was a commanding, physical husband. She wasn't sure what to make of him.

When they weren't discussing new rules and limits, they were having sex. She had lived with Matthew for two years before leaving him. Her husband had been younger and as inexperienced as she had been. Her husband's sexual knowledge had grown. He admitted that being barracked with men who bragged about their sexual exploits had him doing a lot of reading of banned sexual manuals. His prowess and stamina had increased along with his muscles, stubbornness, and unreasonable demands.

Kara was in a conundrum because she secretly didn't want to stop Matt. Once he started kissing her, one thing led to another. They were spending hours every day having sex. She couldn't believe how often they were satisfying their hunger for each other. The frequency of sex wasn't something women discussed among themselves. She didn't think the hours they spent having sex could be classified as normal. There was nothing else to do in the little cabin. They talked, he read, she sketched, and they had sex.

She was responding to Matt's sexual demands. He wasn't the sweet gentleman he'd been before. Now he was a demanding and exhaustive lover, although he gave as much as he demanded. If they weren't having sex or trying to keep themselves occupied, they were arguing.

There was a knock, and Kara looked out the window to ensure it was Matt. It was, and she stepped back as he came into the cabin. "We'll be back in New York tomorrow afternoon."

"Then what?"

"Then we start living as a married couple again," Matthew said.

"At your place?"

"No, I think yours will most likely be our destination. My apartment is small and convenient for work, but living in the same high-rise where you work has drawbacks. I've spent more evenings reviewing my law cases in the past year than enjoying life. It's become only a place to crash for a few hours of sleep.

"It makes more sense to live at your place. Do you have a problem with our living there? I probably should review your Aunt's will, the paperwork involved with her investment in the hotel, and the suite's ownership. We can revise our plan later if the Wolcott suite doesn't work. I want to see those books you found in your aunt's bedroom. Although, in principle, I disapprove of my wife being exposed to pornography."

Kara rolled her eyes. "You are beyond that book, and I didn't read it. The photographs were embarrassing enough."

"What goes on between a husband and wife should never be embarrassing," Matthew said, moving over to her. He sat down on the bed and kissed her. "I will miss having access to my beautiful wife day and night. Don't tell me you haven't enjoyed it. I've seen your face and felt your reactions."

Her unbuttoned shirt was open, and Matthew pulled her to him. His fingers removed the shirt off her shoulders and let it fall. Then he kissed her and laid her back on the mattress.

"I think you're becoming more beautiful with each passing hour," he whispered, and there was no resistance from her. He suckled her breasts while tossing his clothing aside.

"You're mine," he whispered while savoring her lips and breasts, moving further down and pushing her knees apart. This had embarrassed her several days earlier, but not now. Oral sex was something he had learned from several banned books passed from soldier to soldier. He didn't mind revealing that secret to his wife.

Kara knew what was coming next, and there was no doubt that she enjoyed every second of it. She felt his flicking tongue on her most sensitive parts and closed her eyes. Even she couldn't pretend she wasn't affected as she moaned.

She could feel Matthew moving over her. "Open your eyes! I want you to see what we are doing."

Kara opened her eyes to the triangle of dark hair on his chest. Her eyes trailed downward, and her eyes widened at his size. He was big, and she always wondered how he would fit, but he did. She felt a throb between her legs and realized her husband had done it again. He'd seduced her and turned her into a wanton woman.

"Oh," she gasped.

His fingers slid inside, pumping, stretching, while he trailed a line of kisses over her stomach and suckled her nipples again.

"Tell me what you want!" he demanded, pushing her legs apart. He knew what she wanted, but he wanted to hear it.

"You!" Kara begged. "I want you inside me!"

"Yes," Matthew agreed with a smile. "Those words will never pass your lips unless spoken to me!"

Matthew pounded into her sex, filling her, yet she wanted more from him. He continued to sink into the depths of her womanhood.

"Oh!" Kara couldn't stop thrashing on the bed in response to an orgasm. This was the moment that made everything worthwhile.

She was aware of a weight shift. She was turned over and positioned on her knees, and her husband thrust into her again. This was a new position, which her husband had shown her, and she liked it. He rode her hard. His hand spanked her across the bottom and then again.

"Oh!" she squealed. She was already sore, but she was also feeling something else. Her body was preparing for another orgasm. It was happening again. Kara could feel it coming, and she'd endure the temporary discomfort of his spanking hand to experience those few minutes of ecstasy.

"Oh!" she moaned as her body bucked, and Matthew became a wild man following through on what she'd asked of him.

Matthew knew what was happening, and he timed it perfectly. When Kara orgasmed, he pounded into her harder. He let himself go when she bucked for a third and last time. Lying stiff for a minute, he was swamped with what he suspected were the same feelings her body was experiencing. He collapsed and held her closer while discretely disposing of the condom. "You're my wife, Kara, all mine."

Kara closed her eyes. She had been a captive to Matthew in the little cabin for four days. During that time, they'd spent hours talking. They spent hours having sex, and the sex they were having now was leagues ahead of what they'd done in the past.

She should be happy they were going back to the city the following day. She would be returning to her apartment and to what was familiar. Alice and Thomas would return from their honeymoon in a couple of days.

What worried her was she didn't know what lay ahead for her. Matthew had been honest about what he expected of her. Matthew wasn't asking her to give up her dream of being a fashion designer and boutique owner. He wanted to control their personal lives, and she didn't know if she could give up her independence in exchange for phenomenal sex.

Matthew kissed Kara and stretched out on the bed beside her. He gave her a light spank across the bottom.

"What was that for?"

"Because I love your bottom," Matthew said. "I appreciated it before, but now I love it."

"Is this part of your fixation with spanking my ass?"

"Part of it, but ass isn't a word I want coming out of your mouth. It shouldn't be in your daily vocabulary with a dozen other swear words. I expect you to behave and act like a lady. Women who swear in public are vulgar."

"I'll have you know I am the embodiment of a lady," Kara exclaimed.

"Really? What do you call running around dressed as a Hoyden? Driving like a maniac and terrifying a community on the weekends?"

"It wasn't like that," Kara complained. "I was bored, and Alice was busy getting reacquainted with Thomas. Then she went off on her honeymoon. I hired an instructor to teach me how to drive. Maybe he didn't do a good job of it."

"Am I to conclude that Alice has been your guide to using common sense all these years?" Matthew asked.

Kara looked uncomfortable with his words. "Sometimes, maybe. She wouldn't let me drive the ambulance most of the time in London, although I qualified in training. They drive on the opposite side of the road! Alice has been my best friend and confidant for a very long time. She's been there for me, and I can depend on her. We've taken care of each other for a long time."

"You have grown up, but traces of the spoiled girl I married still exist. I don't remember you being so argumentative," Matthew said. "I will only tolerate those traits so far."

"Because of your rules?"

"Exactly," Matthew said. "You already know the consequences for not obeying them. I've become very fond of your backside."

The trip back to Manhattan was uneventful and not as fast as Kara would have preferred. She was still dressed as a boy, and Matthew went to his place first. His apartment was in the same building as the attorney's office where he worked, on the eighth floor. It was small but functional. The entire apartment wasn't as large as her living room. Matthew pulled several suits from his closet and packed them in suitcases, setting them by the front door to be carried downstairs to the car. He picked up his mail and selected several hats from a hat rack in his bedroom.

He asked Kara to check the refrigerator to see if any old food needed to be thrown out. While she was busy in the small kitchen, he put what was left of the box of condoms he'd purchased into a box with other medicine cabinet things and reminded himself to buy more. Kara hadn't asked him about using protection but had seemed pleased when he'd produced it.

Kara entered the bedroom, looking around the room and then at him. "How long have you lived here?"

"Since the government unit I worked for was disbanded. I was a decoder long before President Wilson declared war. I joined the army five months after you left and served until our units weren't needed anymore. I returned to my law firm and my job. My entire enlistment was stateside.

"It's been a miserable life without you. My friends tried to get me to go out, meet girls, and go on blind dates. Some of the guys even questioned if I was a Nancy Boy. They didn't know I was married, and I wasn't interested in going out with just any girl. From the moment I met you, I knew there was only one woman for me."

Kara chewed on her lower lip. "How are we going to make this work?"

Matthew went to her and pulled her against him. "We're both tenacious and bull-headed. But, we will forget the past and forge a new future." He kissed her. "If we could bottle and sell what happens when we are together, we'd be instant millionaires."

"Or jailed for indecency," Kara said.

"We're going to try this marriage again," Matthew said firmly. "Agreed?"

She nodded as he kissed her again. Kara felt that internal throb in her private parts again.

Matthew sensed a change in her mood. He kissed her again, and she returned his affections.

Several hours later, Kara left the bed and padded into the tiny bathroom in his apartment. Stepping into the bathtub, she pulled the shower curtain around the tub. She had made do with washing herself at the cabin and ignored the nasty tub. She turned on the shower nozzle, and it felt wonderful.

Matthew stepped into the tub to join her and rubbed his body against her. "We've got one part of our marriage figured out."

"We weren't this open about sex before. We didn't even get undressed in front of one another before. How did you learn so much?"

"I told you, it all comes from listening to horny, bragging guys," Matthew admitted. "They get very graphic, as were the books passed around. Are you complaining?"

"Only about my sore bottom. I haven't sat comfortably for days."

"You like being spanked during sex," he whispered in her ear. "You'll learn to avoid the other kind of spanking by being a good girl."

Kara wanted to complain when they were seated again in his roadster. The small car was stuffed with his suitcases and several boxes. Matthew said he'd bring more of his belonging over as he settled into Aunt Selina's suite at the hotel. Unfortunately, the lease on his apartment had just been renewed, and he wasn't allowed to sublease without the permission of the building manager. The Wolcott Hotel signed Matthew into the registry as Kara's husband.

Management had simply handed over another key to the suite, and the bellboys took his luggage upstairs. Matthew relinquished his car keys to a valet who would park his car in Kara's empty garage and leave the keys at the main desk for retrieval.

Matthew looked around the luxurious flat when the hotel staff left. He'd only been there twice. Once when he'd met Kara at a party. The other time was when they'd told Selina they had driven to Elkton, Maryland, to be married because there wasn't a waiting period after paying for the license. "Selina lived well. Anyone could get used to living like this," Matthew said.

"This is nothing compared to her flat in Paris. It's gone now. The building was bombed. We heard through some friends of hers that the Paris flat had been destroyed by mortar fire. Aunt Selina was killed during a bombing. She refused to leave when we did, convinced that the French would drive the Germans out of Paris and that she would join us later in London," Kara said.

"Alice and I went ahead, and she was killed in a bombing three weeks later. The Germans bombed our building in London in one of the last air raids. Luckily, we were at our jobs and weren't home."

Matthew looked around the apartment. "So, are you rich; or filthy rich?"

"Rich, on the edge of filthy rich," Kara laughed. "But I can't be foolish with my inheritances. Alice and I are using part of it to launch our fashion line. If all goes well, we'll make a decent profit by the middle of next year."

"We have three more days to relax and enjoy before I have to return to work," Matthew said.

"You really don't expect me to be a typical housewife, do you?" Kara asked.

"Typical, no," Matthew said with a smile. "A good wife, yes. We have to learn to live with each other again. Both of us are different from what we were before. You have to tell me if I'm doing something that bothers you. And, no, that does not include my spanking your bottom.

"My first request is that you rid yourself of those Hoyden clothes. I've seen the closet full of clothing in the bedroom. I know you have beautiful clothes, and I want you to look like the beautiful, talented woman you are. I'm burning that thing you wear to flatten your breasts. It goes in the fireplace!"

Kara smiled, but she didn't argue. "Throwing it in the trash will do. The fireplaces are gas, and even I know that burning anything in them is dangerous. I only dressed as a boy because it gave me more freedom."

"You never have to hide who you are, Kara. You are a beautiful, intelligent, and talented young woman. I was always proud that you married me. But you're not getting behind the wheel of a car until you get some more driving lessons!"

Matthew moved against Kara, and she followed his lead. They were dancing to music from a New York City Radio Station. It was a Saturday afternoon, and they were practicing. They had decided to go to a dance pavilion with a live band in Central Park. They hadn't danced together in years.

Kara was wearing one of her own fashion creations, and Matthew did not like her choice of dresses. The neckline was a deep V slash between her breasts, and the skirt was short.

He stood back and insisted she move and twirl. He shook his head.

"Absolutely not. It's too short and too provocative. When you bounce, everything bounces because you are not wearing a brassiere. When you twirl, the skirt rises above your knees. Go change!"

"This dress is going to be one of our best sellers. Everyone thinks so," Kara argued.

"It's fine, but I don't want my wife displaying what only I should have the privilege of seeing. I don't want strange men gawking at my wife!"

"You're impossible!" Kara exclaimed, stamping her foot.

"Do you want to go or stay here?" he asked.

"I want to go, but..."

"We're not going if you don't change," Matthew warned. "I will not approve of you wearing that dress in public!"

Kara stomped out of the room and pulled a dress she'd designed several years earlier from her closet. It wasn't on the cutting edge of new fashion and wouldn't show her knees or cleavage, with a longer length and square neckline. She was frustrated but knew arguing wouldn't do her any good. She knew dresses in her design line were pushing the unwritten codes of morality for women's fashion. The only way to challenge those codes was by breaking them.

The war had changed women, especially young women. Women were no longer willing to allow fathers, brothers, and husbands to dictate their lives, including how they dressed. Kara loved the new independence she'd gained. But, now Matthew was insisting on her following his rules.

Matthew and Kara had been living in her apartment for a few days. He only had one more day before he had to return to work. He had taken her to his office and shown her where he worked. Most of his office colleagues had been surprised by his announcement that she was his wife. His silence didn't surprise Kara. She had rarely spoken of her marriage herself.

Living in Aunt Selina's luxurious flat was undoubtedly better than the cabin. They had more conveniences and unlimited hot water. Long hot baths were essential to Kara, especially now when her bottom was tender so often. The self-contained suite included a kitchen, although calling for room service was easier.

They were better dressed when they ventured out, but in the privacy of the flat, they were still spending a lot of time wearing only their robes.

Matthew followed her into the bedroom and watched as she changed. He gave her a smile and a thumbs-up at her choice. As Kara disappeared into a large closet, Matthew wandered around the room. He'd been especially pleased with the gigantic-sized bed in her bedroom. However, his thoughts often pondered about her aunt's escapades in it. Kara's aunt had been a liberated spirit, often teetering on the edge of vulgarity. Women hadn't trusted her around their husbands for good reason. She was known for her affairs and didn't differentiate between single and married men.

Matthew pulled a chest drawer open and was shocked by what he had discovered. It was full of sex toys and implements of different sizes. He closed the drawer and opened the one below it. In it were paddles, flat-backed hairbrushes, and other things that could be used for the same purpose. Matthew slapped one of the paddles against his hand.

"Some of that stuff is scary," Kara said, coming out of the closet. "The show-all books I told you about are in the next drawer. I always knew my aunt was free with her favors, but I didn't expect those things. I don't know how some of those things work. I haven't gotten around to disposing of them yet. I'm afraid someone will find them if I throw them in the trash! That would be embarrassing."

"How old was Selina?" Matthew asked.

"She would never admit to her age, but she was sixty-two," Kara said, turning around so he could button her dress. "She looked younger, and she dated younger men. She was quite adventurous."

"I'll say," Matthew agreed, and he picked up another paddle. "I may keep some of these paddles and hairbrushes, although my hand seems to do the job quite successfully."

"Really?"

"Absolutely," Matthew whispered, and he nuzzled her ear. "You can't fool me anymore. You like it when I spank you."

"I do not!"

His response was a sharp crack across her bottom, and she sucked in her breath. "Not the spankings you've been given for being smart-mouthed and insolent. The ones I give you during sex turn you into a wild woman," Matthew smirked.

"I..."

Smack! His hand left a sting across her bottom.

"I'm not flamboyant like my aunt!" Kara protested.

"Whatever works, I'm all for it. As long as it's only for me," Matthew said, stepping behind her and trailing kisses down the back of her neck. He lifted her skirt and rubbed her bottom.

"What about going dancing?" she mumbled.

"It's open every weekend. Isn't this more important? We don't need to go out as long as we enjoy ourselves?" Matthew asked.

Kara looked over her shoulder and straight into his eyes. "Help me out of this dress!"

Chapter 6

"YOU'RE LIVING WITH MATTHEW AGAIN?" Alice exclaimed in surprise when Matthew and Thomas left the hotel suite to return to the townhouse.

Alice and Thomas had returned from their honeymoon to discover a broken water pipe in the second-floor bathroom. Luckily, his neighbor had discovered the leak and had shut the water off, but not before considerable damage had been done.

Alice had suggested they go to Kara's suite for the night, as it was late by the time they'd arrived in New York.

Kara went to the kitchen and pulled out a bottle of wine. She searched several drawers before finding a corkscrew and a box of cookies.

"We've been living together for several weeks," Kara said, nodding. "We haven't killed each other yet."

"Don't even joke about that," Alice scolded.

"We were more or less trapped on Long Island together for the first week. We've talked a lot about what happened."

"Have you forgiven him?"

"Mostly," Kara said. "Matthew wouldn't want me saying

this, but his mother was bat-shit crazy. He has considerably more sympathy for her than I do. Matthew was thrown into a situation he wasn't prepared to handle when his father committed suicide. He didn't realize his mother was insane. Actually, he didn't *know* either of his parents. They were virtually strangers because they sent him to boarding school when he was eight years old.

"Matthew found his father's diary while clearing his parents' home. Wilber Douglas kept Matthew away from his mother as much as possible. He arranged for his son to go home with schoolmates during school breaks. Matthew rarely visited his home from the boarding school. When he did, it was only for a few days at Christmas, Easter, or a week before the next school year started."

"Didn't he think there was anything odd about not spending time with his parents?" Alice asked.

Kara shrugged. "His father would take so-called business trips and visit Matthew on the sly at his school. Matthew was told that his mother loved him, but she was sick and didn't have the stamina to spend time with a rambunctious boy. He was a child and thought that meant Blanche was sickly. The only people who knew she was mentally unstable were Dr. Hillsboro and the servants, who were well-paid to put up with her behavior," Kara said.

"That was one of the reasons I didn't quit," Alice said. "When his father died, Matthew was slapped in the face with a reality he wasn't prepared to handle."

Kara nodded. "He was trying to please his mother and me, and the devil is in the details. Matthew never suspected how unstable she was until it was too late. He never expected his mother would try to kill me and our unborn child. I didn't like the bitch, but I didn't think she would go that far either!"

"I was your accomplice in running away. Is he going to

be able to accept our working together and being friends?" Alice asked.

"He doesn't have a choice about it," Kara said firmly. "You saved and supported me through one of the roughest ordeals of my life. We've depended on each other through a World War! You are more than a best friend. You are my sister and my business partner. My friendship and love for you is non-negotiable."

Matthew sat across the table from a man he'd been good friends with since his secondary boarding school days. They had lost contact after school but had run into each other when Matthew was assigned to the McKim, Mead & White account. Thomas tipped his beer mug, and they clacked the glass mugs together. Thomas was drinking beer. Matthew had ordered it, but he would drink very little. "In a couple more months. This will be illegal," he said.

"It's an idiotic decision, but the amendment passed," Thomas agreed. "The Prohibition Amendment will be considered a huge mistake in a few years. No law will stop anyone from making, selling, or drinking liquor. The law doesn't stop anyone from buying the ingredients needed to make alcoholic beverages. Those idiots in Washington think that if they give the women this legislation, they'll back down on the right to vote. It won't happen, and the 19th Amendment is already before Congress. It's going to pass. Mark my words. Women are going to win this time."

"I believe it," Matthew said. "I hear all the scuttlebutt at the office, and I believe women should be given the right to vote. They've proven themselves during the war. If they can run businesses and pay taxes, women should be treated equally under the law."

Thomas tipped his beer mug again and agreed. "How do you feel about Alice and Kara opening a fancy dress shop?"

"My wife is a different person from the innocent girl I

married. She's a grown woman. She and Alice faced a war far more dangerous than anything we faced in the States. I still can't believe she was a trained medic and a bomb spotter. I accept the fault for those lost years. I never stopped loving her, and I still do. We've decided to give our marriage another try, but I'm setting up rules this time."

"What kind of rules?" Thomas asked.

"Rules that might be difficult to explain," Matthew said, pushing his beer toward Thomas and holding his hand up to signal the waitress. He ordered a Coca-Cola instead.

"Our marriage wasn't working on many levels before. I was just getting my bearing on being an adult, and I didn't know how to handle a wife, especially a young, spoiled one. We've been apart for almost five years, and in that time, we have matured. I had two great mentors during my service in the Army. You haven't met them yet, Colonel Simon Rathforth and Major Harry Warner. They helped me grow up and gave me a lot of advice on being a husband. They taught me a different way of becoming the head of my home."

Thomas looked around to make sure no one was listening. "Would that be the principles of *Domestic Discipline*?"

"You've heard of it?" Matthew asked doing the same head turn for eavesdroppers.

"I was raised with those principles," Thomas said. "I intend to practice it in my own marriage."

"Does Alice know?"

"Of course," Thomas said. "One of the tenets of being the head of our house is that the couple doesn't keep secrets. She wasn't happy about learning that I believed in spanking as a discipline, but with her background, she accepted it.

"Alice grew up with a father who whacked on her mother, her, and her brother whenever he felt like it. She lost them in the cholera epidemic of 1909. From what I've heard, though, he acted more out of meanness than discipline. She didn't know there were rules or a name given to a man spanking his wife. She's read the literature, and we've discussed it. She has agreed in theory, although there haven't been any incidents that required practicing it yet. How is it working in your relationship?"

"So far, so good," Matthew said. "I think Kara is more outspoken and reckless than Alice."

Thomas laughed. "I wouldn't bet on it."

When the men decided they'd given their wives enough private time to talk, they returned to the Wolcott Hotel.

Thomas and Alice spent the night and accepted Matthew's offer to live in his apartment at the Cahill building until the townhouse could be repaired, as long as the building manager agreed. The newlyweds said their good-nights and disappeared into the guest room.

Matthew glanced at the empty wine bottle but didn't say anything until after their guests left. "I thought you said you didn't drink?"

"I don't drink hard liquor or beer," Kara said with a shudder. "Ick! I'm afraid Alice and I have gained an appreciation for good French wine. Aunt Selina has a well-stocked wine closet that has aged well in our absence. We would have to be heavy drinkers to put a slight dent in Aunt Selina's stockpile. Mr. Harrison, the hotel manager, told me there is a wine cellar in the basement for the permanent residents. Selina's is full and locked, although I haven't seen it."

"Don't spread it around that you have a stocked wine cellar. It would be asking for trouble," Matthew warned. "Is everything okay between you and Alice?"

"Of course," Kara said. "We've never had a problem between us that we couldn't resolve."

On his lunch hour the next day, Matthew joined Thomas, Alice, and Kara in his apartment to finish packing his things. He'd received permission from the building manager, explaining that he wasn't subleasing. He was helping a friend who needed a place to stay until their home was fixed. It helped that Mr. Cahill, Matthew's boss, owned the building. The Markhams could use the apartment until the townhouse was repaired. The manager had agreed and promised to add their names to the building security logs.

"Are we going to join Thomas and Alice *dancing* this evening?" Kara asked with an alluring smile. They had planned to go dancing several times. So, far they hadn't made it to a club. *Dancing* had become a somewhat code word between them, meaning one or the other wanted to have sex.

"They are newlyweds, and they don't need us hanging around," Matthew said, drawing his wife into a kiss.

Later that evening, Matthew sat in bed and pulled Kara over his lap.

"I haven't done anything wrong!" she protested.

"This is maintenance," Matthew said. "Who is the head of our house?"

"You are," Kara said.

"I am, and you agreed to certain principles of our life-style, didn't you?"

"I wasn't given a choice," Kara protested, and she felt a sharp smack across her bare bottom.

"Wrong answer!"

"All right! Yes, I did," Kara said aloud.

"Spanking will be a regular part of our married life," Matthew said, re-positioning Kara over his lap. He stroked her beautiful buttocks and ran his hand up her back and down to her bottom. He gave her another spank. His wife's figure was on the edge of thin, but somehow she had perfectly filled out breasts and bottom. He loved her figure. He loved her, and they had settled in together without too much conflict.

"Did you know Thomas and Alice have adopted domestic discipline as a lifestyle too?"

Kara twisted around. "You're kidding!"

"I'm not. Thomas told me they had agreed to it long before he was shipped home. His parents practice D/D, and they have a good, strong marriage. One he plans on modeling his own marriage on."

"I still think it's a kinky idea," Kara exclaimed, yipping at another stinging spank. "Oh! Okay! Okay! Apparently, my aunt was into it too, with all those paddles and hairbrushes she had stored in the dresser."

"I'll only use those if I need to remind you of our agreement," Matthew said. "This spanking is maintenance to remind you to behave yourself. Have you set up a maintenance calendar, as I asked?"

"Not yet."

"That's going to cost you," Matthew said.

Kara knew where this routine of questions was going to lead. These spankings were to remind her that her husband was in charge, and he wouldn't let her forget it.

"Let's get on with it," Matthew said, peppering her bottom with several harder spanks. "How do you feel about maintenance spankings?"

"I hate them, but you insist I need one weekly!" Kara squeaked.

Matthew spanked her bottom again. "They are for your own good and to remind you of who is in charge. You like it when I spank when we are having sex, and don't deny it. Who is in charge?"

"You are," Kara agreed again, and several hard whacks

descended on her backside. Matthew spanked her bottom until it turned bright pink.

Kara could feel the sting on her bottom. She also felt a throbbing building in her lower regions. She didn't remember longing to have her husband inside her in her younger years. Kara had decided to allow Matthew's so-called dominance over her as long as he continued fulfilling her sexual needs. This time around, Matt wasn't the pushover he'd been before. Now he was a husband in charge, and she liked it even if she had to be careful about sitting down occasionally.

Alice rushed through the front door of the storefront they'd rented to launch their new shop. It was pouring down rain outside. She shook the water from her umbrella and put it in an empty box.

"Did we get our deliveries today?" she asked.

Kara looked up from her task. "They arrived on time, but I haven't had time to check them yet."

"I'm sorry I'm late, but Thomas dragged me to a warehouse this morning. He said I had to decide on the kitchen tile and linoleum flooring. I hope I picked the right one."

"Which one did you pick?" Kara asked, having seen the samples.

"The pale green and white tiles. The new kitchen cabinets will be painted a slightly darker green. Why can't he make these decisions? He's the architect, and he knows more about these things. I don't!"

Kara smiled. "He wants you to be happy with the choices. You will spend a lot of time in the kitchen cooking, although Thomas has bragged about his barbecue expertise. What is it with this sudden interest all men have in barbecuing?" Suddenly she changed the topic. "Am I to assume the insurance company has finally paid for the damage?"

Alice shook the rain off her coat and hung it up to dry. "The check was in yesterday's mail. I'm sure Matthew's threat to take them to court had something to do with it. They've been procrastinating for weeks! And, the interest in barbecuing is because every magazine and newspaper has pictures of men with aprons and chef's hats on their heads in front of very costly man toys."

Kara laughed at her friend's remarks and stood back from the sign she was painting, and Alice joined her.

"It's perfect," Alice said, looking at the script. "Is it the right size?"

Kara & Alaïs Couture Designs

"I measured three times," Kara said. "And then measured again to make sure. The outside sign is twelve inches longer than the inside sign on the wall behind the register counter."

"The signs are beautiful, but giving my name the French spelling implies that I'm French," Alice said.

"Our clothing line is influenced by French Couture. After four years of being deprived of European fashion, our grand opening will be a success. I just know it," Kara said. Then she took a deep breath and added, "I hope!"

Alice giggled, went to hop on a stool, and changed her mind.

"Trouble in paradise?" Kara asked.

"Why do men have to be so obstinate?" Alice asked.

"Why are you asking me?" Kara questioned.

"You've been married longer," Alice claimed.

"The first two years don't count," Kara said. "We were different people back then. We were young and stupid. Sometimes it feels like it was a lifetime ago. We have the memories but only try to remember the good parts. Matthew is definitely a different man now."

"Thomas is the same, but he seems more masculine. His father is very influential," Alice said. "Don't get me wrong, his parents have been wonderful, but I don't think they approve of our opening this boutique. We will be pushing the limits of what is considered a conventional manner of dress for women. On top of that, my in-laws want grandbabies."

Kara nodded. "Matthew and I discussed that too, and he feels the same. But as I've told him, what we design and what we wear are two different things. Our designs aren't obscene, and women will not go back to wearing shapeless skirts to their ankles and corsets.

"We discussed the baby issue, too, and we're not ready for children yet. I love the man Matthew is now. He has matured, and I'm proud of his success. I think he's proud of what we are trying to build. At least, he claims to support our endeavor. Our only problem is his mindset to follow the tenets of Domestic Discipline. It's become a religion to him, and what's worse is that Selina practiced it."

"No!" Alice exclaimed. "She couldn't! Selina was the most independent woman I've ever met!"

"She was also what most people would consider immoral. She left an entire dresser full of sex toys and things Matthew considered obscene," Kara admitted. "I think even he was embarrassed by some of the things we discovered. He was so funny, not letting me see some of the things. He did keep some of the books and several paddles. He doesn't know that I've already been through the dresser, and I've already looked through most of the books. I was curious."

Kara looked over to Alice. "That's a secret I don't want to be shared. If he knew, Matthew would probably come after me with one of those paddles."

"Thomas' father gave him a paddle as a private wedding

gift," Alice said. "He hasn't used it yet, but he has admitted that he isn't averse to using it if he thought I deserved it. We're going to visit his parents this weekend."

"How did we both end up with spankers?" Kara whined.

"Apparently, it was inherited in Thomas' family," Alice said.

"I get to meet the people who indoctrinated my husband this weekend," Kara complained. "Matthew considers two military officers his role models.

"Excuse me?"

Kara and Alice jumped at the unexpected voice. They turned to find a well-dressed woman navigating her way through the shop filled with boxes and naked manikins.

"I'm sorry," Kara said. "We're not open yet."

"I can see that," the woman said, looking around. "My name is Beatrice Bonanutchi. I'm a fashion columnist for The New York World. I don't mean to be nosy, but I am always looking for new shops opening."

"Hello," Kara said, embarrassed because she'd worn overalls. "We are opening a boutique, but we are several weeks from opening."

"I can see that," Beatrice exclaimed. "What kind of merchandise do you plan on selling?"

"French-inspired Couture," Kara said. "I'm Kara Douglas, and this is my business partner Alice Markham. We studied in Paris before it became too dangerous to remain there. We were evacuated to London and spent the war working and supporting the war efforts. When it was safe to come home, we did. Our goal is to open a French-inspired boutique here in New York City."

"Oh my goodness," the columnist exclaimed. "I'm so excited, and I want to hear your stories. Who did you study under?"

"Coco Chanel, Madeleine Vionnet, and Jean Patou and

Poiret," Kara said. "My aunt was a New Yorker and a world traveler. She knew the top designers and wore couture. She introduced us to her favorite designers. We worked and learned under their direction. They were just beginning a new revolution in fashion when the war started. They wanted to liberate women from the constraints of corsets, layers of petticoats, and heaving bosoms. Women need liberty and comfort in their dress as much as men."

"We are following in their footsteps," Alice said. "We can't afford to be singularly Couture, one of a kind, but we will be Couture. Our designs will be limited, and our quality will be the best. We hope most of our sales will be through appointment."

"Oh, I'm so excited," Beatrice Bonanutchi exclaimed, grasping her chest. "I'm going to talk to my editor, and I'd like to feature you and Alaïs and this new boutique in my column." The columnist looked around at the empty racks. "My readership will be excited. And I promise a feature column will make your opening a success!"

Kara and Alice looked at each other. They nodded and smiled.

"You must give us time to finish our boutique and our designs. Everything we sell will be under our label."

"That sounds wonderful," Beatrice Bonanutchi exclaimed. "My readers will anxiously wait for your salon to open. Could I at least see a few designs and interview you about what you did during the war?"

"When we get closer to our opening date," Kara suggested. "Hold on, I received our business cards just this week." She rummaged behind the counter and produced a box of business cards. If you give us your number, we'll give you a heads-up on our opening date."

"Thank you," Beatrice Bonanutchi exclaimed, clapping

her hands. “That will give me time to clear the article’s date with my editor!”

Kara and Alice followed the woman to the door, shook hands, locked the door, and watched as she sauntered away. When they saw the columnist hail a taxi, they turned to each other, held hands, and jumped up and down like excited children.

Chapter 7

MATTHEW REACHED across the front seat of his car and squeezed Kara's hand. "Why do you look so worried?"

Kara took a deep breath and then let it out slowly. "What if they don't like me?"

"Why wouldn't they?"

"Because they know I'm the woman who caused you a lot of grief over the past five years!"

Matthew pulled into a parking lot and turned to her. "I've given them a truthful explanation of what happened, and I didn't spare myself from the blame. I've spent years going over and over every hour of that day. I've thought of many scenarios of what I could have done differently. The problem is that no matter how hard I try, the result is the same.

"My mother had a mental breakdown, and I can only thank Dr. Hillsboro for recognizing it. I thought you were safe, and I had to deal with her. I've told you this before, and I mean it. I don't blame you for running away.

"The Rathforths and the Warners are good people. They're a bit older than us. The Rathforths are in their fifties, and the Warners are in their mid-thirties. I couldn't have picked better friends and sometimes parent substitutes."

Kara nodded. "I'll be nice." She straightened her feathered headband nervously, and Matthew took her arm. The door was opened, and suddenly they were surrounded by small children shouting at her husband.

A tall man towering several inches over Matthew waded through the children. "Let them in. Give them a chance to breathe!" he scolded.

"Sir," Matthew exclaimed, offering his hand.

"It's just Harry now," the man said with a smile. He turned his attention to Kara. "This must be the lovely Kara I've heard so much about. Kids! Settle down!"

"I apologize for my children, but they are excited to see Matthew again. Come in, come in. These stairstep boys belong to me and my wife, Sharon. Boys line up."

The boys rearranged their order, but the little girl held out her arms and was picked up by her father. "Kara, these are my boys, Jason, James, and John, and this lovely little lady is my daughter Cora Jean." He set his daughter down. "Kids! Go outside to play! It's grown-up time."

The children grumbled but followed their father's orders as Matthew and Kara were ushered into a living room, where a large man poured a drink from a bar cart.

"I'm sorry I didn't get the door fast enough," the man said. "I'm Simon Rathforth, and..." he turned his head and smiled as a woman joined them. "This is my wife, Deloris."

"So you're Kara," the woman said, offering her hand. "I'm finishing the preparation for the barbecue. Why don't you join me in the kitchen?" She gave a dismissive wave toward the men. "Let them catch up, and we'll get acquainted. Harry, you shouldn't leave the barbecue grill unattended while the little ones are in the backyard."

Kara followed Deloris into the kitchen, where every surface was covered with bowls and platters of food.

"Excuse the mess," Deloris said. "The Warners were supposed to help, but Harry's mother, Lily, fell yesterday and hurt her shoulder. She's seventy-five, and Sharon had to rush over to help her."

"I'm not much of a cook, but is there anything I can do to help?" Kara asked.

"Everything is ready," Deloris said with a grin. "Sharon and Lily will be here any minute. The men planned this barbecue, and they'll take credit for it, but the only part they are responsible for is the meat on the grill." She pulled a chair from the table for Kara to sit in and leaned back against the counter. "So, how are you and Matthew getting along?"

"So far, so good," Kara said. "Sometimes we agree, and other times have opposing views."

"Honey, that is marriage, in a nutshell," Deloris laughed. "What was it like living in the midst of the war in London?"

"Terrifying. Every day you woke up knowing it might be your last day or the last day of your friends or their families. One of the side effects was that I grew up fast," Kara admitted. "I was there with my best friend, and we joined the American Red Cross and the VAD efforts. VAD was the Voluntary Aid Detachment of civilians.

"Men will also be credited for winning the war, but women did more than their fair share, at least in England. More in some cases."

"I apologize," Deloris said. "I shouldn't have brought up the subject. I prayed daily that my husband wouldn't be called to the front, and Sharon did the same. Oh, that's Sharon, Harry's wife, pulling into the driveway now. It looks like she brought Lily. Let's go help them."

Kara followed her host to the car, was introduced, and

then her hands were filled with more bowls and platters of food.

The Rathforths and the Warners were obviously good friends, and Kara and Matthew were brought into the friendship. The women loaded the two picnic tables on the patio with food while the men began to cook hotdogs, hamburgers, and steaks on the grill. It didn't take long before everyone was filling their plates and enjoying the outdoor feast.

Matthew had wanted Kara to meet his friends and mentors. He kept his eye on her, watching her interact with the families, and was glad that she was accepted by his friends.

Kara fit in well with the women. There were five children present ranging in age from five to fifteen. The Rathforths' youngest son was a boy of fifteen named Daniel. He was in a military boarding school most of the time. Their two older sons had already left home. One lived in Virginia, and the other in Florida.

After the meal, the younger kids wanted to play kickball, and teams, including the grown men, were decided. Kara shook her head. She hadn't dressed for sports. She helped the two mothers take the foods that might spoil in the heat and stored them in the refrigerator.

Then they went outside to watch the game. While the mothers were cheering their kids, Kara was watching Lily Warner. The older woman was stretched out in a lounge chair, but she seemed to be uncomfortable. One of the younger children stopped the game and asked for a treat; Deloris and Sharon went inside to bring the desserts to the table.

Kara walked over to Lily Warner and sat next to the senior woman. "Is your shoulder bothering you?"

"A little bit," Lily said.

"I think more than a little bit," Kara said with a smile. "Try doing this."

While the dessert was being devoured, Sharon looked around. "Where is Gran?"

"She's over there," Harry Warner said. "Kara is with her. What are they doing?"

The adults watched as Kara demonstrated a move, and Lily copied her.

"Should Mom be doing that?" Harry asked.

"Kara was a Red Cross medic during the bombing raids in London," Matthew said proudly. "She wouldn't do anything to hurt someone."

"Mom, are you feeling all right?" Harry Warner asked as his mother walked toward them, rubbing her shoulder.

"Better than I have all day," Lily exclaimed. "Kara showed me some stretching exercises, and my shoulder feels better!"

"Only do them three times a day," Kara said firmly, excusing herself to go inside the house.

"Well, what do you think of Kara?" Matthew asked his friends.

"I think she's a lovely girl," Sharon said. "The shop she's planning on opening will be out of our league. She said the designer dresses could cost hundreds of dollars, and one-of-a-kind couture dresses could be a thousand or more."

"A thousand dollars for a dress?" Simon Rathforth exclaimed, looking at his wife. "Who would pay that for a dress?"

"Lots of high-society women in New York and wealthy women all over the country," Matthew answered. "They want the best and are willing to pay for it. A newspaper writer from The New York World is writing an article featuring the grand opening. Hopefully, that will give the shop a boost. This is Kara and Alice's venture, and I only know what I overheard."

Matthew squeezed Kara's hand on the drive back to the Wolcott Hotel. "What did you think of my friends?"

"I liked them, but the more important question is... did they like me?"

"They adored you," Matthew said, and then he grinned. "Although Simon and Harry are as ignorant about couture as I was before I started listening to you and Alice. I thought Simon would choke when he heard the prices for your dresses. But I was in shock because you're still running around dressed like a boy!"

Kara laughed. "Only when I'm working in the shop. We still have a million things to do before the grand opening! "

"I don't want you doing anything dangerous," Matthew scolded.

"It's silly to hire a repairman for things we can do ourselves."

"I'll come over after I leave the office," Matthew promised. "Make a list."

Matthew kept his word. He drove and parked his car as close as possible to the shop every evening. The problem was he never knew when he would complete his work or when the last client would leave the office.

Thomas' hours seemed to be more regular. He would pick up Alice between five and six in the evenings. He would help with jobs traditionally done by men, and then they would go to their townhouse. Once there, Thomas would inspect whatever work had been done by hired contractors, then, he and Alice worked on the rooms that hadn't been water-damaged, painting and wallpapering. Alice sometimes got calls in the middle of the day and had to leave to meet with delivery men.

Kara understood that Alice was busy and didn't blame

her for wanting to get her new home fixed. She and Thomas were starting a new life together. She hadn't had to do that because there was very little in Aunt Selina's penthouse that either she or Matthew wanted to change.

Still, she was left without a third set of hands.

Matthew snuck a peek at the wall clock that was behind his client. He'd listened to Mr. Grover Bristol complaining and listing his wife's faults for the last hour. Divorce wasn't Matthew's specialty, but Mr. Cahill, the senior owner of his firm, had asked him personally to take on the case.

"You are claiming that your wife is cheating on you," Matthew said. "Where is your proof? Infidelity, on either side, will make it a cut-and-dried case. Can your wife produce anything as a counterclaim before a judge?"

"Well, you know women," Bristol exclaimed. "She'll probably claim I'm catting around."

"Are you?" Matthew asked.

"I'm a man," his client blustered. "It's different for men. If she won't put out, I have the right to find a woman who would!"

"In other words, you've been unfaithful," Matthew said. "Does she have proof?"

"She might," Bristol said. "If she does, what will that mean to my finances?"

"How long have you been married?"

"Twenty-six years," Bristol admitted.

"Did she help you establish your plumbing business when you started it? Was she involved with running the business?"

"She didn't do that much," Bristol claimed. "She took care of the billing and ordered supplies."

"How many years?" Matthew demanded.

"Eleven," the man in front of him said, frowning.

"Did you have children during those years?"

"Two girls and a boy, but what's that got to do with anything?"

Matthew sat back in his chair. "Let me put this into perspective, Mr. Bristol. You founded your business with your wife's assistance for over a decade. In addition to working, your wife was married to you and having your children while you were out doing the actual plumbing jobs. During this time, she also cleaned your house, fixed dinner, and saw that your children were being raised properly.

"After almost thirty years of marriage, you have been unfaithful to your wife. You've found some sweet young thing that hangs on your every word and makes you feel like a big, important man again. Now, you want to dump your wife and continue to own all your assets."

"You can't speak to me like that," Bristol bristled.

"I'm not wrong, am I?" Matthew asked. "Go home, Mr. Bristol. Stop at a phone booth, call your girlfriend, and break up. I guarantee that your sweet little adulterous girlfriend is only after your money! Then phone your wife and tell her to dress up because you're taking her out to dinner. Stop on the way home and buy some flowers, or better yet, stop at a jewelry store and buy her a piece of expensive jewelry.

"When you're in that restaurant, take a good, long look at your wife. She may have wrinkles and gained some weight, but take a good look at yourself before you claim she's not as pretty as she used to be. She's the woman who has spent most of her life supporting your business, you, and your children. You should treat her like the Queen she is and not a piece of trash that you want to throw away. Now get out of my office. I've listened to your bullshit for damn near an hour, and my Queen is waiting for me."

"What is this?" Bristol demanded.

"This is my telling you to go to Hell," Matthew said. "If I hear that you're trying to screw over your wife, I will ensure she has the best legal team in New York City to protect her! I will change your status, and you will learn what it's like to be cast aside and left very poor. Good day, sir!"

Mr. Bristol slammed out of Matthew's office.

Matthew made a note to call the private detective his company used to monitor clients he'd just thrown out of his office. He was clearing his desk of confidential files and locking them in his desk when there was another knock on his door.

"Come in!" he shouted. His secretary had left more than an hour before.

Mr. Irving Cahill, the firm's owner, stepped into his office.

"That didn't take long," Matthew said, expecting to be censured by his boss.

"Did you throw him out on his ass?" Mr. Cahill asked.

"I did, sir."

"Good. Mrs. Bristol is a friend of my oldest daughter. I knew you could handle him. Are you sure you don't want to handle divorce cases?"

"They aren't my specialty, sir," Matthew said. "It would probably cost the firm revenue, as I'm usually on the side of the underdog."

"How is your situation working out with the return of your wife?" Mr. Cahill asked.

"Surprisingly well, sir. Kara is about to open a women's boutique," Matthew said, glancing at the clock again. "I'm sorry, sir, but I'm late to pick up my wife."

"I won't hold you any longer," Mr. Cahill said. "Call my secretary for an appointment. You've been doing a good job, and it's time to discuss your future in the firm."

"Thank you, sir," Matthew said.

As his boss turned to leave, Matthew stopped him. "Sir?"

"Yes?"

"Why did you send Bristol to me?" Matthew asked.

Irving Cahill gave a huff. "He's typical of men my age. He wants his youth back and thinks he can get it by divorcing his wife and family for a pretty young woman, a third his age. I've been married to my wife for thirty-one years, and I love her more now than I did when we said our vows. I may be old-fashioned, but I believe marriage should last until *the death do you part* happens."

"Was this a test, sir?"

"Integrity doesn't need to be tested, son," Mr. Cahill said, leaving the office. "Real integrity stands on its own!"

Matthew didn't wait for the elevator. He ran down the five levels of stairs, reviewing the words from his boss. He was over an hour late to pick up Kara, not that either of them clocked nine to five hours.

The problem was Kara didn't have a shut-off switch. She would keep working until he picked her up. Matthew was fumbling for his key when the front door to the shop opened on its own. He stepped inside, but all he saw were boxes and clothing racks.

"Kara?" Matthew shouted.

"I'm here! Help!" was a muffled reply.

"Where?" he demanded

"Over by the dressing rooms," Kara shouted.

Matthew fought his way through a maze of boxes to an area where several clothing racks were overturned, along with a stepladder. "Where?" he demanded again.

"Under the rack with the green dresses," Kara answered.

"Jesus!" Matthew exclaimed when he realized the weight of the wooden stepladder was holding down the racks that had turned over. He lifted the ladder, folded it, and set it against a wall, righted a stand with gold-colored dresses, and raised the rack with the green ones.

Kara was at the bottom of the pile, and she sat up.

"Are you hurt?" he demanded.

"No, I've just been stuck under there for a little while," she responded.

Matthew pulled his wife to her feet, inspecting her for any signs of her being hurt. He tilted her face upward and discovered a bruise on her chin and a bump on her head. "What happened?"

"One second, I was hanging up dresses; the next, I was caught under the racks."

"The ladder fell over and trapped you," Matthew said. "Do you need to go to the emergency intake?"

Kara looked into a mirror and inspected the lump on her head and the scratch on her cheek. "It's just a bump," she assessed, and then said, "Ouch!" when her husband touched it gently.

"Has the electric icebox for the back room been delivered?" Matthew asked. "You need to put ice on that goose egg."

"I'm okay," Kara insisted, still looking in the mirror. "The refrigerator is here, but the ice tray didn't ship with it. I've already complained to the company. They were supposed to deliver it today, but didn't. I can comb my hair over to hide the bump."

"I'm taking you home," Matthew said, looking around at the showroom that was in disarray. "Come on, I have to take you home and ensure nothing else is broken. Tomorrow is Saturday, and we'll sort this out if you feel up to it." He checked the locks on the back doors, closed the curtains on the windows, and locked the shop door, checking it twice.

When Matthew opened his eyes the following day, he winced upon seeing his wife's face turned toward him.

"Is it that bad?" Kara exclaimed, rolling out of bed and disappearing into the bathroom as Matthew followed her

"I look like I've gone a few rounds with Jack Dempsey!" Kara wailed.

"Turn around?" Matthew said gently, inspecting her naked body. "You bruise easily. There are only a couple of bruises on your back and shoulders. There's one on your bottom that I didn't put there, although I might add a few later for you working alone. Turn around," he instructed and continued with his inspection. "How many times have I warned you about working alone?"

Kara covered her face with her hands after looking in the mirror.

"Stop it!" Matthew said, peeling her hands from her face. "You're a trained medic, and you should have known there would be bruising."

"I can't go out looking like this," Kara exclaimed.

"Call Alice and tell her to meet you here, not at the shop. With all that makeup on your dressing table, you should be able to hide the worst of it."

"Good idea!" Kara exclaimed, and she dashed out of the bathroom.

Kara dressed in women's trousers, a relatively new way for young women to dress, primarily due to the influence of Hollywood movies and women working in factories.

"Thomas will drop off Alice on his way to their townhouse to inspect the latest work this morning. When he's done, he'll join us later to help tame the mess in the boutique," Kara said. "I called down for a room service breakfast."

"Good, that will give us time to talk," Matthew said.

Kara gave him an exasperated look. "Are you going to make a big deal out of a silly accident?"

"Yes, I am," Matthew said firmly. "I've asked you not to

work alone in the shop several times. What would have happened if you'd knocked yourself out? What would have happened if I'd been later than I was? I know Alice and Thomas have a lot going on right now. So do I, but I won't allow you to take a chance of getting hurt. I want you to hire someone to help. I don't care if it's a man who can do the heavy lifting or a woman to help you with all the frilly stuff. But you are not going to be working alone again. You have one week to hire someone, or I'll call an agency to send someone over."

"I can't just make unilateral decisions like that without Alice's input. We're equal partners."

"I'm your husband," Matthew growled as there was a knock on the door. He walked toward the door but stopped beside Kara. He gave her a hard swat across her bottom. "Neither the front nor the back door was locked! Anyone could have walked in, robbed the place, and done *God Knows What* to you! Don't fight me on this because this rule has become law, and I'm sure Thomas will agree. I will not be ignored. Am I making myself clear this time?"

Kara rubbed her stinging bottom. "Yes," she mumbled.

The knock on the door sounded again, and Matthew let the hotel employee in with the breakfast cart. He tipped the employee, and when the door closed, he returned to Kara. "Tonight's maintenance spanking will include discipline. You've been pushing the limits, and it will stop."

Chapter 8

"CAN we afford to hire a salesperson when we haven't opened the doors yet?" Kara asked.

"We don't have a choice," Alice said, opening a box. "Matthew says there has to be a second person here at all times, and you heard him talking to Thomas. Now my husband has agreed and thinks it's a good idea.

"When Matthew told Thomas about you getting hurt, I could see that both of our husbands were concerned," Alice continued. "Hiring a sales clerk before the opening isn't a bad idea. It will give her time to become acquainted with the merchandise. I'm assuming you want to hire a woman."

"Of course," Kara exclaimed. "Men in fashion may be normal in France, but I don't think it will go over well here. Plus, it would free us for one-on-one appointments with our clients. I still don't like Matthew's chauvinistic attitude," Kara said.

"Would fighting him gain you anything?" Alice asked.

"No, so I guess we'll have to put our heads together and write an advertisement for the New York World," Kara said. "I just hate when he's right all the time!"

Alice laughed. "Thomas and I have had a few tussles since we said our I do's. Marriage is marriage, and although we'll have equal rights under the law soon, don't expect men to give up their advantages."

"It's not fair that they always have the upper hand," Kara grumbled.

"As long as that hand doesn't land on my backside, I'm quite happy with Thomas," Alice laughed.

Kara laughed with her friend, and then she looked around. The storefront was beginning to look more like a high-end boutique. That was because Matthew and Thomas had spent most of the weekend following her and Alice's instructions on what needed to be done. She pulled a sheet of paper from under the counter and began writing down the qualifications required for a salesperson.

Matthew designated Friday or Saturday evenings for D/D maintenance, whichever was convenient. It was a time set aside to openly discuss any issues they were having. Maintenance usually meant Kara would have a tender bottom the following day from a spanking. Matthew's analytical mind never forgot even the slightest infractions of his rules. From swearing to outright mutiny, misbehaving was punished by him spanking her bottom. And, for what he considered severe misbehaviors, her husband brought out a paddle and left her bottom bright red and stinging.

Aside from her husband's ridiculous beliefs in D/D, Kara was pleased with how she and Matthew got along. He was doing well in his law firm and willing to help in the shop with what he called *men's* work. That meant painting walls and carrying boxes he deemed too heavy for women to lift.

The boutique's grand opening date seemed to make time fly by faster. Three weeks from their planned opening date, Kara called Beatrice Bonanutchi, the feature writer, and arranged for her to interview them. The advertisement for a sales clerk position was delivered to the *Daily News,* although there hadn't been any responses.

Miss Bonanutchi spent several hours talking to Kara and Alice. She asked questions about their backgrounds and training. She was given a few insights about when they lived in France and London during the war. Beatrice took copious notes and oohed and aahed over the garments on the racks.

"My readers are going to adore your designs," the writer gushed.

"The Grand Opening of our boutique will be one week after Paris Fashion Week and two weeks after New York's Fashion Week. We did this deliberately, as we are the up-starts. We believe in our products, but it's up to the ladies of our city to decide if they will like our styles."

"Once our fashionable ladies see what you have to offer at Kara & Alaïs Couture Designs, the boutique will be a hit," the reporter promised.

Kara and Alice were dressed in their designs for the photo shoot. When the reporter finally left, Kara locked the door and popped the cork on a bottle of French wine. They kept the bottle out of sight and drank from coffee cups.

They were enjoying the wine when there was a knock on the front door.

"Our customers can't wait!" Alice laughed as she went to answer the summons. Kara quickly removed the evidence of their drinking, although it wasn't illegal yet.

Alice returned, followed by a girl who didn't look to be past her teen years. "Kara, this is Claudina Gallo. She's here about the job."

"I must have missed it in the paper," Kara said. "I've been looking for it, and I was expecting a phone call, not a walk-in."

The young woman looked nervous. "Actually, the ad hasn't been printed yet."

"Then how did you know about it?" Alice asked.

"I saw it when it crossed my desk," Claudina said. "I know it was wrong to hold it back, but I really want this job! I work at The New York World and hate my job. I want a job in fashion."

The young woman looked around the shop and burst into tears. "This is what I want to do. I want to learn, and I want to design. I have sketches I've done, and I was told I have talent." She fumbled with a thick folder and pulled out a handful of drawings. "I just need a start and someone to believe I can do it!"

"Calm down, and we'll listen," Kara said gently. "Why don't you come into the backroom, and we can talk. Alice, double-check the door locks, please. We don't want to get into trouble again."

The young woman was settled at a small table and offered tea.

"Let's start by introducing ourselves," Kara said when Alice joined them. "I'm Kara Douglas, and this is my partner, Alice Markham. Tell us a little bit about yourself, Claudina."

"I know you won't want to hire me after I've barged in here, but I want this so bad! I had to try!" Claudina cried.

"You're good," Alice said matter-of-factly. She was looking through the sketches. "Why didn't you simply answer the advertisement?

Claudina swiped at her tears and dug into the satchel she was carrying for a handkerchief. "Because if the paper had run the advertisement, there would have been a line of qualified applicants. Women who have probably worked in high-end shops, and I have no experience. I can't compete with them. All I've ever done is type the ads for the print-setters. It's the only job my father would allow me to have because he can always keep an eye on me. I'm sorry!"

"How old are you?" Kara asked.

"Twenty-one last month," Claudina said.

"You look younger. Your father can't stop you from working if you're over twenty-one," Kara said.

"Through intimidation, he can," Alice said. "Has he always been strict and demanding?"

The young woman nodded.

"Are you still living at home?" Alice asked, and there was another nod. "Is he taking the money you earn?"

The girl nodded again. "He says he's saving it for my marriage."

"Is there anyone you could live with if you moved away from your father?" Kara asked.

"I have a friend, Emma," Claudina said, nodding. "She has a bedsitter and said I could bunk in with her."

"Does she have a phone?" Alice asked.

There's a phone in the lobby of the building. Everyone shares it."

"How did you get away from the paper today?"

"I told the woman in charge of our department that I was sick," Claudina answered.

"Do you have any experience in retail?" Kara asked.

"I worked for a couple of weeks at a five and dime. I ran the cash register there before my father made me quit," Claudina said. "I'm sorry. It was a mistake to come here. If you give me back my sketches, I'll go away."

"Have you tried to leave home before?" Alice asked.

"Several times, but he's sent the police to bring me back," Claudina said.

Kara and Alice exchanged looks and silently came to a decision.

"He could do that when you were underage. If you are twenty-one, as you say, he can't. Do you have any other relatives?"

"No, it's only him and me. I lost my mother when I was twelve. It's only been my father and me. I'm sorry for wasting your time."

"You're not wasting our time. Why do you want to work in a dress shop?" Alice asked.

"Because I want to design dresses. I've read every fashion magazine published. I get them from the public library. I've taught myself how to make alterations and to mend clothing."

Alice took a deep breath. "If you have proof that you're twenty-one, we will help you. "Do you want to go home and back to the same job?" Alice asked gently.

"Goodness, no. I've been reading fashion magazines since I was a little girl. It's all I ever wanted, but my father wants me to marry. I don't want to be forced into a marriage I don't want."

"Alice and I have both been in tough spots before," Kara said firmly. "If you want to change your circumstances, we are willing to help, but if you want help, you must first help yourself. You have to prove you're of age because we don't want to get in trouble with the law."

"Call your friend, and make sure the offer of sharing her bedsitter is still available," Alice said. "Then go home for your things. Take your birth certificate or a birth record if you can find one. Try to slip away unnoticed. Spend the night if need be. Tomorrow when your father goes to work, plead sickness again."

"Tell him it's a female problem," Kara interrupted. "That usually sends men into a frenzy to distance themselves."

Alice laughed. "It does work," she told Claudina. "Leave a note for your father, and mail a letter to your work supervisor resigning. Drop off a letter at the nearest police station telling them that you are a legal adult and leaving your home by choice. If you're of age, your father can't send the police out looking for you."

"We need proof of your age," Kara said. "You look younger than twenty-one, but I know what that's like because people have told me that my whole life."

"I know where my father keeps important papers, "Claudina said. "I've seen my birth certificate in the box."

"If you come to work here, you'll be missing in plain sight," Kara agreed. "A new haircut, some makeup, and you'll be hard to recognize."

"Why would you do this for me?" Claudina asked.

"There was a time when I had to run away," Kara admitted.

"Me too, and women need to look out for one another," Alice agreed. "My father was a lot like yours. I'm sure he meant well, and he thought he was protecting his family. But, in reality, he was smothering us. I didn't have the natural talent you possess."

"Yes, you did. You just hadn't had a chance to develop it," Kara interrupted. She turned to Claudina. "If you don't show up by mid-week, we'll know you've changed your mind." She closed the scrapbook of designs. "These are good, really good, and I would feel terrible if this was a talent wasted."

"I'll be here," Claudina gushed. "To prove it to you, I'll leave my designs here. They mean the world to me! I'll be here or call and tell you what's holding me up. Thank you, and I'll be the best clerk ever! I really will!"

"I believe you, and we're willing to help," Kara said. "But, you must be willing to work as hard as we do."

"I will," Claudina exclaimed. She looked around the storage room and the clock. "May I use your phone?"

"It's on the counter in the shop," Alice said.

"I have four hours before my father is due back home,"

the young woman said excitedly. She jumped from her seat and ran into the other room.

Kara followed, listened behind the curtained doorway, and returned to Alice. "She's talking to her friend. Goodness, what is this going to cost us?"

"She's a beginner, so she'll earn about eleven or twelve dollars a week," Alice said. "More important is what our husbands will think about helping this girl? If she's lying, we will be in deep trouble."

"We're not hiring her until she shows us proof of her age," Kara said firmly. "We're hiring a clerk who is interested in learning the trade. Her personal problems are not our business."

"I agree," Alice said firmly. "But, if this backfires, we will both get skinned."

"Excuse me," Claudina said, knocking on the doorframe. "I'm leaving now. My father won't be home until after seven o'clock. Emma's coming with me to help me pack my things."

"Don't forget the letters and the proof of your age," Kara warned.

"I won't," Claudina exclaimed with a happy smile. "I'll see you tomorrow." She turned to leave and then turned back. "What time should I be here?"

"Nine in the morning," Alice said.

"On the dot," the young girl exclaimed and rushed out of the shop.

Thomas looked around the shop and nodded his head in approval. "The shop looks ready for a grand opening to me! That short dress and the hat display look great in the window. When are you opening the curtains?"

"As soon as we finish organizing the storage room and back room," Alice said. "All the deliveries have come in except for the fox fur wraps and the silk stockings."

"Have you hired a clerk yet?" Thomas asked.

"As a matter of fact, we did," Alice said. "She's supposed to start tomorrow."

"I was hoping you would hire a man," Thomas said.

"So was I," Matthew said, entering from the shop's back room.

"If you haven't noticed, this is a women's boutique," Kara said, smiling at both men. "Women don't feel comfortable undressing with men around."

"Note taken," Matthew agreed. "Is there anything we need to do? Lift or carry?"

"Yes," Kara said. "Two sewing machines were delivered this afternoon, and we'd like to have them moved upstairs. We've decided to use the upstairs room for making our one-of-a-kind couture dresses."

Matthew and Thomas removed their suitcoats and uncrated the heavy machines. They carried them upstairs and stifled their swearing.

"Anything else?" Thomas asked.

"No, we can go home now," Alice said, kissing him.

"I had good news today," Matthew said as he opened the car door for Kara. He walked around the car and got in the driver's seat. "Mr. Cahill called me into his office today. He's promoting me to a Junior Partner position in the Cahill, Gordon & Reindel Law Firm."

"What does that mean?"

"More status, more work, and harder cases," Matthew said, smiling. "That's what I've been working toward since I returned to the firm. Now that the war is over, the International London branch will reopen. There will be some shifting of positions as we lose men to that facility."

"They aren't considering you for a London assignment, are they?"

"No. Most international assignments are given to attorneys who speak several languages. I don't. But it means I have a better chance of promotion here."

"You've never been to Britain," Cara said. "The accents are hard to understand, and they exaggerate them further when talking to a Yank!"

"Well, I'm not going to worry about that," Matthew said, laughing. "There's plenty of work to go around. It might mean that I'll be later to pick you up in the evenings."

"I could buy another car," Kara said. "I still have the insurance payout from the Silver Ghost."

"No," Matthew said simply and firmly.

"I know how to drive," Kara complained. "I have a license!"

"A New York driver's license is little more than an identification card. You don't have to know the road rules or even prove you've ever driven a vehicle to get one. I've seen you drive. You're a menace, a danger to yourself and anyone sharing the road."

"I'm not that bad," Kara complained.

"No," Matthew repeated firmly. "Either Thomas can take you home, or you can hail a cab if I'm running late. For that matter, call Mr. Daniels, the concierge. I'm sure he'll be able to make arrangements for you."

"I like to drive," Kara complained. "I drove all the time when I lived in London."

"You drove an ambulance. Your patients wanted you to get them to the hospital as quickly as possible, as long as they arrived alive. You're still driving like that, and from what I saw of your driving, it was reckless," Matthew said. "The next time we go to Long Island, I'll let you drive. Maybe you can change my mind."

Not wanting to start the weekend with an argument, Kara didn't push the subject. The time they'd spent together lately had been sparse. Their evenings had been busy. She was busy working in her study. Matthew's work was usually spread out over the kitchen table. She'd awakened several times in the middle of the night to find her husband working on his law case while she slept.

Chapter 9

MATTHEW PULLED into an empty parking space, and Kara gave him a quick kiss and jumped out, giving her husband a wave and watching as he maneuvered his way back into traffic. A cab swerved around him, honking impatiently.

She held her breath for a second, but there was no crunch of metal. New York City did have a traffic problem and a reckless, impatient driver problem. Walking down the sidewalk toward the boutique, Kara saw Claudina Gallo dart from behind a parked truck. She was carrying a small suitcase.

"Are you okay?" Kara asked the young girl as she unlocked the front door.

Claudina nodded, but she was obviously scared. She followed Kara inside. "I'm just scared my father will try to stop me. Last night, he said I should cook dinner for a young man he wants me to meet."

"Get inside," Kara said, stepping aside. Then her mouth dropped open as Alice turned into the alley beside the shop and parked in the only parking space allotted to the shop, next to a delivery platform.

"Hi," Alice said. "What's wrong?"

"Thomas hands you the keys to his car, but Matthew won't let me drive at all!" Kara complained.

"You're a terrible driver," Alice said matter-of-factly. "I know it, and you know it. You just won't admit it. I'll be driving myself to work from now on, and I'll be able to pick you and Claudina up in the morning and take you home after we close the shop. Thomas was issued a truck by his company because he's supervising two large projects near Battery Park. Did our waif show up this morning?"

"She's already inside," Kara said. "She looks scared out of her wits."

"I was the same when I first left Weehawken. Thank goodness for secondary night classes," Alice said, looping her arm through her friend's with a wide smile. "Let's go see what trouble we can get into!"

Claudina had laid out several papers on the glass cosmetic/jewelry counter. There was a diploma from a primary school. There was also the required birth certificate.

"That's enough proof for me," Kara said. "Are you ready to begin training on how to be a clerk and a dressmaker?"

Claudina nodded her head. "Emma was wonderful, helping me to pack my things. She called her boyfriend, and he drives a taxi. We were in and out of the apartment in no time."

"But, you're still scared?" Alice guessed. "If you're over twenty-one, your father can't force you to live at home or force you into a marriage you don't want."

"I know," Claudina nodded, but her face crumpled.

"I know. I know," Alice soothed, hugging her. "You love your father and don't want to leave, but he hasn't given you any other choice, has he?"

"I'm afraid of being caught and recognized," Claudina said, wiping her face.

"We can take care of that," Kara said. "With makeup, the right hairdo, and the right clothes, he won't recognize you. What's your middle name?"

"Elizabeth."

"What is your grandmother's maiden name?" Alice asked.

"Berkley," Claudina said, catching on. "Oh! I can change my name. I've always wanted to be called Elizabeth, but my father insisted I go by Claudina because I was named after his father. I never met my grandfather."

"All right, Elizabeth Berkley, it's time for the caterpillar to change into a butterfly," Kara said.

An hour later, Kara and Alice looked at each other and clapped their hands. Then they turned the newly named Elizabeth to face a full-length mirror.

"Oh my, is that me?" Elizabeth gasped.

"That's the new you," Kara agreed.

Elizabeth ran her finger through her short hair and stroked the feathered headband.

"Is there anything you want to change?" Alice asked.

Elizabeth smiled. "I've always wanted to have blonde hair like yours. Can that be done?"

"Yes, but it's a lot of upkeep, expensive, and it could damage your hair," Kara said. "I've heard horror stories about women losing all their hair from the chemicals used."

"You don't need blonde hair to be beautiful. I don't think anyone will recognize you now," Alice said.

"I love it. I look so different and modern," Elizabeth exclaimed. "I can't believe it's me."

"It's you," Alice said with a smile.

"I don't mean to sound ungrateful, but how much will I earn? I have to pay half of the rent of the bedsitter."

"How much were you earning at the newspaper?" Kara asked.

"Ten dollars a week, but they always gave it to my father."

"We can afford eleven," Alice said. "As you learn, your salary will go up. Do you think that's fair?"

"More than fair," Elizabeth said.

"We have a week before the grand opening," Kara said. "In that time, we'll show you how to work the cash register and how to greet and help customers. You'll need several dresses equal in quality to the one you're wearing. We have to represent the fashions we're selling. And we need to find you some better shoes!"

Elizabeth looked down at her bare feet.

"Try this shoe on," Kara said, removing one of her shoes.

Elizabeth tried to slide her foot into the shoe, but it was too tight. "My feet are too big," she said.

"Actually, I think they might be the right size," Alice said, looking at her partner. "Are you thinking about Selina's shoes?"

"I am," Kara said. "There is a huge box of Selina's shoes in the back closet, along with her pre-war clothing. They are too big for me and too small for you. They might fit Elizabeth. It's worth a try. I kept most of the dresses because we can cut them down to size for our use, and now for Elizabeth. The fabrics are so beautiful that I didn't want to discard them. We can bring them in with us in the morning."

Kara looked down at her outfit of loose women's trousers and a loose blouse. "If we're going to sell couture, we have to dress it and represent it. I'm going to miss my trousers."

"Then we'll have to include wide-legged trousers in our designs," Alice said. "Just because the war is over doesn't mean women will want to give up their trousers."

"That's an excellent idea," Kara agreed. "I'll start working on the designs."

All three women practiced transactions on the cash register. Kara and Alice pretended to be customers, and their new hire was instructed on greeting customers and potential buyers. She even practiced answering the phone with the boutique's name. The time went by fast. Before they knew it, it was quitting time.

"Should I leave my new clothes here?" Elizabeth asked.

Kara exclaimed. "The outfit you are wearing is yours now, and tomorrow we'll take you over to my place, and we'll go through my aunt's shoes and clothing that we can give you. She was about your size, so we shouldn't have to alter them much. Alice, can you drive Elizabeth home, pick her up in the morning, then come by my place?

"It sounds like a good idea to me," Alice said. "Elizabeth is going to need her own make-up too."

"Again..." Kara said. "I have loads of makeup. I went a little crazy when we returned to the States, and it was available." She turned to Elizabeth. "Alice and I spent the nearly five years of the war in England."

Elizabeth nodded. "I know. I read the article, Miss Bonanutchi wrote for the paper. I thought that if you were brave enough to volunteer during a war, I should be brave enough to stand up against my father. Only I wasn't. I tried to talk to him about going back to school or getting an apprenticeship to be a seamstress.

"He laughed at me and said I wasn't smart enough. He said I didn't know what was best for me, and he did. Why can't he believe I know what is right for me?"

"Because he's a typical father of his time," Alice said. "My father was the same. Many girls are raised in an environment where the father figure is always right. Most don't have the fortitude to go against their families. I was there myself a long time ago. We don't want you to worry, Elizabeth Berkley. You are safe with us."

Matthew was late arriving home, but he had great news.

"Kara!" he shouted when he walked through the suite but saw no sign of his wife.

"Back here!" was a muted response.

Matthew found Kara in the third bedroom, surrounded by piles of clothing, shoes, and hats. This was a room they were planning to turn into an office for him.

"Did a hurricane hit this room?" he asked.

"No, this is actually the first step in clearing out this room so you can have an office," Kara exclaimed, popping up from behind a large box. "Our new hire showed up for work this morning, and we think she will work out fine, except she doesn't have an appropriate wardrobe. Elizabeth is about the same size as Aunt Selina, so passing on some of these beautiful things to her makes sense."

"I hope she works out," Matthew said. "I have some good news."

"What would that be?" Kara asked.

"I was given the lead on a case today, and I'm probably going to need this room as a home office because there will be a lot of overtime, and I don't have to do it at the office."

"What's the case about?" Kara asked.

"The structural collapse of the DeLuca building three years ago," Matthew said. "The building was only twelve years old. During the demolition, structural errors were discovered. The failures had been noted by inspectors three years before the building collapsed. Improper materials were responsible, and the list of violations is a mile long. The citations were ignored. Eighteen people were killed when the building collapsed. Twenty-nine were seriously injured. The suit was filed against the DeLuca brothers by the families who lost their family members or were injured."

"That's horrible," Kara said. "Can you prove the owners knew they built an unsafe building?"

"That's my job," Matthew said. "They are guilty, although they will try to claim innocence. I intend to make them pay for their negligence." He pointed to the boxes. "Is there anything I can do to help clean up this mess?"

"No, Alice, Elizabeth, and I will work on this tomorrow morning," Kara said.

"Good, because I want to take my wife to dinner," Matthew said. "Believe it or not, I'm tired of the fancy food from downstairs. I want a pizza with everything from Lombardi's."

"That sounds good," Kara agreed. "Can I wear my trousers?"

"It's casual, but I don't know if it's that casual," Matthew said.

"Then give me five minutes to change," Kara said.

Matthew followed her to their bedroom and closet. His wife's statement of five minutes meant twenty to thirty minutes. He'd already accepted that she would change outfits several times when she dressed for any occasion. When Kara was stripped down to panties and a bra, he nudged her.

Kara threw her head back against his chest. "It's either me or pizza."

"Can't I have both?" Matthew asked.

"Not when Lombardi's serves the best pizza during the evening dinner rush," she teased. "You can have me later."

"Deal," Matthew said. He rubbed his hand across his chin. "While you're getting dressed, I'll spiff up. It's been a long day."

When Matthew joined his wife, she wore what the magazines called the 'flapper look.' A straight shift covered her knees, and her hosiery was out of sight beneath her dress. They had already had several discussions, and he had been firm about a respectable girl wearing garters under the skirt and out-of-sight. He did not like the rolled-down stockings look.

He and Thomas agreed to their wives wearing the fashionable Couture dresses they designed in their shop. But, they also insisted that when they weren't in the shop, the more laid-back look of a blouse or cardigan with a pleated skirt was more appropriate for everyday wear. There was a little more leg showing than Matthew would have preferred, but as he'd been told, times were changing. Women's fashions were challenging the status quo. The war had put women to work, and women working was a direct defiance of the old male guard of the past. Men couldn't lord over their wives as the breadwinners.

Matthew didn't think he was old-fashioned. He just didn't want other men looking at his wife. Between him and Thomas, they tried to handle the areas where strength and knowledge of traditional male skills were needed.

Thomas was the master of all trades, but Matthew tried to help when his minimal skills with tools could save his wife from taking on the projects. He knew she could do most things but didn't want his Kara hurt.

Lombardi's was full of customers, as it was most of the time. They ordered drinks and went out on the balcony to enjoy the cacophony of voices, talking and laughing, with music in the background. It was an hour before their number was called, and they slid into a cozy table with only two chairs. A waiter finally brought their drinks, and they ordered a pizza.

It was hard to talk and be heard over the loud voices. A large man wearing a bandana tied over his hair and a stained apron came to their table."

"Matthew, my friend!" The large man exclaimed loudly. "Why has it taken you so long to return?"

"I've been busy, Sal," Matthew shouted over the noise of someone turning up the sound of music. "This is my wife, Kara. Kara, this is Sal Bianchi. I helped him on a legal matter last year."

"You saved my home from those cheats!" Sal bellowed. He turned around to all the people at the surrounding tables. "This man is a good lawyer! Not a cheat and not a blowhard. He saved my home from being taken from me by cheats! This is a good man to trust!"

"Sal," Matthew protested.

"No! You are my friend and the best lawyer in the city. Follow me! You get the best seats in the house. Follow me!" He scooped the wine glasses off the table and turned to Matthew. "Come, come! I owe you. My whole family owes you, and we don't forget our debts or our friends!"

With little choice, Matthew with Kara followed Sal through the crowded restaurant.

Sal went up several stairs and opened the door to an enclosed booth with a small table inside. "Sit, enjoy. I'll bring your food."

"We've already ordered a pizza," Matthew said. "It should be coming out soon."

"I'll find it," Sal said, shaking Matthew's hand again. "I'll take care of you and your beautiful wife! Anything you want, you ask. It's yours!"

"You don't owe me anything, Sal," Matthew said.

"You're my friend," Sal exclaimed. "What is mine is yours!"

"You've made a conquest there," Kara said with a smile.

"He's a good man," Matthew said. "He's the sole supporter of his family, and that's sixteen relatives. He was coerced into signing for a loan that jeopardized the ownership of his home. It took strong-arm tactics, but the matter was finally settled out of court. He knows now not to sign anything without an attorney's advice first."

"Was he a pro bono client?"

"He was," Matthew admitted.

The wait was a long one, and finally, a knock on the cubicle's door, and Sal opened it. He set a large pizza tray on the table, along with a bottle of wine. Then he stepped out and unloaded a tray of appetizers and other dishes.

"Sal, we can't possibly eat all of this," Matthew protested.

"Try, and what you can't, I'll pack it to go! Eat! Eat and enjoy, my friend!"

"If we eat all this, they'll have to take us out in wheelbarrows," Kara laughed.

Matthew picked up the bottle of wine and turned the label so she could read it. "Is this a good one?"

"It is," Kara admitted. "But, I'm only good for two small glasses; otherwise, I'm drunk, and you're driving."

"We'll leave it unopened," Matthew said. "Dig in."

Dinner was delicious, but they had four times more food than they could eat in days. It was nice to have the privacy of the booth. After they had finally convinced Sal that they couldn't eat another bite, he had the table cleared and refused any payment from 'his God-sent attorney'!

They left the restaurant with two large grocery bags, a bottle of wine, and a promise to return the dishes.

"What are we going to do with all these leftovers?" Matthew asked as he drove into the garage at the Wolcott Hotel. "It would take a week for us to eat all this."

"I have an idea," Kara said, directing him to a door they didn't usually use and down a hallway. She knocked on a door, stenciled *Maintenance*, and it was opened by an older man in coveralls.

"Mrs. Douglas, is something wrong?"

"Not at all, Mr. Groban," Kara said with a smile. "This is my husband, Matthew, and we just came from Lombardi's. My husband knows the manager, and he loaded us with far more food than we could possibly eat. I thought your men might like a treat."

"We'd appreciate it," Mr. Groban exclaimed. "Not many ever think about the crews that keep this place running. Even as a little girl, you always brought my men candy and snacks."

"You didn't tattle on me when I snuck away from my nanny," Kara teased.

"What were you doing that he didn't tattle on you?" Matthew asked as they walked to the private elevator.

"I was given a tricycle by one of Aunt Selina's male friends when I was a little girl. The only problem was I wasn't allowed to ride in the suite. Selina called and asked maintenance to remove it. I followed them to the basement maintenance area crying. That's when I met Mr. Groban. He dried my tears, gave me chocolate, and put my tricycle in his office. He would let me ride it in the hallway outside his office when I could slip away. Depending on who was watching me, I disappeared quite often."

"Poor, little rich girl," Matthew said. "Aunt Selina wasn't the best parent."

"I've never denied it," Kara admitted. "She didn't either. But she took me in, and in her own way, she cared for me. She lived by her own terms, and very few women can claim that."

Matthew stopped her and tilted her chin up to face him. "Complaints?"

"I resent the rules," Kara said honestly. "But not enough to toss you out of my life again. I'm going to take a shower."

Kara stepped into the oversized bathtub and pulled the curtain around so she could use the shower attachment. She wasn't surprised when Matthew joined her. He kissed her deeply, turned her around to face him, and nudged her with his sex. His height prevented them from having face-to-face sex standing up. Instead, he turned her around and bent her over. She steadied herself with her hands against the tiles and spread her legs apart as he plunged deep into her. Kara loved it when her husband was commanding during sex. There was no doubt about who was in charge, and she liked it that way.

She also knew Matthew had kept several sex manuals when he'd gone through the illegal books from Selina's dresser. She knew where he'd hidden the books he hadn't sent out with the trash. Kara didn't care where Matthew learned his skills as long as it wasn't from another woman.

Kara gasped at the fierceness of his taking her, but she enjoyed being taken.

She couldn't help a moan when he withdrew, but a second later moaned again as he entered her arse. This was a new method of sex, and it had taken a few tries before it became a favorite. The sensations she felt inside were incredible, although they never brought her to the point of having a climax. Even so, they both enjoyed it.

Kara always knew when Matthew was getting close. His stiff erection became rigid and hard. Thrusting into her, he accepted what she gave willingly. Suddenly Matthew withdrew from her body. He disposed of a condom and replaced it with another. Then he entered her sex again.

He plundered her with his hardened penis, driving her to an orgasm and then another. Her husband pounded his sex into her until he finally let himself come with a masculine growl.

Laying his forehead against her naked back, he pulled her against him and turned her around to face him.

They kissed and laughed and dried each other with

towels. Matthew carried Kara to their bed with a sweep of his arms. She knew his conquest of her body would continue. There had been many improvements and changes in their revised sex life and marriage. His possession of her had been irksome at first. Now she realized it was one of many ways he expressed his love for her.

Chapter 10

KARA RAN to open the door to her flat with a slice of cold pizza in her hand.

"Ugh!" Alice exclaimed, coming in and making a face. She was followed by Elizabeth.

"I like cold pizza." Kara waved her hand toward the kitchen. "There are three slices left."

"For breakfast, no thanks," Alice said.

Elizabeth was looking around at the suite in awe. "This is where you live?" she whispered.

"It was an inheritance from my aunt," Kara said. "I was dragging out a bunch of boxes last evening and this morning." She led the way into the third bedroom. "Matthew is gone, so you can strip down to your slip."

"We should start with the shoes," Alice suggested.

"Those are in boxes, marked shoes," Kara said, spinning around and opening two large boxes. "I know everything looks like chaos, but really it's organized.

"What size are you?" Alice asked Elizabeth looking into the large boxes.

"A size seven and a half or an eight," Elizabeth said.

Kara dove headfirst into a box and stood up, holding up three sets of black high heels.

"They fit," Elizabeth said, standing up to walk in the shoes, although she was wobbling.

"Let's try this another way," Alice suggested. "First, Elizabeth can try on a dress or a suit, and then we'll find the best shoes to go with it. Elizabeth, don't break a leg. Wearing high heels takes practice."

Elizabeth was a good fit for most of the professional-looking suits. They only needed a tuck around the waist for a better fit.

The dresses were more of a flapper style, shifts and showing a hint of the girl's knees if she raised her arms.

"Perfect!" Kara exclaimed. "You look like a professional clerk!"

Elizabeth looked around the room. "I appreciate you doing this for me, but I don't have room for all these things. I share a room with my friend Emma, and the closet is small."

"Don't worry about it," Kara said. "We'll box the things we're giving you, and they can be stored in the room above the shop. You can alternate your wardrobe anytime you want."

Elizabeth turned back to the mirror. "I can't dress like this in my neighborhood. I'd stand out like a sore thumb."

"That's not a problem," Alice said. "You can wear your usual clothes and change when you get to work.

"I feel bad for Elizabeth," Kara told Matthew, picking up a box to carry to the front room. Thomas had promised to bring his truck by the following day. All the things given to Elizabeth and the boxes of clothing made of rare silks and other materials would be reused.

"I appreciate you turning this room into an office for me," Matthew said, picking up a heavy box. Mr. Groban had already offered help from his maintenance crew to move everything to the loading dock in the morning. "Don't forget to give me Elizabeth's birth certificate and the other papers that prove she's of age. I'll have photographs taken of them tomorrow at the firm. She doesn't look twenty-one, and if her father disapproves of her actions, it might become a problem."

"She has proof of her age," Kara said.

"Documents can be forged," Matthew said. "It never hurts to be cautious."

"Alice said the neighborhood she's living in isn't the best," Kara said. "I was tempted to offer her the room on the third floor."

"Don't," Matthew said firmly. "You don't know her that well, and don't leave her alone in the shop. For the time being, keep her off the cash register."

Kara wanted to protest, but Matthew's stern look made her nod in agreement. It was true. They'd known Elizabeth only a few days. Kara didn't want to believe the young woman was lying, but sometimes the people you trusted could let you down. No one knew that better than her husband.

"All right, I'll talk to Alice, and we'll keep an eye on her," she promised.

The following week flew by. A sign in the window counted down the days to the Grand Opening. There was so much left to do that they didn't believe they would be done in time, and then suddenly, they were done and ready. Alice and Kara checked the lists several times and hadn't missed anything.

Beatrice Bonanutchi ran a small reminder advertisement at the end of her column, and the phone was already ringing.

Most women asked if they could preview the couture designs. Each call was answered politely, and they were told that private sessions could be arranged, but only after a visitation to the shop."

Alice, Elizabeth, and Kara arrived at the shop an hour early and thought it was strange that all the parking spaces alongside the sidewalk were lined with expensive vehicles until they realized the women in the cars were waiting for the boutique doors to open.

Elizabeth ran upstairs to redress while Alice and Kara checked their makeup and deportment. Kara filled the cash register, and Alice went to the display window pulling the shutters aside. She could already see young women exiting their cars and looking at the window displays.

Elizabeth joined them. "Do I look all right?"

"Perfect from head to toe!" Kara said.

Alice picked up the last two signs from the counter and handed one to Kara. They walked to their positions at the front door and the window display. At exactly nine o'clock, they replaced the countdown signs with OPEN signs and opened the door.

In the first few hours, they knew the shop would be a success. Kara and Alice manned the floor, introduced themselves, and, with Elizabeth's help, pointed women in the right direction for their needs. The three dressing rooms were constantly full, and rarely did a customer not purchase the dress or outfit they'd tried on. Several women came into the store, introduced themselves, and made private appointments that would begin the following week, sometimes looking at the merchandise and giving their size for a 'hold' on the garment or asking to look in the *couture* book of designs.

It was a busy day, and fifteen minutes before closing, Kara rang a bell and announced that the shop would be closing. There was a rush of women to check out, and two women were arguing over the last black sequined flapper dress on a rack. Alice intervened, and Elizabeth was sent upstairs to find the sequined shift in the correct size.

When the sign on the door was turned over to CLOSED and the display window shuttered, Kara went into the back storage room and came out with a bottle of wine and three glasses. "Ladies, we deserve to toast our success!"

With the customers gone, they took a short break. Then Kara and Elizabeth went upstairs and began to bring down more merchandise. Alice emptied the cash register, went into the small office space to count the receipts, and then joined them after locking the money in a hidden safe. Replenishing the stock took them more than an hour, in addition to straightening items on display and cleaning the dressing rooms.

"We made a hefty profit today," Alice said when Elizabeth went upstairs to change clothes and remove her makeup. "I'll tally what we sold today, but we can't expect this kind of a crowd every day."

"You two can leave," Kara said. "I'll mop my way out the door when Matthew arrives.

"That's not going to happen," Alice said. "Elizabeth can leave, but Matthew and Thomas agreed that we wouldn't be left alone here. Our husbands have been accommodating thus far, and I don't want to cross Thomas. If Matthew is going to be late, he'll call, and I'll drop you off at the hotel."

Elizabeth said goodbye and left, then Kara and Alice brought out their sketchbooks and began to make a list of what designs they would produce next. They were working with a woman who had a small sewing shop. With five seamstresses, the shop could create high-fashion designs as needed.

Matthew was on time, and he congratulated everyone on

their success. Locking the shop and metal security doors, he turned to Kara. "Your grand opening was a success!"

"We also have six private appointments next week," Kara said with a smile.

"No one complained about the prices?" he asked.

"Women who can afford couture don't quibble about the prices," Kara said. "They loved our designs. The women who didn't purchase are waiting to see if our designs meet their one-of-a-kind expectations."

"I'm still shocked that women will pay that kind of money for a dress. You can buy a dress at Macy's for under three dollars!" Matthew exclaimed.

"A horrible little housewife dress with huge pockets, or it comes with a matching apron," Kara said. "Our clientele, for the most part, don't cook or have to pinch pennies."

"Will there ever be a time when you want to be a housewife and a mother?" Matthew asked, as he turned into the garage area behind the Wolcott Hotel. He turned to face her.

Kara was silent, and he exited the car and opened the garage door. Then he came back and drove the car inside. They entered the hotel from a rear door, made their way to the top floor by private elevator, and entered the apartment.

"You haven't answered my question," Matthew said.

"I'm not sure of the answer," Kara said. "There was a time when I was happy being your wife and expecting our baby. Then I was a walking wreck for months. It was Selina who introduced me to high fashion. It was couture that captured my imagination. And then there was the war, and no one knew if they would survive from day to day."

"Kara..."

"I don't blame you anymore," she interrupted. "We were both young, stupid, and victims. There is a part of me that has blocked off what happened. I don't want to think about it. I'm also not the child that I was back then. Alice and I have worked hard to build the shop, and regardless of your newfound rules, and male confidence, I won't give up what we have achieved.

"I'm not saying a child would be unwanted, but many working women have someone care for their children while working. I've never been responsible for children, so I don't know how I would react if I got pregnant. We've been using protection, and I trust you not to deceive me or sabotage the prophylactic. If we decide to have a child, it has to be mutually agreed upon."

Matthew pulled her into a tight hug. "Thank you for being honest. I wouldn't deceive or trick you, but sometimes women get pregnant despite using condoms. They could have a small hole or tear. We were both victims, and I've never totally forgiven myself."

"We can't turn back time," Kara said. "We can only look forward."

"Forward," Matthew agreed, giving her a kiss. "I hate to say this, but I need to spend an hour or two on my new case."

"Good, because my creative mind has wanted to get to my sketchbook all day, but we were too busy. I'll call downstairs and order dinner. Any preference?"

"Surprise me," Matthew said. "I'll spread out my papers on the dining table. It will have to do until I can get Thomas to help me move my desk here."

"According to Alice, Thomas is swamped with work," Kara said. "His schedule is worse than yours. That's why he gave Alice his car to use."

"I know what you're thinking, and the answer is no," Matthew said. "We'll make time Sunday for a driving lesson, but you're not getting behind the wheel until I know you'll be safe! You're too familiar with driving on the wrong side of the road."

It was nearly midnight before Matthew tossed a handful of papers on the table and retired to the bedroom. He expected Kara to be sleeping, but she wasn't there. Going to the room she used as a studio, he found her asleep, with her head pressed against a drawing.

"Sweetheart, wake up," Matthew said, giving her a gentle shake.

"Ummm," was her only response, as he suspected it would be. Kara had always been a deep sleeper. Pulling her from the chair, he lifted her into his arms and carried her to their bedroom. Laying her in the bed, he left her and went into the bathroom for a washcloth. She had an imprint on her cheek of the design she'd been working on.

Kara woke up to her husband cleaning her face. "What?"

Matthew held up the washcloth to display the ink on the cloth.

"Oh," Kara exclaimed. "What time is it?"

"Past time for you to be asleep, although you won't be thinking of sleep for a while," Matthew promised as he unbuttoned her blouse, revealing that she hadn't bothered with wearing a brassiere. Her breasts were gloriously naked.

"Oh," a now awake Kara gasped as he demonstrated why she wouldn't be sleeping. Suddenly, she was wide awake.

Matthew trailed a slow path downward, removing her trousers and underwear. When she was naked, Kara became his play toy. He played with her breasts and worked his way down her body. It didn't take long before she was writhing with lust and wanting him to take her. She stroked his manhood, although he was already stiff and in need.

Knowing it was late, Matthew wouldn't delay what they both wanted. As her legs wrapped around his waist, he plunged into her.

It didn't take long before Kara responded with an

orgasm. Matthew rolled her over, not losing their linked bodies, and his wife didn't disappoint him. She began to rock against him, riding his sex. As she rocked, he thrust upward, filling her completely. When he was about to come, he switched their position again. This time he placed her legs over his shoulder and drove into her until both of their bodies seized.

His orgasm was over quick enough, but he wouldn't stop. He knew Kara could have multiple orgasms and wouldn't deny her sexual responses.

Matthew pumped and worked Kara's sex until she finally relaxed and moaned. She was hot, sweaty, and tired. She was spent, and he was satisfied.

As they separated, Matthew pulled her from the bed, and they entered the bathroom and stepped into the tub. Turning on the shower, he soaped her body and turned her around to face him, pulling her into a long kiss.

Kara stepped back and went to her knees. She took him in her mouth and rolled her tongue around the head of his penis.

Matthew closed his eyes as he felt his body reacting again. He'd never expected this, and he was fully aroused in seconds. The wet slide of her tongue was more than his control could endure. He was pulsing with the need to come again. Pulling her back to her feet, he turned her around and bent her over the tub edge. With a deep thrust, he was inside her again. He thrust into her, and it took a few seconds for them to gain control again, and he pulled her upright and into his arms. They stepped under the water spray again, and he held her steady as she stepped out from under the water.

Drying off, they returned to the bedroom and straightened the sheets and blankets before climbing into the bed and holding each other.

"Where did you learn that?" Matthew asked.

"From a book Aunt Selina had hidden in her closet. The title is *Ideal Marriage: Its Physiology and Techniques*. Did you like what I did?"

"It's every man's dream, but I didn't expect it," Matthew whispered. "I loved it."

"That's what counts," Kara said. "If you touch me down there, I don't see why I shouldn't reciprocate."

"You amaze me," Matthew said. "Thank you." He didn't get a reply and looked down to find Kara asleep. He kissed her forehead and closed his eyes.

"Kara!" Matthew's shout opened her eyes.

"What?"

"We forgot to turn on the alarm," Matthew exclaimed, jumping out of bed.

"Damn it!" Kara exclaimed, jumping out of bed and dodging his hand aimed at her bare bottom. She ran into her closet.

Matthew was on the run too. They were running a half-hour late. He managed to get dressed before she did and filled his pockets with the personal items that he left in a tray on his dresser every night when he went to bed.

It was a kiss-and-run morning with no time for breakfast. As Matthew passed Kara on his way to the front door, she stopped him long enough for a kiss and handed him a mug of coffee. "Thanks. Don't plan on working Sunday. You need a day off, and we'll head north for a driving lesson." With his hand on the doorknob, Matthew stopped. "Oh, and Rathforths invited us to a barbecue around six o'clock. I told him I had to check with your schedule first."

"I'm clear," Kara responded. "I have to get downstairs. Alice will be here any second! I have to get my sketchbook!"

"Shoes, too," Matthew said with a smile.

Kara made it downstairs in time, so Alice wouldn't have

to try to park, but it took her three false tries because she'd forgotten things she needed, including shoes. She was laughing at herself because she wasn't usually a scatterbrain.

The second day at the shop was as profitable as the first day. The shop was five customers short of the Grand Opening day, but the sales receipts indicated the women spent more than the previous day. The lunch hour was bustling. It was a long day, and after the door closed for the last time, they repeated the previous day's restocking and cleaning.

"Well, Elizabeth, have you found your calling?" Alice teased when the young woman finished filling a rack of dresses.

"I love this job," Elizabeth exclaimed with a wide smile. "I just wish I didn't have to hide from my father."

"I don't know how to work around that," Alice said.

"Take the train to Prospect Hill," Kara suggested. "Go to the post office and ask for a mailbox. I read somewhere that it costs about three dollars a year. You can write your father and assure him that you are safe and well. You don't have to give the post office your real address, and you will be the only one who retrieves mail from your box."

"That's a good idea," Alice said. "Write a letter to him, so he won't be worried, and you should be honest with him. Tell him why you left your job and what you want to accomplish, but don't give him too many details."

"You don't have to give him details," Kara repeated. "But definitely remind him that you are an adult and wish to be treated as one."

"Post offices close at five p.m.," Elizabeth said. "I'd have to take part of a day off."

"Give us a week," Alice said. "The store will settle down, and we'll be able to spare you then. Since this is our idea, you won't be docked."

Elizabeth hugged Alice and then Kara. "I still can't believe how you've taken me in. You're my heroes."

Kara looked over to Alice. "We understand because we've been in your shoes. Not exactly the same circumstances, but we understand desperation. Alice has been my hero for years."

Alice laughed. "And, you're mine, so we're even. Now let's go home. Hopefully, my husband will be home on time."

Chapter 11

KARA BACKED the car up a good quarter of a mile, including a sharp turn, stopped, and then did a perfect three-point turn. She backed the car again, pulled onto a paved road, and turned to Matthew with a smug smile.

"Has Alice been giving you driving lessons?" Matthew asked.

"No, I told you I was a good driver," Kara claimed.

"Not from what I witnessed before," Matthew said.

"It's not my fault if people walk off the sidewalks without looking where they are going. They're reading the newspaper or talking to someone, and then they swear at the drivers when they are the idiots who walk into traffic!"

"It's the driver's responsibility to look out for the idiots," Matthew said. "If you hit someone, guess who will be sued?"

"People, even idiots, should be responsible for their own safety," Kara exclaimed.

"I agree, but as the driver, you are responsible for looking out for pedestrians. That's how the law sees it," Matthew said. Large raindrops splattered on the windshield, and Matthew turned on the wipers, a new vehicle invention he'd paid extra for when he'd bought the car. "Let's switch places. I'll test you in bad weather later. I was impressed today. I'm going to drive back to the grocery store we passed. There is a telephone booth there, and I'll call the Colonel and ask him if he still wants us to come to dinner. It doesn't look like it will be an outdoor barbecue. Winter is beginning to set in."

Matthew made the phone call and returned to the car. "Dinner is on, but it won't be outside."

Kara and Matthew dashed from the car to the porch, and Daniel must have been watching for them because he opened the door.

Deloris was right behind him. "Come in, come in!" she exclaimed. "Simon is on the patio. He refuses to give up on the idea of steaks on the grill now that they are available again. Matthew, why don't you join him. Kara, you can keep me company."

The kitchen table was loaded with food as it had been their last time there.

"Everything is ready except for the meat," Deloris exclaimed. "I read the article in the newspaper about your boutique opening. How is it doing?"

"Grand opening week was unbelievable," Kara said happily. "And, our second week did almost as well. The private consultations will begin this week, and our calendar is full. We've hired three new seamstresses and two beading experts who will work from their homes."

"What does Matthew think about the boutique?" Deloris asked.

"Well, he doesn't like it that I'm working at home in the evenings," Kara said honestly. "But, he's working on a difficult case, so he has been working at home too, so he can't complain. We cleared the third bedroom in our apartment and turned it into a home office for him."

"I admire young women with your spunk," Deloris said.

"I've tried several times to get Simon to allow me to get a job, but he wants me to be a stay-at-home wife and mother."

"Did you work during the war?" Kara asked.

"No. Simon wanted me to keep an eye on Daniel," Deloris said. "He just turned fifteen, but even at thirteen, he could have passed for eighteen. Keeping the younger boys from lying about their ages and enlisting was difficult. It was my duty to make sure our youngest stayed in school. Our older two enlisted. David became a pilot, and John joined the Navy. I still don't know what they did or where they were sent. Neither will talk about it. I volunteered through our church as much as possible. "

"Deloris!" Simon Rathforth shouted from the patio. "Bring me a meat platter!"

Deloris turned around, grabbed a large platter, and hustled outside. Simon Rathforth came into the house carrying a full steak platter, followed by Matthew, and set it in the middle of the dining table. At the same time, Deloris returned to the kitchen and began taking all the other dishes to the dining room table. Kara followed her with several more dishes and continued to help. The women made several trips back and forth, and Daniel joined the men sitting at the table.

"Have a seat," Simon said to Kara while Deloris filled glasses with iced tea. "I see you've picked up the habit of wearing trousers."

"They were comfortable and were necessary during the war. Wearing a dress and looking pretty for men during the bombings would have been stupid," Kara responded.

The Colonel frowned at her response. "Yes, Matt told me about that. It's hard to believe Britain allowed women in those jobs. As Americans, our duty was to protect our families."

"The United States wasn't separated from the war by a

twenty-mile span of water," Kara said bluntly. "Americans didn't have Zeppelins flying over and dropping bombs."

The Colonel frowned, but he nodded. "You're right, but now that the war is over, women should return to their homes and children. Matt was telling me about you opening a shop. After being separated for so long, do you think that's wise?"

"Obviously, my partner and I do. We've only been open for a short time, and so far, we have been successful. Our personal appointments begin this week. We'll find out soon enough how our *couture* designs will be accepted."

"Maybe you should go to the shop, Deloris," Simon said.

Deloris smiled. "I'd love to, but I don't think we can afford it. The dresses begin at fifty dollars and can be as high as a thousand dollars."

"Are you serious?" the Colonel exclaimed. "That's ridiculous!"

Kara shrugged and turned her attention to Deloris. "I've been admiring the paintings on your walls. They're beautiful."

"That's my wife's hobby," Simon interrupted. "She wastes a lot of time painting."

Kara opened her mouth to protest, but she got a bump under the table and a head shake from Matthew. She turned to Deloris. "I'd be honored to display your paintings in our shop. The paintings I've seen are wonderful."

"Deloris doesn't have much time for that nonsense," Simon said. "She has responsibilities to her family."

Kara looked down at her plate and then stood up. "Excuse me, I'm feeling ill suddenly." She stood and walked down the hall toward the bathroom.

Matthew knew that Kara was about to explode. He knew she believed in the Women's Suffrage Movement in Britain and the U.S. She hadn't joined the Suffrage moment in New

York because Congress ratified the 19th Amendment only a month after her arrival. Matthew skillfully changed the subject but was watching the clock on the dining room wall. When fifteen minutes had passed, he pushed his chair back.

"I'm going to check on my wife. If she's feeling ill, I'll have to take her home," he said and went down the hall. Knocking on the door, Kara opened it. "Are you all right?"

"No, I'm not. I don't want to be around that obnoxious man! He's crude and offensive!" Kara hissed.

"He's also my former Commander," Matthew said. "I've already made excuses for you, so we can leave. Hold it together for a few more minutes, and we'll leave."

Kara nodded, and they returned to the dining room.

"I apologize for ruining your dinner, but I need to go home," Kara apologized, addressing herself to Deloris and not the Colonel. "It's not your food that's made me ill. It's a reoccurring medical problem. Thank you for inviting us to your home."

Matthew apologized, and Simon Rathforth stood and shook hands with Matthew. Simon moved toward Kara, but she sidestepped and bent down to retrieve her purse from the floor.

Once in the car, Kara sat back against the seat and closed her eyes. "If their marriage is an example of how you want our marriage to be, I'm not willing to go there! I know he was your Commander in the Army, but Colonel Rathforth is one of the most insufferable men I've ever met. He treats his wife like a servant!"

"He's not that bad," Matthew said. "He's old school."

"He's unbearable!" Kara exclaimed. "Deloris cooked every dish of food on that table except the steaks, and he had the nerve to take credit for it. *He* boasted that *he* has the best barbecue dinners in the neighborhood! All that man did was put raw meat on the grill and turn it over! It was *Deloris do this*, and *Deloris do that*, and then he had the nerve to complain to her that the potato salad wasn't made with deviled eggs, and she'd forgotten to clean *his* golf clubs!"

"I agree he wasn't on his best behavior!" Matthew agreed.

"The nerve of him. I would have told him what he could do with his golf clubs. I would have wrapped one of them around his head! Then he had the nerve to complain about Deloris wasting her time painting while he's out chasing a little white ball around for hours! She's an outstanding artist!"

"I agree," Matthew said gently. "I've never seen this side of him, but it's not our business to interfere."

"How could you not see that he's awful?" Kara asked.

"He was my Commanding Officer," Matthew said. "He was in charge. When he gave orders, they obeyed. Plus, he treated me quite well as a junior officer. Now that he's retired..."

"He's still acting like he's in the Army," Kara said, finishing his sentence. "I feel bad for Deloris! I'm surprised that he doesn't expect her to salute!"

"I agree that the Colonel was overbearing today. There's a period of adjustment to being a civilian again."

"He'd better adjust faster if he wants to stay married," Kara exclaimed. "Because today he was a jerk!"

"They've been married for over thirty years," Matthew said. "I went to their anniversary party. Everyone had a good time, and they seemed happy. What goes on in their marriage is not our business."

"He's a bully!"

"Please, calm down," Matthew said, reaching for her hand and squeezing it. "We've had a great weekend. Don't let the Colonel spoil it."

Kara took a deep breath and exhaled, and then challenged him. "It's stopped raining. Let me drive back to the city."

Matthew pulled the car over to the side of the road. "Only if you stay three full car lengths behind the vehicle ahead once we cross the city line and drive slower than the speed limit."

"If I drive any slower, we might as well walk!"

"The speed limit sign on this road is twenty miles per hour. It will be fifteen once we cross into the city," Matthew reminded her. "Your choice. I'm only trying to keep you safe."

"Men!" Kara exclaimed, but she scooted over to the driver's seat when her husband got out and walked around the car.

The drive back to New York City was uneventful, although Matthew pointed to the speedometer several times. When the car was parked in the garage, Kara handed the keys to Matthew. "How did I do today?"

"Much better than the last time," Matthew said.

"Good enough for me to buy a car?"

"You don't need a vehicle," Matthew said. "When would you drive it? As it is, we have very little time together."

"That's true," Kara agreed. "But, I liked feeling free."

"You aren't free, and neither am I. You're my wife," Matthew said, upset with her words.

"I know that," Kara said. "I love you, Matthew. You know I do, but I'm not the child you married. My innocence was trampled on a long time ago. Living and surviving in London all those years made me more independent than most women. Listening to Simon today made me angry. My instinct was to offer Deloris a way out."

"Kara..."

"I know," she interrupted. "She probably wouldn't accept it. Deloris has been taught to serve her husband and children her entire life. It's not wrong if she's happy with that lifestyle. But I felt a tiny bit of rebellion in her today when we discussed her art. I'm giving you a fair warning. If she comes to me and needs help to get away from Simon, I won't refuse."

"Like you did with Elizabeth?"

"Women have to stand up and support each other because most men are hanging on to old traditions and are unwilling to change. Women getting the vote is only the beginning of our new journey into equality." Kara smiled and stood on her tiptoes to kiss him. "I'm delighted that my husband doesn't fit into the category of obnoxious asshole."

Matthew laughed, giving Kara a swat across the bottom, as he did when he heard her swear. "I'll give up a lot for your independence, but I'm still in charge of our love life. Are there any objections?

"Not a single one, so far," Kara agreed.

The first personal appointment for Kara & Alaïs Couture Designs was on Monday afternoon. Mrs. Alverta Barker was a writer. She wrote fiction stories and book reviews in the foremost magazines and publications in New York City. She socialized with high society and had been a friend of Aunt Selina.

Once the niceties had been observed, the women got down to business. Both Kara and Alice's sketchbooks of evening dresses were shared. Mrs. Barker narrowed her choices to three and gave them deadlines on when she needed them. She was only concerned that the dresses she bought had to be unique. Mrs. Barker didn't hesitate at the prices.

With the transaction completed, Mrs. Barker was

escorted to her limousine, where her chauffeur had been waiting for two hours. Elizabeth had worked in the shop alone, with Alice slipping out occasionally to check on her.

"Any problems?" Kara asked, returning from locking the door and turning the Open sign over to Closed while Alice pulled the drapes on the window display.

"One woman complained that the prices were too high and wanted to bargain about the price," Elizabeth said, shrugging. "I apologized but told her this was a boutique, not a thrift store. Another woman was disappointed that we don't carry fur coats."

Alice shook her head. "They're too expensive, and we don't have the room to display them."

Elizabeth giggled and explained when her employers looked at her with questioning eyes. "You just sold three exclusive dress designs for almost three thousand dollars, and then you say fur coats are too expensive."

"You have a point," Kara said, opening a bottle of wine and pouring three small glasses to celebrate. "Drink up. We only have until January to enjoy this openly."

"My father and his friends have been stocking cases of beer and liquor ever since the amendment was passed," Elizabeth said. "One of his friends was building a still in his basement."

"He better not get caught," Alice warned.

"Matthew says Prohibition is a huge mistake," Kara said. "The wealthy have been stockpiling the good liquors and wines. People have been drinking spirits since the beginning of recorded time."

"Thomas hasn't been stockpiling, but he's not happy about giving up his occasional beer with his male friends," Alice agreed. "His father has quite a collection of what he calls 'the good stuff,' although my mother-in-law isn't happy about it." She raised her glass. "To our success today!"

"Success!" Kara and Elizabeth repeated, clinking their glasses together.

"Okay, let's get busy," Kara said. "I'm going upstairs to gather the materials needed to make the patterns for Mrs. Barker's dresses. I'll start working on the off-shoulder black evening dress with sequins and fringe at home."

"I can start on the red silk," Alice said. "We have all the measurements. Once we have the preliminary fitting appointment, we can get started.

"Is there anything I can do?" Elizabeth asked.

"We'll start you on the alterations to what we sell in the shop," Alice said. "That's where most designers start. You have to work up the ladder."

"Yes, ma'am," Elizabeth answered.

Matthew called and said he was going to be late. He had several witness interviews to do before he could leave the office and a lot of paperwork to complete. A few minutes later, Thomas called Alice and said he would be several hours late because he'd been called to a construction site on the opposite side of the city.

Kara had already told Matthew she would go home to the hotel, so Alice told Thomas she was going there to work for several hours.

"We're on our own this evening," Alice said, turning to Kara. "Why don't you get the bolt of muslin out of the stores upstairs, and we'll work on making the pattern for the black silk for a few hours. Alverta Barker and I are almost the same size. She's a little thicker in the hips." She turned to Elizabeth. "Can you phone Emma and tell her you'll be late?"

"Yes, I can call her before she leaves her job," Elizabeth exclaimed with a huge smile that she was being included by her employers.

It was an evening of women working together and enjoying themselves. Kara ordered sandwiches and snacks from room service. Making a pattern true to size from a sketchpad required a lot of measuring and pinning. Alice spent most of her time standing on a chair in her slip with Kara, measuring and cutting a pattern in muslin.

When the telephone rang, it was Thomas, and he told Alice he was on his way home.

Alice stood still while the pattern pins were removed. "Goodness, it's almost eight o'clock." She dressed and left with Elizabeth in tow to drop her off at her boarding house.

"I'll keep working until Matthew gets home," Kara said, closing the door after her friends. She returned to the workroom and didn't look up until there was a knock on the door.

"Are you still working?" Matthew asked.

Kara looked over at the clock, and it was after midnight. She got up and stretched. "Alice and Elizabeth were here until eight. How did your evening go?"

"Busy," Matthew said, and he looked exhausted. "I need a shower."

Kara entered the bedroom to find Matthew sprawled across the bed on his stomach. He was naked with his face buried in a pillow.

"Did you eat dinner?" she asked, crawling across the bed to reach him.

"Ordered out, but it was never delivered," Matthew groaned.

"There are several sandwiches left over from the cart I ordered earlier for the girls," Kara said.

"Good, because I'm famished." Matthew turned over and captured her with a kiss. Then he rolled out of bed, pulled on his robe, and headed for the kitchen. Removing the cover on the service tray, he picked up a sandwich and smiled. "Meatloaf, one of my favorites."

"There are two untouched salads," Kara offered. "And a

roast chicken sandwich. We have fresh milk, iced tea, and lemonade in the refrigerator.

"Iced tea sounds perfect," Matthew said, pushing the cart closer to the small dining table.

"How did your meetings go?" Kara asked.

"Better than I could have hoped for," Matthew said. "One of the secretaries working in the office with the building manager was aware of the complaint letters. Gladis Gilbert overheard a conversation between the manager and the DeLuca owners. Frank DeLuca ordered the manager to destroy all the complaints except minor nuisance complaints. She also overheard that she was to be fired for questioning the manager over the complaints and because she knew too much. The DeLucas were going to fire her and replace her with someone who didn't know so much. Or, as she quoted to me, *someone they could trust.*"

"Did she go to the police?"

"No, she did better, at least for my case," Matthew said. "When the owners and the manager left that evening, expecting her to lock up, she reviewed the files. Gladis Gilbert gathered all the legitimate complaints and inspector reports. She carried a three-inch thick folder out of the building and hid it at a relative's house. She might have planned to use it for blackmail, but I don't care. It's proof the DeLucas knew about the structural problems."

"If she stole the paperwork, can you use it?" Kara asked.

"I don't know yet. Mrs. Gilbert did have permission to take work home. Work that she didn't get paid for doing. That should work in our favor. She was given notice, but the new hire was delayed in taking the job. Nine days later, the building collapsed. All the manager's staff got out of the building in time. It took a week for the fire department to declare all the occupants were accounted for. Eighteen people died, and thirty-five were hospitalized.

"Three days after the rubble was declared clear, there was a fire in what was left of the manager's office. The DeLuca brothers were trying to destroy evidence that they knew the building was unsafe.

"My witness handed me a landmine of proof against the owners and the manager. The DeLuca brothers knew the building wasn't safe and didn't do anything about it except to evict the occupants if they complained."

"So, you'll win your case."

"If the evidence is accepted in court, there's no chance of their winning," Matthew said. "In addition to the families of the victims who were killed or hospitalized, we have over two hundred occupants who lost all their belonging when the building collapsed. How did your day go?"

"We got an order from Mrs. Alverta Barker today for three couture dresses. If she likes our work and recommends us to her friends, there's no turning back!"

Matthew didn't know who Alverta Barker was, and it was too late to get into a long discussion about dressmaking. He just nodded and congratulated his wife.

Chapter 12

WHEN MATTHEW ROLLED OVER, he glanced at the clock and shot upright. "Kara!"

"What?" she mumbled.

"We forgot to turn on the clock alarm again," Matthew exclaimed, scrambling from the bed. "We're going to be late!"

Kara rolled over and followed him into the bathroom. He grabbed his razor, and she jumped into the tub and turned on the shower. There was no time to spare as Alice was expected to pick her up in less than a half-hour.

Matthew's morning schedule wasn't as rigid, but his company did frown on lateness, regardless of how late the lawyers worked the previous evening.

Kara was trying to get dressed. She ran into the kitchen and turned her back to Matthew so he could button the back of her dress. As he did, she was hopping on one foot and pulling on stockings, and trying to get the seams straight.

"Stand up," Matthew said, and he cocked his head to view the hemline of her dress.

"It's exactly five inches below the knee," Kara smirked.

"Keep it that way," Matthew said, handing her a coat while she jammed her feet into her shoes. "Here, I buttered some toast for you. You need to eat."

"Wrap it in a napkin, and I'll eat it in the car. Alice is probably waiting for me!" Kara exclaimed. She ran into her studio and grabbed the large shopping bag she'd filled with her work the night before. She kissed Matthew, grabbed the toast he was offering, and ran out of the suite.

Matthew put two more slices of bread in the toaster and looked over his shoulder. The bedroom door was open, and the room was a wreck. The bed hadn't been made, and there was discarded clothing taken from the closet that Kara had decided against wearing. She usually tried on four or five outfits before deciding what to wear. He headed into the bedroom, hung the clothing back in the closet, and returned several pairs of shoes to where they belonged. He went into the linen closet, removed a set of sheets, and set them on the bed. Next, he went into the bathroom and put the used towels into a hamper.

Returning to the kitchen, he took the time to drink a cup of coffee before pulling on his coat and picking up his briefcase. Then he did something he hadn't done before. He called the front desk and asked for maid services to clean the apartment. Matthew didn't know the terms of the penthouse occupation, but he did know all the services provided in the hotel were included. He couldn't scold Kara about leaving the apartment disheveled when he had no time to straighten it himself.

Kara jumped into Alice's car. "I'm sorry for being late. Matthew didn't get home until almost midnight. I finished the pattern, but I need you to try it on before I start sewing the muslin."

The week went by quickly. There were three more private appointments with wealthy patrons. Two of the three picked designs from the drawings. The store wasn't quite as busy, but they were making a decent profit and had already reordered stock dresses of very high quality that carried their label.

Kara and Alice took turns working in the upstairs rooms. The dresses took three to five hours of sewing time, and that was to make the dress in muslin. Then the client would try on the dress. They would make any alterations needed, and then it would be disassembled and used as a pattern for the expensive materials. Only the couture dresses were sewn by Kara and Alice. They had an assembly of associate seamstresses who worked out of their homes under their label. Some women specialized in adding buttons, beads, feathers, and fringe embellishments.

Kara was helping a shopper when the bell rang over the door, and she looked up. Deloris Rathforth and Sharon Warner entered the shop. "Excuse me," Kara said to the shopper, and she motioned for Alice. "I'll have my associate help you."

Kara greeted her guests. "Hello, I wasn't expecting you. Are you interested in our fashions?"

"No," Deloris said, and her face blushed. "I wanted to apologize for my husband's behavior. He was upset about the weather and had a bit too much of the drink."

"There's no need for you to apologize," Kara said sincerely.

"That's what I told her," Sharon said. "Simon is a bit much to take sometimes. We're working on him!"

Kara laughed. "Why don't you come in and look around?" She looked around and whispered. "I can give you a good discount."

"Actually," Sharon said, but she was interrupted.

"I can ask her," Deloris said, although she looked uncomfortable.

"Ask me what?"

"You said my paintings are good," Deloris said. "I know you were being nice, but..."

"Your paintings are beautiful," Kara said. "I'm no expert, but I meant it when I said they are professional level."

"We brought you some of her paintings," Sharon interrupted. "You said you would love to display them in your shop."

"Where are they?" Kara exclaimed.

"In the car," Sharon said. "We can bring them in."

"Let's get them," Kara said. She followed the women to a car, and between them, they carried the canvases into the shop and leaned them against the check-out counter. While ripping off newspaper wrapped around them. A few customers moved closer to see what was going on.

Kara pointed to two large paintings of the Eiffel Tower. "I want those. One for our living room and one to hang in the shop right over there!"

"I painted those from pictures in a magazine," Deloris admitted shyly.

"This one is going on the wall right over there as soon as I pay for it," Kara said.

"Oh, I wouldn't ask you to pay for it," Deloris said. "I thought you could use them to decorate the shop."

"You're not asking. I'm insisting," Kara exclaimed. She turned to the women who were listening. "Don't you think these paintings are incredible?" Heads nodded.

"I want this one," Alice said. "I love the rustic covered bridge with a fall background."

"I... I... couldn't," Deloris whispered.

"Deloris," Kara scolded gently. "You are a talented artist. If you don't want to sell your paintings, I will proudly hang them on the walls. But, if you want to sell them, I assure you they won't be here for long."

The paintings had drawn most of the customers' attention. The boutique customers crowded around, looking at the canvases.

"Are these for sale?" a latecomer asked.

Alice looked to Deloris, who had tears in her eyes, but she nodded. Alice turned to the customer. "Three hundred dollars for the large canvases and one hundred and fifty for the smaller ones."

Within a few minutes, seven of the ten paintings were sold. The women walked out with both clothing and newspaper-wrapped paintings.

"Wow," Sharon exclaimed. "We didn't expect that to happen!"

"I can't believe it," Deloris exclaimed. "I never thought my hobby was worth anything."

"I've been trying to convince you for years," Sharon scolded.

"You've earned one thousand three hundred and fifty dollars in less than an hour," Alice said. "That's proof that you are a talented painter. "Now, you have to bring us more to hang on our boutique walls."

"We'll be happy to display and sell them for you," Kara agreed. "Even if you don't want to sell them, I hope you'll let us borrow them for decoration."

"I can't believe it," Deloris cried.

"Believe it," Kara said. "Goodness, it's almost closing time. Would you ladies like to come to dinner tonight?"

Both Deloris and Sharon shook their heads. "We have to get home to our families," Sharon said.

Alice went to the cash register and counted out what was owed to Deloris.

"No, no," Deloris exclaimed. "I brought them as a peace offering, not for you to buy them. I don't mind selling the other paintings, but the ones you and Kara picked are gifts."

"I offered," Kara said. "And so did Alice and our customers. My paintings will be hung on the wall behind the counter and in my living room, so I can look at them daily."

"And my painting will be a birthday present from my husband," Alice said. "Thomas keeps telling me to buy something I want, and I found it in this painting!"

A clock on the wall began to chime.

"It's time to lock up," Alice said.

"We'll get out of your way. May we speak in private?" Deloris asked Kara.

"Of course," Kara said, leading the way to the office.

"I know you were upset when you left our home. I married Simon when I was sixteen, and we've been together for thirty-three years," Deloris said. "You're young, and you have a different outlook on marriage than women of my age. Simon was in the Army for twenty-seven years. He has spent his entire adult life serving his country. He's having a hard time settling into a civilian world. We've had good times and bad times during our years together. Trust me when I say that I love my husband. He can be bullheaded, but he's also a good man. I don't like doing it, but sometimes I just have to sit him down and vent all my anger and frustration until we can settle our differences.

"I want to thank you for today. I didn't come here to find a vocation at my age, but I'm willing to give it a try. As my husband has to accept change, so do I. Sharon is teaching me how to drive, although I'm not very good yet. I'll have her bring me back with more paintings. I have stacks of them stored in closets and the attic."

"Please do," Kara said, looking around the boutique at the framed newspaper articles about Haute Couture fashion shows. "If you have paintings of Paris, London, or Italy, I would love to see them."

"I have quite a few, especially of the fountains," Deloris admitted. "I always wanted to go to Europe."

"It was beautiful, but give them a few years to rebuild," Kara suggested sadly.

Alice dropped Elizabeth off a block from where she shared a boarding house room with her friend Emma. The newspapers claimed the neighborhood wasn't the best, and crime was rising. When Elizabeth entered the building, Sharon drove into traffic.

Elizabeth checked the mailbox for any mail, turned to take the stairs, and stopped.

"Don't run, Claudina," Marcio Giordano said. He was sitting on the stairs. "I'm just here to find out why you ran away and if you're okay."

"My name is Elizabeth now, and I ran away because I had no choice!"

"No choice in what?" Marcio asked.

"Anything and everything," Elizabeth said. "Our parents decided we would be a couple when I was six years old!"

"We were just kids," Marcio said. "They don't mean any harm with that kind of talk."

"I was thirteen when I came home from school, excited about my first crush. My father was furious and told me I was already promised to you! Nothing has changed, Marcio. My father hasn't stopped reminding me daily that I was going to marry his best friend's son," Elizabeth said. "I'm sick of being told what I am supposed to do with my life! It's my life!

"My father wouldn't let me continue with my education. He forced me to work at the newspaper, and I've hated every minute I've been there. He has taken my earnings ever since

I left school. He claims he's putting the money aside so we won't be strapped for money after we marry. I never agreed to marry you and I won't marry until I establish a career. And who I marry will be my choice!"

"I'm sorry," Marcio said. "My parents have been saying the same things, but I thought they were just messing with us. I like you, Claudina... sorry, Elizabeth, but we haven't even dated. Geeze, you've been more of a kid sister."

"Exactly," Elizabeth said.

"I'm sorry," Marcio said. "I do know your father is going crazy worrying about you."

"I left him a letter," Elizabeth said coldly. "It explained why I quit my job and left the way I did. I'm twenty-one years old. Old enough to make my own decisions."

Marcio nodded. "I'm sorry. I won't tell your father that I've seen you. I just wanted to make sure you were okay. You are okay, aren't you?"

"I have a good job, and I'm learning a trade," Elizabeth said stiffly.

"Have you told your father how you feel?" Marcio said.

"Of course I have," Elizabeth exclaimed. "He ignores what I say and tells me he knows what is best for me. He doesn't know what is best for me.

"If you tell my father where I live, I'll never forgive you, and I will run again. He has no right to force me to do anything!"

"I won't. You have my word," Marcio said, although he looked concerned. He stood and walked to the door before turning back. "If you need help with anything, call me. I'm still living with the folks. I mean it, anything at all." He cracked a lopsided grin. "It was my job in school to scare off the wise guys and keep them from messing with you."

"I never thanked you for that," Elizabeth said softly. "Unfortunately, my biggest bully has been my father."

Elizabeth went upstairs to the small room she shared to a note on the table from Emma. The message said Emma had gone to care for her younger brother and sister, so her mother could work a double shift. Looking out the window, Elizabeth watched Marcio walk away and allowed herself a few tears. Then she opened the bag she'd brought home and began to repair the dress she'd been given. A cigarette burn had damaged the dress before the No Smoking signs had been posted in the shop. There were three warning signs in the shop now. If a dress was carelessly damaged, it was considered sold to the person who damaged it.

Alice called the signs 'the live and learn' policies.

Whatever the policy, Elizabeth didn't care. She'd been given a dress that cost more than she earned in a month. The dress was several sizes too large, but she was going to cut it down to her size, and she had her boss's permission to use the sewing machines upstairs, on her breaks, or when the shop wasn't busy. Running her fingers over the expensive material, Elizabeth smiled. She loved her job and her employers, but they didn't replace her father and all the neighbors and friends she'd known all her life. Marcio's mother had been a second mother to her, but she believed that being a wife and mother was a young woman's ultimate goal. Elizabeth didn't think of herself as Claudina anymore. She was Elizabeth Berkley, and the next time she saw Kara's husband, she would ask him how to make her new name legal.

Kara and Alice were pleased with Elizabeth's work on the dress and helped her work out a few problems she hadn't anticipated. Overall she was encouraged to use her talents. When Elizabeth had six new dresses in her closet. She purchased a new streamlined coat at Macy's and a Cloche hat. Then she went to a thrift store and bought a badly damaged coat for the fur collar that was in good shape and added it to her new coat. When the first frigid day of winter came, she was prepared and stood on the corner sidewalk waiting for Alice to pick her up.

"Nice," Alice said, approvingly of her outerwear.

From that day forward, Elizabeth never dressed down in her neighborhood.

Deloris and Sharon returned to the boutique the following week with the backseat of Sharon's car filled with paintings. Kara purchased two more paintings for the bedroom in the suite. The very explicit art Aunt Selina had hung on the bedroom walls had been taken down by Matthew when he'd moved in. He'd declared them indecent and sent them back to the gallery where they had been purchased with a reminder that New York City had decency laws. Now they were enjoying views of Venice and Milan. The rest of the artwork was displayed in the boutique, and it wasn't unusual for clients to walk in for clothing and walk out with clothing, accessories, and paintings.

Deloris also had the boutique take ten percent of the price of the paintings. Although Kara and Alice protested, Deloris told them a gallery would have charged her more.

The boutique was doing far better than expected but also took more of their time than expected. With high sales, more seamstresses were needed for a quicker turnaround on the most expensive brand items.

Matthew's liability case was going well, and it was now a matter of waiting for a court date. He was coming home at a decent time, only to find his wife late or working in her studio. The building that Thomas was supervising was on schedule with no problems, and he was coming home on time, only to discover Alice working on a sewing machine.

The only issue within both marriages was that there was never enough time together. It was a problem that Matthew and Thomas decided needed to be fixed. Matthew called Thomas, and they agreed to meet at Lombardi's. Matthew called Sal Bianchi and asked if he could use one of the booths for a private meeting. The way Sal laughed, Matthew guessed that Sal thought he was meeting a woman, but he couldn't have been more wrong.

"Pizza?" Sal asked when Thomas entered the private booth.

"Everything except onion, sardines, and olives," Matthew said, looking over to Thomas.

"Sounds good to me," Thomas agreed, but he questioned the large man in an apron. "Do you have any Irish Stout?"

"I can find you some," Sal said with a smile. "Get it while you can."

Over pizza Matthew and Thomas discussed their mutual problem. Their wives worked too hard and put in too many hours at the boutique. They agreed they were proud of their wives' success, but Alice and Kara averaged working fourteen to sixteen hours daily. Elizabeth was keeping shorter hours, but that was because she wasn't a designer or a professional seamstress. The men discussed the problem and decided on a strategy that hopefully wouldn't get them kicked out of their marital beds.

Matthew carried the leftover pizza home and slid it onto the kitchen counter. There was no evidence of Kara calling room service for her dinner. He went straight to her work-room, and she was bent over a sewing machine. Walking over to her, he bent down and kissed her. "It's time to shut down. Did you stop long enough to order something to eat?"

Kara was going to lie, but her stomach growled in hunger. "I thought about it but was having problems with the sewing machine, and I forgot."

"Come on," Matthew said with a nudge to her shoulder.

"I only have..."

"Now," Matthew insisted, giving her a firmer nudge. Once in the kitchen, he slid two pieces of pizza onto a plate and poured her a glass of iced tea. He waited until she'd finished half of one of the pieces.

"This has to stop," Matthew was firm.

"What has to stop?" Kara asked.

"Working two shifts a day," Matthew said. "You've lost weight that you can't afford to lose. You are pushing yourself too hard at the shop."

"We're doing great," Kara protested.

"I agree, but you need to hire more help," Matthew said firmly. "What's the purpose of becoming successful if you can't take the time to enjoy it?"

"You work long hours!"

"I do, but only when I need to," Matthew said. "You and Alice are putting in twelve to sixteen hours a day. It's not worth it if you're working yourself to death. You're in the shop at seven in the morning and don't leave until six. That's an eleven-hour day. Then you come home and work an additional four to five hours. Enough is enough."

"We have commissions to finish," Kara said. "I've explained this to you before. If we're going to make a dent in the fashion world, we must put all our efforts into it!"

"I want you to succeed," Matthew said. "But not at the expense of your health or our marriage. We haven't had time to go to the show, go dancing, or have dinner with our friends. We haven't been talking because you don't like to be interrupted when you are working, and you are always working.

"It's one thing for you to sketch the drawings. It's another for you to work yourself into the ground. You need to hire more seamstresses, finishers, or whatever you call them, to work upstairs or in their homes. Put hiring signs in the boutique windows and advertisements in the newspapers. You need more staff."

"I know, but it takes time to train them," Kara said.

"Time you're going to take," Matthew said. "Shop hours I can handle. I can also handle your drawing all the time. The actual sewing needs to be done by others. The sewing machine is going back to the shop. Thomas and I will be watching both of you closely."

"You talked to Thomas?" Kara exclaimed.

"Yes, and we discussed it," Matthew admitted. "He's as worried about Alice as I am about you. Both of you need to slow down."

"Why didn't you talk to me first?" Kara demanded.

"Because you have a habit of not listening," Matthew said. "We are standing firm on this matter, Kara. We want our wives to enjoy their lives and stay healthy!"

Chapter 13

WHEN ALICE PULLED into the delivery lot behind the hotel, Mr. Groban, the maintenance foreman, followed Kara, carrying a Singer sewing machine encased in a wooden carrying case. He opened the back door, and Elizabeth moved a similar case to the middle of the seat, so there would be room for it.

"You too," Alice whispered.

Kara nodded, but she mouthed the word 'later.' She didn't want to talk in front of Elizabeth. Once they were in the boutique, Elizabeth was tasked with straightening the racks, and they carried the heavy sewing machines upstairs, where they could speak privately.

"Did Thomas give you hell last night?" Kara asked.

"A long lecture that turned into an argument," Alice admitted. She looked over her shoulder at the stairs and rubbed her backside. "And, you know what, when we had words."

"They planned it," Kara said angrily.

"We do need to hire more seamstresses," Alice said. "We've been doing great in the boutique, but I don't want to fight with Thomas. I don't want the boutique to cause problems in my marriage."

"We'll advertise," Kara agreed. "If we call in the ads today, they should appear in the Sunday paper. The dresses we are working on can be finished here." We'll take shifts working up here and downstairs. We don't have to be on the floor all the time."

"You still look upset," Alice said. "Please don't let the boutique come between you and Matthew."

"It's not the shop," Kara denied and took a deep breath. "Well, maybe some of it is, but when things like this crop up, it makes me angry! I'm a grown woman who has been making my own decisions for a long time. I don't complain when Matthew has to work late!"

"This is your second chance with Matthew," Alice said. "He's a different person than what he was before. I haven't heard many complaints."

"I'm a different person too, and I haven't made many complaints," Kara admitted. "But when he gets on his high horse, something in me just wants to fight back! It doesn't make sense, but that's how I feel."

"Could it be because you couldn't fight back before?" Alice asked.

Kara shook her head. "I hope not. We have talked about what happened in the past. I thought we'd put it behind us."

"Thomas and I have what we call 'time-outs'," Alice said softly. "We stop arguing, give ourselves time to calm down, and rethink our stance on whatever has become an issue. I told him before we married that I wouldn't tolerate living with a tyrant, and I meant it. I left home at fifteen because of that kind of behavior from my father."

"I'll go write the advertisements for the newspapers," Kara said. "Then I'll work upstairs for a couple of hours."

Checking in with Elizabeth, Kara went into the small

office. She sat tenderly because the previous evening had been a 'maintenance' night. Despite what Matthew called *putting his foot down*, he insisted that maintenance night was needed because it had already been trimmed down to twice a month. Kara didn't mind and even looked forward to the sexual spankings Matthew did while they were intimate. But the maintenance spankings were different. They were Matthew's way of claiming authority over her, and she didn't like it.

She wrote two ads. Cleared them with Alice and called them in to the newspapers. They were advertising for seamstresses and finishers. Then she went upstairs and worked on the dress she was trying to finish before the last scheduled fitting.

Kara was subdued for most of the day. Something was bothering her, and it was evident to her friends. Alice dropped Kara off at the hotel but squeezed her hand before letting her out of the car. "Are you okay?"

Kara smiled and nodded. "I will be, one way or another."

"Don't do anything foolish," Alice whispered.

"I won't," Kara promised. "And if I do, I know my best friend will stand by me."

When Matthew entered the suite, he looked toward the studio his wife used for a workroom. The door was open slightly, and he pushed it open to see if she'd brought the sewing machine back, but she hadn't. She was sitting at a worktable sketching.

"I see that you listened," Matthew said.

Kara turned and gave him what he interpreted as a solemn stare. "You were right. Alice and I were putting in too many hours." She turned her attention back to her drawing.

"What's wrong?" Matthew asked.

"What's wrong is your cockamamie ideas of marriage,"

Kara said bluntly. "I'm not your servant, your lackey, or a child. I walked around today with a sore bottom because you think you have a right to whack on my ass simply because I'm a woman. It would have been different if I'd done something wrong, but I was doing exactly what you've been doing for the last couple of months. You've been preparing for your class-action suit. I've been working toward making a name for myself in fashion. Just because you're a man doesn't mean you own me."

"I was trying to make you see that our marriage needs equal time and effort," Matthew interrupted.

"Not only by me," Kara said firmly. "I know you think the philosophy of your former officers is how a marriage should be run, but I didn't appoint you to be my Lord and Master. You didn't give me a choice, and I've realized I'm unwilling to accept your rules. I want an equal marriage. You can complain about something I'm doing, but you don't have the right to dictate to me. I can do the same. Either we reset the rules to this dictatorship, or it's not going to work. I survived quite well without you for five years in far more dangerous circumstances. I can do it again."

"Kara, I love you," Matthew exclaimed.

"I love you too, but I won't tolerate being treated like a troublesome child! You demanding total control smacks of your mother, and I won't allow that again."

"I was looking out for your best interests," Matthew said.

"I'll bet Simon Rathforth thinks he's doing what is best for Deloris too, but all he's done is damage her self-esteem and self-confidence. Did you know that he refuses to allow her to drive? She had to depend on friends, taxis, and buses while he was being posted to different assignments. Sharon has taught her in secret, and Deloris will get her license."

"Is that what this is about?" Matthew asked. "Your driving?"

"No," Kara snapped. "It's about men thinking women are idiots and incapable of making decisions! If I want a car, I'll buy one! You admire how the Colonel handles his marriage. I don't!

"Sharon is more liberated and chooses to be a stay-at-home mom while her children are young. She has firmly told Harry that she will return to teaching when her children are old enough to be in school, and that's coming up soon.

"Deloris married at sixteen. She was a child! Deloris didn't have a chance to finish school, and she's never had a chance to be anything but a housewife. She admits that she spends more time on her artwork, but it's because Simon treats her so horribly. He keeps telling her she's wasting her time, but painting is the only thing that keeps her sane!"

"That's their problem, not ours," Matthew said.

"It's my problem that those men are your mentors!" Kara exclaimed. "I'm done with the *maintenance* spankings. If I haven't done anything wrong, I don't want you whacking on my ass!"

"All right, and please calm down," Matthew said. "I want you to succeed, Kara. I really do, but I don't want you exhausting yourself at the boutique."

"I'm not," Kara said. "I phoned in advertisements for the employment pages. It might take a while to fill the positions, and we have dresses that must be completed by their due dates. We will hire some assistants, but it may take a while."

"That's all I ask," Matthew said. He leaned over and kissed her. "You really don't like the Colonel do you?"

"No, I don't," Kara admitted. "He's a dictator, and Sharon says he's been worse since he retired. Deloris never had a bank account before Sharon went with her to the bank. She's been depositing her painting earnings into her account. The balance has been growing, and she doesn't want him to know about it!

"Sharon doesn't think much of Colonel Rathforth's behavior lately either, but she thinks the world of Deloris. I think Deloris is preparing to leave him, and I don't blame her."

Matthew pulled Kara into his arms. "Would she throw away thirty years of marriage?"

"Why not?" Kara asked. "He treats her like a servant, not his equal. And, if you tell him that I'm selling her paintings in my shop or anything else I've told you, you will go from being in hot water with me to being in boiling water. Do you understand?"

"Yes," Matthew said. "Okay, you've had your say, and I have been listening. Maybe I came on too strong when we got back together. But, I still believe a man should be the head of his family, whether it's only a couple or a family with kids. Someone has to be in charge and have the final say. The same principles work in most corporations, companies, shops, and relationships."

"It doesn't mean you get to be a tyrant," Kara said.

"I agree. We are on equal footing in most things. But, I'm also not denying that sometimes I may have to put my foot down within the confines of our relationship, and the result will be setting your bottom on fire."

Kara's chin jerked upward, and her eyes flared with anger.

"You are brilliant at what you do, tenacious and obstinate. Don't deny it," Matthew said firmly. "I'll pass on the maintenance spankings, but if I think you deserve a spanking, I won't hesitate. Those are my terms."

"I can live with that," Kara conceded. "I think."

"What about spankings during sex?" Matthew asked. "You like those spankings. I think it spices up our love life."

Kara nodded. "I do like those, as long as they don't get too hard."

"Agreed," Matthew said. "Are we okay?"

"Promise me that you won't go tattling to Colonel Rathforth? What Deloris decides about her marriage is her business."

Matthew held up his hand. "I swear, I won't. Now, how about going downstairs to the restaurant for dinner? My treat."

"That's silly," Kara said. "Why pay for what comes free? We can order from downstairs and enjoy our meal in our pajamas, or naked if we please."

"Now that sounds too good to pass up," Matthew agreed with a wide smile.

Running down the stairs while trying to pull on her coat one-handed, Elizabeth stopped and set a grocery bag in front of her 1st-floor neighbor's apartment door. She finished buttoning her coat before ringing the doorbell and ran outside, darting behind the side of the building.

Mrs. Edith Jordon was a widow who had lost her job several weeks earlier. Although Edith was supposed to start a new job, it didn't start for another week. She was struggling to make ends meet with three children to feed.

Elizabeth didn't see the young man across the street run between moving vehicles and down the sidewalk.

Marcio turned the corner of the building at a run and almost plowed over Elizabeth. "Are you all right?" he demanded.

"Of course I am," Elizabeth exclaimed. "What are you doing here?"

Marcio Giordano ran his hand through his hair and looked sheepish. "I've been keeping an eye on you. Just to keep you safe until your ride gets here."

"Why wouldn't I be safe?" Elizabeth asked.

Marcio looked uncomfortable. "I overheard some smart-ass wannabe thugs making comments about you. It's the way you dress now. They think you're hoity-toity. I told them to leave you alone, or they'd answer to me. When you came running out of the building, I thought something was wrong."

"Thank you for looking out for me, but I was only dodging my neighbor," Elizabeth said with a smile. "She's having a hard time, and I left a bag of groceries at her door. I had to ring the bell and run. It might have been stolen if I left it there and didn't ring the bell."

Marcio smiled. "That sounds like something you would do. You're looking really good Claud... I mean Elizabeth. The new job seems to suit you."

"It does," Elizabeth said, walking to the corner where Alice would pick her up.

Marcio walked alongside her.

"Are you still working with your father in the plumbing business?"

"Only for a short time," Marcio said. "Then I'm going to the new Police Academy for training."

"You're going to be a policeman?"

"Yeah," Marcio said. "I don't want to be a plumber. The City Police Department has been going through what they call a professional reorganization, and there will be twice as many policemen hired to protect New York City. There will be more police precincts.

"The Police Commissioner, Theodore Roosevelt, has promised that all policemen will be trained to follow a set of rules set by the commission, or they would be fired and replaced. There won't be any more policemen knocking people around just 'cause they feel like it. Even if a crime is committed, there will be rules on how to handle it. Citizens can file complaints if the police use violence against them. Becoming a policeman will become a profession, and the uniform will be removed from men who can't pass the new requirements. If I can stick with it long enough, there will be a pension when I retire. It's either the police academy or rejoin the Army," Marcio said. "I served in the Military Police in France during the war before the Army gave our units a name. I spent a year at Camp Mills, and I liked it. That's why I want to be a policeman."

"It sounds like you know what you want. It was nice talking to you. Thanks for coming to my aid, even though I wasn't in danger. Here comes my ride."

"Can I come by sometime and talk with you?" Marcio asked. "Maybe go on a date? I've kept my promise. I haven't told anyone that I've seen you."

Elizabeth fumbled in her purse and came out with a business card. "Call me during the day, but my need for secrecy still stands."

"I haven't told anyone, and I won't," Marcio promised.

"I have to go," Elizabeth said when Alice pulled over to the curb. She jumped into the vehicle and gave Marcio a wave.

"He's cute," Alice said. "A boyfriend?"

"No," Elizabeth said, looking over her shoulder. "For now, Marcio is a friend. He's entering the new Police Academy we've been reading about in the newspapers. It's a twelve-week program, but he doesn't think it will be difficult because he served in the Military Police during the war and at Camp Mills."

"My husband was stationed in Camp Mills before he was sent to England," Alice said. "They might know each other."

The advertisements were in the Sunday papers, and appointments were set up for women who wanted to interview. They were asked to bring samples of their work to the shop, and Alice and Kara hoped to hire at least five women to work out of their homes.

By the end of the week, Kara & Alaïs Couture Designs had several new employees. The shop was a success, and Beatrice Bonanatchi stopped by one day with a photographer. She wanted to do a follow-up story and had photographs taken of Alice and Kara in front of the boutique's display window.

Kara and Matthew had settled into a routine. There were still evenings when Kara or Alice took work home, but they were careful to not let the shop interfere with their marriages.

Matthew was making an effort to enjoy what New York City offered. Friday and Saturday evenings were set aside to go to well-known restaurants, cabarets, and Broadway shows. They especially enjoyed Silent Films with Charlie Chaplin, Lillian Gish, and Clara Bow. Most of their evenings were just the two of them, but Alice and Thomas joined them occasionally.

Christmas was approaching, and that meant parties and celebrations. The shop was already ahead of what they knew would be a busy season. The theme for this holiday was post-war extravagance. Bright-colored dresses pushed the limits of the hem lengths, and V-neck plunges exposed a hint of breasts, and off-the-shoulder sleeves were popular. Lots of costume jewelry and dresses with fringe were purchased. The fastest-selling dress was covered in red sequins with a white fox collar and hem. It wasn't a couture design but sold for nearly half the price.

One afternoon, a short, heavyset man entered the boutique. This wasn't common, although several men had come into the shop for advice and made purchases for their wives and girlfriends. This man wasn't concerned with the women's dresses. He was looking at the paintings.

"May I help you?" Kara asked.

"Yes," the man exclaimed. "Who is the artist?"

"Who is asking?" Kara asked.

"I apologize," the man said. "I am Mr. Nathan Wallace of the Wallace Art Gallery on Madison. One of my clients told me about the artwork being displayed here. Who is D. Rathforth?"

"The artist is a friend," Kara said.

"I would like his name and information on how to contact him."

"*She* exhibits here because she is a friend," Kara said. "I will pass your information to her. Whether she wants to engage in business with you is up to her."

The man looked around the shop and shook his head. "This representation of the artist's work is amateur. My gallery would be able to display her work professionally!"

"That's up to her," Kara said. "I'll be sure to pass on the information."

Mr. Wallace took his time walking around the shop and inspecting the paintings. When a woman coming out of the dressing room looked shocked at seeing him, Kara tapped him on the shoulder.

"Mr. Wallace, this is a women's shop. I must ask you to leave. You're making my clients uncomfortable."

"Oh, I didn't realize," he exclaimed. He went to the door immediately, but turned before opening the door. "Please tell D. Rathforth I will expect a call."

"He's an obnoxious little man, isn't he?" Alice said.

"Pushy," Kara agreed. "But I'll tell Deloris about his interest the next time she comes in."

Kara tossed the bag she'd brought home onto her work table. The radio wasn't on, and that was the first thing Matthew did when he came home. She was disappointed until she entered the bedroom and heard the shower running in the bathroom. Matthew was home. Stripping off her clothes, she walked into the bathroom naked and stepped over into the tub.

To say her husband was pleased was an understatement. Matthew pulled her body against his, kissing her while his hands roamed over her body. His hands stroked her breasts, and she felt his erection hard against her belly.

His lips slid down her throat, and he bent down to slide his erection between her legs, but they were too mismatched in height. Pinning her against the wall, he lifted her body, but they nearly fell. Turning off the water, he grabbed a towel, tossed it to the floor, and lifted her out of the tub so she wouldn't slip.

Kara quickly toweled off, and he was doing the same. Matthew turned her around and bent her over the sink counter. Spreading her legs apart, he thrust his engorged cock into her, and he wasn't gentle. He was taking her hard and deep, the way she liked it. When he moaned, she pleaded with him, "Not yet! Not yet!"

Matthew knew what she wanted, and he was going to provide it. He pulled her off the counter, swept her into his arms, and went straight to their bed. He was still large and hard. "My turn, sweetheart!"

Kara didn't have to be asked twice. She straddled his hips and rode him like a rocking horse she'd had as a child. Kara rode him until they switched positions again, and he began plunging into her. She could feel her body reacting again.

"Kara." Matthew's voice was raw and gritty.

"Yes!" she responded, and he filled her as her body tightened around him.

"Oh!" Kara exclaimed as he withdrew and turned her over on her belly. He took a buttock in each hand, pulled them apart, and inserted himself.

"Oh!" she breathed when he began to bury himself to

the hilt and pounded into her. It was rough, but Kara didn't care. She was sure she would be sore when he finished, but again she didn't care.

Matthew wore her out, and she loved every second of it. She had another climax, and so did he, before he removed himself. Kara wished he hadn't, but he was temporarily spent.

"You enjoyed that, didn't you?" Matthew said.

"I did," Kara admitted. "It was fantastic. What set you on fire?"

"I left the office early, and I was reading one of Aunt Selina's illegal books," Matthew admitted.

"I'll take my chances," Kara whispered as she kissed him. "It was worth it!"

Chapter 14

MATTHEW ROLLED over in bed and squinted at the clock.

"Holy smokes!"

"What?' Kara mumbled.

"We forgot to set the clock! Again!" Matthew exclaimed.

"What!" Kara sat up in bed and frowned at the offending alarm clock. Then she rolled out of bed and made a run for the bathroom. Matthew was a few steps behind, and he grabbed his razor. They didn't have time to complain as they rushed to get dressed.

Matthew raised an eyebrow at the wide-leg trousers Kara was wearing.

"We're expecting a shipment of new items this morning, and I'll be doing most of the unpacking," she explained. She glanced at the clock, pulled her husband down to her level, and kissed Matthew long enough to make his toes curl. "You might want to sneak that naughty book in your briefcase and see what else you can learn." Then she ran to her studio, grabbed her leather portfolio, and was out the door.

Alice was waiting when Kara ran out the back door of

the hotel. "I'm sorry. I'm sorry! We forgot to turn on the alarm!"

"We haven't been here long," Alice said. "I was a little bit late myself, there was an accident blocking traffic, and two drivers were having a fistfight over who caused it. The police arrested both of them, but we were stuck there until they cleared the street."

"Let's hope it's not going to be *one of those days*," Kara commented.

Later that afternoon, Alice left Elizabeth in charge while she went into the small office to make a pot of tea. Drinks weren't allowed in the boutique, but those rules didn't apply to the owners or the employees. Alice carried a cup of tea into the store room, where Kara unloaded boxes.

"You jinxed us," Alice said to Kara. "It has been one of those days. We've had two returns. One had obviously been worn. The sign on the back of the cash register clearly states that returns must have all original tags intact and no damage. Two out of three tags had been removed. She claimed the sign was put up after she purchased the dress. I told her the sign had been there since we opened. I hate people who are liars and cheats! That was a sixty-five dollar dress!"

"There will always be cheats in retail," Kara said, looking flustered.

"Are you feeling okay?" Alice asked.

"Not really," Kara said, pushing her hair out of her eyes. "I've been sick twice this morning."

"Are you pregnant?"

"No," Kara said. "Although sometimes I'm sick on the first day of my cycle."

"Go upstairs and lie down for a little while," Alice advised. "We can handle everything down here."

"I'll be okay," Kara said. "It's the curse of being a

woman, but I'd rather be sick than pregnant. Besides, Matthew has been using protection."

"Don't you want children?" Alice asked.

"Not right now," Kara said honestly. "I want the shop to be stable first. We've discussed it, and Matthew is okay with delaying kids for a while." Kara looked up from her work. "Am I going to lose my partner anytime soon?"

"No," Alice said. "And I don't believe that crap about a woman going into hiding because she's pregnant. I've already told Thomas I'm a working woman, and having children may mean I have to cut back on my hours, but it won't stop me from being a designer and businesswoman."

"Matthew and I had the same conversation," Kara said.

Later that afternoon, Nathan Wallace called twice, asking for Deloris' phone number. Alice told him firmly that she had been notified. What she did with the information wasn't her business.

Kara completed the unpacking of the new inventory. She steamed the wrinkles out, tagged them, and was pleased with their latest designs and the quality of the outsourced sewing. Then she went downstairs to the office and picked up her sketchbook. A few hours later, Alice looked in and over her shoulder at the drawings.

"Did our conversation inspire you?" Alice asked, looking at sketches of flapper-style dresses with sheaths draped across the stomach at angles to disguise a maternity bump. "These are interesting, and I think they would sell. I especially like this one with wide-leg trousers and this long jacket. Together they look almost like a floor-length dress! They look very modern."

"I'm going to sketch a version of the floor-length for our couture line with beading," Kara said, smiling.

"That's a great design. I think women would like it

because it would cover a multitude of sins for larger women, even the ones who aren't pregnant," Alice suggested.

"I hadn't thought of that, but you're right," Kara nodded. "If I can get the drawings to our suppliers by next week, we might be able to get a limited supply in by Christmas."

"I have a question," Alice said.

"What would that be?" Kara asked.

Alice smiled. "Are you free Saturday night?"

Kara nodded. "I think we are. Matthew tries not to bring too much of his work home over the weekends, although he's said his hours will get worse as the DeLuca trial gets closer. Why?"

"Because Thomas has tickets at The Cotton Club. He wants to go there for dinner and dancing before prohibition starts. It's supposed to be elegant, and they still serve liquor. The client who gave him the tickets claims it's the place to be."

Kara laughed. "I don't doubt it. I'll call Matthew before we close. He has wanted to go there, but we always get side-tracked."

There were only two customers in the shop. One of them was in a dressing room, and the other woman was taking items from the racks and taking them into the private dressing rooms.

Elizabeth watched the shop while Kara and Alice were in the storage room. Her job was to remain at the cash register counter. If a shopper needed assistance, she was to call for help. When the phone rang, she answered with the shop's title, only to discover it was Marcio.

"I don't mean to interrupt your work, but I was wondering if you'd go out with me Saturday?" Marcio asked. "I can borrow my friend Mack's car, and we can go somewhere. I don't have much time before I report for my Police training."

"I'd like that," Elizabeth said. "But we can't go anywhere in the old neighborhood, and you must keep your promise."

"I have," Marcio said. "But you should write and tell your father you are okay."

"I have written to him several times," Elizabeth exclaimed. "I had the letters mailed from Long Island, and I don't owe you an explanation."

"Okay, okay," Marcio agreed. "I'll pick you up Saturday evening around six. Wear something casual, and we'll go to Coney Island."

"I'm looking forward to it," Elizabeth said, hanging up the phone. She looked up when both women emerged from the same curtained cubicle. As the women passed the register, they were carrying shopping bags with logos of other stores. That wasn't unusual because many women brought bags into the shop. Elizabeth looked in a mirror positioned so she could see the dressing rooms without leaving the register. The curtains hadn't been closed, and no dresses were hanging on the hooks. She looked to a rack where one of the dresses she admired should have been, but it hadn't been returned either.

Dashing through the storage room door, Elizabeth ran through the room, screaming. "Watch the register! Two thieves just stole some dresses!"

Alice ran into the shop. Kara followed Elizabeth through the back door that led to the alley. Turning the corner, she saw Elizabeth running after two women carrying large shopping bags, screaming, "Stop them, Stop them. They are thieves!" She caught one of the women and tackled her, screaming for someone to stop the other woman. The other woman dropped the bags she was carrying but was tripped by an aproned clerk sitting on a bench outside a tobacco store.

A policeman's whistle was heard, and Kara saw two uniformed officers running toward them on the sidewalk. Kara joined Elizabeth holding down the swearing woman on the sidewalk. The policeman bent down, kneeling on the young woman's back. Then he forced her to her feet, pulled her arms behind her back, and handcuffed her. A second uniformed officer handcuffed the woman being held down in front of the tobacco store.

Kara was looking through the shopping bags and pulled out several outfits. She asked Elizabeth, "Did they pay for this merchandise?"

"No," Elizabeth exclaimed, trying to get to her feet.

At the same time, one of the women swore and claimed that they did pay for the dresses.

"Let's take this back to your place of business," the first police officer said.

Kara turned to follow, but stopped when Elizabeth got to her feet unsteadily.

"You're hurt!" Kara exclaimed.

Elizabeth raised her skirt and displayed scraped bloodied knees. "My shoes!" she wailed. "They're broken."

"Oh, honey, that's not important," Kara exclaimed, putting her arm around Elizabeth's shoulder to help her walk.

The man from the tobacco shop came running. "Let me help," he exclaimed, and with a swoop of his arms, Elizabeth was carried while Kara carried the bags.

"Oh, God!" Alice exclaimed, opening the door and allowing everyone inside. She flipped the Closed sign over on the door and ran into the backroom. She came back with a folding chair and a first-aid kit.

Elizabeth was seated in the chair, and Alice left the room again and returned with a basin of water and a washcloth.

The policemen had the thieves sitting on the floor while they asked questions of Elizabeth, and Kara identified the clothing.

Both women claimed they paid for the merchandise, but neither could produce a receipt.

The clerk from the tobacco shop asked if he could return to his job before he got into trouble with his boss. The police said they would come to his shop for a statement before leaving. The officers arrested the women and called for a paddy wagon to take them to the nearest police precinct.

Kara followed the clerk outside and thanked him for his assistance.

It took a while, but a paddy wagon finally arrived and took the thieves away. The policemen asked questions, especially of Elizabeth, and asked if she wanted to press charges of assault.

"They didn't assault me," Elizabeth said. "I fell on the concrete and scraped my knees."

"They stole from your business," one of the policemen said patiently. "You were injured trying to catch them. A judge would call it theft and assault. You should probably go to the hospital, so there is written proof."

"We'll take her," Alice said, agreeing.

One of the policemen had been using the shop phone. "You should hear from the police about this matter in about a week. These two have a history of shoplifting and have served time in jail. The charges have been petty theft up to this point. But the prices of your merchandise make this theft a misdemeanor."

"I'm so sorry," Elizabeth said when the police left.

"For what?" Kara said. "This isn't your fault!"

"It was," Elizabeth admitted. "I was on the phone and

should have been paying more attention." She raised her feet and removed her stocking. "Oh, my stockings are ruined!"

"Don't worry about the stockings," Alice exclaimed. "We're more worried about you. I'll get the car, and I'll pull up in front. Your wrist is swelling. You probably need an x-ray!"

Elizabeth shook her head. "I heard those machines make your hair fall out!"

"They don't," Alice and Kara said together.

Elizabeth didn't get an x-ray because the doctor said the damage was only a broken bone in her wrist. It was severe enough to warrant a cast. The scrapes forming scabs on her knees would make bending her knees painful for a few days.

"I think you should come home with me tonight," Alice offered.

"That's not necessary," Elizabeth said.

"I disagree," Kara said. You live in a fifth-floor walkup. How are you going to manage that with those knees?"

"I think you should come home with me, and depending on how you feel tomorrow morning, you might have to stay with us for a few days," Kara said.

"You don't have a spare bedroom," Alice said. "You turned both extra bedrooms into offices for you and Matthew. If Elizabeth has to take off a few days, she'd probably be more comfortable at my house."

"I don't need to stay with either of you," Elizabeth said. "And I won't be missing work! I can't afford to miss several days of work."

"If you are hurting tomorrow, you will stay home and be paid," Kara exclaimed. "You stopped those women from stealing from us, and you'll be given a new dress and stockings for your heroic efforts in stopping them. A new rule is being put into place. Bags from other stores will not be allowed in the dressing rooms."

"If I'd been watching them more closely, I could have stopped them before they left the store!" Elizabeth said. "It was my fault!"

"Don't be silly," Alice said. "We're going to care for you, so you might as well give in. It's two against one!"

It was decided that Alice would take Elizabeth to the hospital. When that was completed, Elizabeth was wearing a plaster cast. Elizabeth insisted they had to stop by her boarding house. Alice ran up the stairs and left a note for Emma. She packed a small bag of fresh clothes for Elizabeth.

Elizabeth planned to return to work the following day, but she was so stiff she could barely get out of bed. Walking was painful.

Thomas was concerned about Elizabeth's injuries and asked her to stay until she felt better, or at least until she could climb the stairs to her bedsitter. It was decided that she would remain at the Markham home. Alice made her breakfast before leaving and promised to check in during the lunch break. Elizabeth was told firmly to let her injuries heal.

Matthew was concerned about the robbery and stopped by to check on the door locks. Kara was opening the shop by herself as Alice would be late. He suggested hiring another clerk, but she shut him down. On any given day, two clerks and two owners would make the shop overstaffed.

Matthew also stopped by the police station and spoke to the Sergeant in charge. The shoplifters had already been sent before a judge. Because they had previous records and the price of the merchandise stolen, the charge of an infraction crime was raised to a misdemeanor. The two women were sentenced to ninety days in the women's detention center.

Kara inspected the stolen dresses carefully. They were unharmed because the merchandise had been hidden in the bottom of the shopping bags. She steamed out the wrinkles and dealt with the customers until Alice arrived.

"How is Elizabeth?"

"Stiff," Alice said. "It has to be expected. She had an uncomfortable night, and I told her to lay in and rest."

"Matthew has already been to the police station. Those women have done this kind of thing before, and they have ninety days to think about what they did. I feel guilty myself. We left her in the shop by herself."

"I know, and one person can't watch all the customers," Alice said.

"Agreed," Kara said.

Elizabeth came back to work three days later. She was still stiff but insisted because Saturday was the shop's busiest day. She also didn't want to miss Marcio when he came to the bedsitter to pick her up for a date. She didn't have a phone number to contact him besides his parents', and she wouldn't call there. Elizabeth didn't think she was up to walking the boardwalk at Coney Island and hoped he would understand.

Kara brought in a high stool, and Elizabeth was told her only job was to sit and operate the cash register. They would handle the customers.

Matthew came to the shop and promised to be Elizabeth's attorney, although she wasn't aware she needed one. Matthew laughed and told her he was teasing.

It was a very long day for Elizabeth, although Kara and Alice insisted several times that she go into the back office and rest. She was feeling better and was stunned when her employers gave her a choice of any outfit in the store for what they called heroic actions. When Alice dropped her off in front of her building, Elizabeth knew walking up the five flights would take a while.

Emma was changing out of her uniform when Elizabeth

entered the room.

"Are you okay?" Emma asked, although she knew what had happened because she'd seen the note.

"I'm feeling better," Elizabeth said. "I worked today. Alice and Kara are terrific."

"Will you be okay by yourself tonight?" Emma asked. "Mom is working a double shift, so I have to stay with the kids."

"Of course," Elizabeth said. "Actually, I have a date."

"Who with?" Emma demanded.

"A guy from the old neighborhood," Elizabeth said. "I've known him most of my life."

Emma looked surprised. "I thought..."

"He's promised to keep my secrets," Elizabeth interrupted. "If he betrays me, I'll deal with it!"

"I've got to go," Emma said. "Be careful!"

"I will," Elizabeth said. After hearing her friend run down the stairs, she closed the door and changed into a wide-legged trousers set her employers had given her. The scabs on her knees were stiff and sore. There was a lot of dark bruising that was ugly. Still, except for the plaster cast on her wrist, most of the damage was hidden.

Watching out the window, she saw when Marcio parked a car on the street below. He ran across the road, and she lost sight of him. Then she heard him knocking.

Marcio was all smiles when the door opened. "You look terrific," he said, and then he frowned. "What happened to your hand?"

"I broke a bone in my wrist," Elizabeth said. "I'll tell you what happened when we get in the car. It's against the rules to have men in our rooms."

"Sure, okay," Marcio said, taking her coat and helping her get the cast arm hand through the sleeve. With his arm around her shoulders, they walked downstairs to the lobby and outside to the car. He looked upward at the snow falling. "I guess Coney Island is out. At the first drop of winter, they close everything down. We could take in a film and get something to eat afterward?"

Elizabeth settled in the car seat but winced when she swung her legs to get in. "That would be better."

"What's wrong?" Marcio asked.

Elizabeth pulled one of the pantlegs up to reveal scraped and bruised knees.

"What happened?" he demanded.

Elizabeth explained. "If you don't want to go out, I understand."

"Don't ever do that again!" Marcio scolded. "If someone steals from the store, call the police, but don't confront or chase after them!"

"That's what both Thomas and Matthew said," Elizabeth admitted. "I've already been scolded."

"Who are they?" Marcio frowned.

"My employers' husbands. Kara's husband, Matthew is a lawyer. He did his own investigation and said the women who stole from us have a record of stealing. Until now, they got away with warnings and minor sentences. This time they picked the wrong store. The judge gave them ninety days in jail."

"Good for him," Marcio said. "Do you feel up to going out tonight? We can go out some other time, but it's my only chance before I go into training. I was called up a week early."

"I'm moving a little slower, but I didn't want to miss our date," Elizabeth said.

Marcio smiled. "A new Lillian Gish film is playing at the Lyceum Theater. We'll have time for dinner if we get tickets for the second show."

"That sounds like a good idea," Elizabeth agreed.

Chapter 15

WHEN ALICE PULLED over to the curb Monday morning, Elizabeth climbed into the back seat.

"Good morning," Alice said. "You're looking better, and you're not limping."

"I feel a lot better," Elizabeth admitted. "Did you have a good time at The Cotton Club?"

"We did," Alice said. "It was amazing! The liquor flowed freely, and the club was wild with jazz music and dancing. It was so out of control that it was embarrassing. We even saw Betty Compton, the famous Broadway showgirl, accompanied by Jimmy Walker. He's got a reputation for being a man-around town. Matthew said it's rumored that Walker is going into politics. How was your day off?"

"Not as exciting as yours," Elizabeth said. "I went to see a film and had dinner with a friend."

Alice pulled into the alley behind the hotel, and Kara came running. She slipped and skidded on the ice on the concrete pavement.

"Be careful!" Alice exclaimed.

"How are you feeling?" Kara asked Elizabeth over her shoulder.

"Fine," was the answer. "My dress is long enough to cover most of the damage."

"We can't push the lengths any shorter," Kara said. "Mainstream clothiers aren't ready for it yet."

"Neither is my husband," Alice laughed. "Thomas says there are parts of me he wants fully covered."

Kara laughed. "Matthew is the same."

It was a busy morning, even as the snow accumulated. Deciding to close early, they were closing out the register and tidying when there was a knock on the closed front door.

Kara went to answer the door and smiled when Sharon and Deloris came in, and both had their arms full of paintings.

"Goodness," Kara exclaimed as the women put down their loads and returned to Sharon's vehicle for more.

"I tried to call several times, but the line was busy," Deloris said. "Simon went to a bowling alley with some friends, so it was a good time to bring more paintings."

"Anytime," Kara said. "We only have three left. Should you be out in this weather? Did you call Mr. Wallace?"

"I did," Deloris said. "He's a pushy man, and I didn't like him, even though we only spoke over the phone. He wanted to charge me for gallery space, and he wanted half of the painting's sale price. If you don't mind, I'd rather continue selling my paintings here."

"We're delighted," Kara said, as Alice chimed in simultaneously, "Of course, we don't mind!"

"We don't have a lot of time," Sharon said. She glanced over at Deloris and then at Kara with a slight jerk of her head.

"I'll get your commission money," Kara said. "Sharon, there is something I'd like to show you."

"Sure," Sharon agreed, following Kara into the office.

While Kara was opening the safe, she turned to Sharon. "What's wrong?"

"It's Simon," Sharon whispered. "He's become more obnoxious than usual. I won't even go to Deloris' house unless I know he's gone. He's treating her horribly."

"Does she need help?" Kara asked.

"She claims he's just having a problem adjusting to his retirement."

"Adjusting as in physically hurting her?" Kara asked.

"I haven't seen any signs of that yet," Sharon whispered. "So far, it's only been verbal. He shouts at her over nothing."

"What is she going to do about it?"

"I don't know. Deloris makes excuses for him, and I know she's embarrassed," Sharon said. "At the same time, I know she's hiding the money she's been getting for her paintings from him. She has a driver's license now."

"Good for her. It sounds like she's taking baby steps and planning something. Is there anyone she can go to for help?" Kara asked.

"The only family she has left is a sister in New Jersey," Sharon said. "If she goes there, it will be the first place Simon looks after coming to my house."

"She has friends," Kara said. "Matthew has an empty apartment he no longer uses but can't break the lease. It's sitting there empty. If she needs a place to disappear, she can stay there."

"Can he do that?"

"He let our friends Alice and Thomas stay there when their house flooded from a broken pipe," Kara said. "Matthew and I have already dismissed a lot of the bunk that the Colonel was preaching on how to keep a marriage together. After the way he's been acting, he shouldn't be advising anyone!"

"I'll tell her, but don't be surprised if she doesn't accept the offer," Sharon said. "They've been married a long time. I know she's hoping that his behavior will change."

"From what Matthew tells me, he has changed, but for the worse. Most women know when it's time to walk away," Kara said. "I know because I was there at one point in my life. Let Deloris know she has friends who will help. She can make a living with her talent, but warn her not to sign exclusivity contracts. She should be able to exhibit her paintings at many studios, not just one."

"I'm not suggesting that she leave him. But someone needs to tell him to straighten up! I'll keep an eye on her," Sharon said. "Men bitch about women going through the change of life, but they won't admit that they do the same. My Harry was planning a twenty-year career with the Army, so we would always have a pension to fall back on. It's not enough to raise a family, but I didn't want to continue teaching while the kids were small. Harry's father was a partner in the furniture store, and he inherited the part ownership when his father died. Harry had something to fall back on.

"Simon has interviewed for several jobs. He's fifty-nine, but he looks older. Simon probably has good management skills but no experience in non-military positions. At first, he was spending his retirement on the golf course. Now he spends it playing pool, poker, and drinking at a local tavern."

After Deloris was paid, they left. Sharon was watching the clock and said they had to go before the bank closed.

"Be careful," Kara warned. "The forecast on the radio is that we may get a foot or more of snow."

"Is the Colonel mistreating her?" Alice asked after the door closed.

"How did you know?" Kara asked.

"She bent over, stacking the canvases, and I was inches

from her. I saw a bruise on her neck, and she was wearing thick makeup on her cheek."

"Bastard," Kara said. "Sharon promised to keep an eye on her."

"Men knocking their wives and kids around is common in my old neighborhood," Elizabeth said.

"It may be common, but that doesn't make it right," Alice said.

"Times have changed, and women have changed for the better," Kara said.

Matthew was late coming home from the office. He kissed Kara, changed out of his suit, and sat down to wait for their dinner to arrive.

"Is something wrong?" she asked.

"The DeLuca trial has been delayed," Matthew said.

"Is that good or bad?"

"Both," Matthew said. "It gives my team more time to prepare. The reason for the delay was we discovered that Judge Bennett, who was supposed to hear the case, was heavily invested in DeLuca Enterprises. He's been suspended, and the case has been turned over to Judge Seinfield. It makes me sick when I discover someone I trusted is corrupt."

"Well, I hate to add to your misery, but your mentor, the Colonel, is abusing Deloris," Kara said.

"That can't be true," Matthew said, shaking his head.

"Believe what you want," Kara said. "It doesn't change the facts."

"He called today," Matthew said. "He wants us to come over before Christmas."

"If I go, it will only be to support Deloris," Kara said.

"According to Sharon, Simon is spending his retirement at a local tavern, guzzling beer, and losing money playing poker and pool. He's not happy and taking it out on his wife."

"Those are not the actions of the man I served under and respected," Matthew said. "Have you spoken to Deloris?"

"Not directly. Sharon says she's in denial," Kara said. "She said Deloris always has an excuse to explain the bruises. She bumped into something, or she fell. Deloris isn't stupid. She might not want to admit what is happening, but she is protecting herself. Simon doesn't know she is selling her paintings, and she's opened a bank account in her name."

Matthew shook his head and took a deep breath. "I'll go Saturday to talk to him while you're at the shop."

"Sharon thinks part of the reason she hasn't left already is Daniel. I told Sharon that Deloris could use your apartment if she needed a place to stay. It's sitting there empty, although she hasn't admitted that there is a problem yet."

"Try not to get involved," Matthew said.

"I am involved. Deloris is my friend, and I won't stand by and allow her to be mistreated," Kara warned.

Matthew held both hands up in surrender. "You're right. When we discussed discipline, wife beating was not what Simon and Harry drilled into me. I'll talk to the Colonel and throw some of his advice back at him. How was Elizabeth today?"

"I had her sitting on a stool most of the day. She's healing. Her understanding of dressmaking is coming along. Her designs are improving, but the math is a problem," Kara said.

"Alice and I were discussing sending her to a Senior High School. Several schools are offering evening courses past the eighth-grade level. Elizabeth's father pulled her out of school when she turned fourteen and got her a job at the newspaper. It's legal, but it's terrible that parents don't think their children, especially their daughters need a secondary education beyond that age."

"The Keating-Owen Act was passed two years ago, but the Supreme Court struck it down, saying it was government overreach," Matthew said. "Protection laws for children will come. It takes time to enact new laws, and it also takes time for people to change." He walked over to Kara and wrapped her in a hug. "We've changed a lot, and both of us have matured. If we want to keep our marriage healthy, it takes time and compromises."

As the Christmas season approached, the boutique doubled its revenue. Party dresses were selling faster than they could hang them on the racks. The pre-ordered couture dresses were being finished in time for holiday galas. For the women who hadn't ordered dresses in time, they *settled* on rack wear.

Kara stormed out of the boutique after a long, slightly heated discussion with a wealthy young woman. She walked down to the nearest deli and ordered lunch. The temporary hires would be working with them for several weeks, part-time. Returning with her arms full, she carried the lunches to the upstairs rooms, where four women were sewing enhancements on the last of the couture designs due before Christmas.

Returning downstairs, she gave the part-time hire a lunch and sent her into the storage area, where a table and refrigerator were set up as a lunchroom. They had hired two temporary clerks for the boutique but had dismissed one of the hires within a few hours.

"Have you calmed down?" Alice asked.

"Was I ever that obnoxious?" Kara asked her dearest friend.

Alice shook her head, laughing. "No, but I believe that

was because of the strict Catholic schooling influence, not Selina's. You handled Mrs. Madison quite well."

"Did she really think you would make her a couture dress in seven days?" Elizabeth whispered. "It usually takes at least two months or more."

"She did," Kara said. "She even threatened that if I didn't, she would spread the word that my boutique was unreliable."

Alice closed her eyes. "And, what was your response?"

Kara smiled sweetly. "I told her to go ahead and try. My husband, who happens to be a lawyer, would sue her for defamation of character, and in the meantime, the Madison Candy Factory would gain a reputation for being infested with rats, and all those fancy chocolates would sit on the shelves, with no one purchasing them during the Christmas season."

"What was her reaction?" Elizabeth asked.

"Shock at first," Kara said. "Then I told her two could play her game. That her threats were meaningless, and she was acting like an ass. I warned her that I *could* end her social status with one phone call and suggested she take her snobby, upstart behavior elsewhere because I wouldn't tolerate it."

"Did she believe you?" Alice asked.

"She did. I saw fear in her eyes," Kara said. "She won't be any trouble to us or the boutique."

Matthew called Simon Rathforth, agreeing to meet him on a Saturday afternoon at a tavern he'd spent quite a bit of time in during his service in the Army. Matthew hadn't seen his advisor since the summer barbecue and was shocked by his appearance. Simon had gained a lot of weight and had a belly hanging over his belt. His hair had changed from salt-and-pepper to full-out gray.

Simon raised his hand from a booth, and Matthew joined him. "Matthew, my boy. How are you doing?"

"Busy," Matthew said as Simon waved at the waitress.

"Have a beer," Simon said, smiling. "That damnable prohibition goes into effect soon."

"I'm driving," Matthew said to the waitress. "Iced tea or soda for me. Whatever you have."

Waiting for the drinks to be delivered, Matthew asked how his retired commanding officer was doing in retirement.

Simon swilled a third of his beer and slammed his mug on the table. "Retirement is a bitch!"

"If you're not ready to retire, you should find something else to keep you busy," Matthew suggested.

"What?" Simon demanded. "Golf wastes my time, and I can't play in the winter. What the hell am I supposed to do? My job was to keep the base running during the war, and I did it! But the war is over."

"Many men are in the same situation," Matthew said. "They came back to jobs that don't exist anymore. The war was difficult, but it was also a time of invention. Factories built machines that replaced workers."

"The world isn't the same," Simon complained. "My boys are grown and have jobs and girlfriends. Except for Daniel, my sons don't need me. Even he doesn't want to come home on his school vacations."

"I'm worried about you," Matthew said gently.

"Why the hell are you worrying about me?" Simon demanded.

"Take a good look in the mirror, sir. You've gained a ton of weight and don't look fit. What will you do when the pubs are closed after the New Year? What does your wife think about you not trying to find something useful and respectful to do?"

"All my wife wants to do is waste her time on those damn paintings!" Simon growled. "She won't take time to even feed me!"

"You don't look like you're missing any meals, sir," Matthew said. "Besides, Deloris kept the home fires burning while you fought in the Spanish American War and this last Great War. She deserves a break to do whatever makes her happy."

"You're too young to understand," Simon growled. "Husbands aren't supposed to be Namby-pamby boys!"

"You told me that to keep a marriage strong, both parties have to give a hundred percent of themselves. Deloris did far more than her share on the home front. She's supported your career and lifestyle for over thirty years. She respects your choices. Maybe it's time that respect was reciprocated."

Simon took a long drink, emptied the mug, and slammed it onto the table. "Lieutenant, you don't know what the hell you're talking about! You've only been back with your wife for six months. That doesn't make you an expert."

"It was Captain," Matthew said. "I don't claim to be an expert, and I'm learning more daily. But I do know I'm proud of my wife. She was in the thick of it in England, and she's created an amazing business since she returned. I'm proud of what my wife did over there and what she has accomplished since coming home."

"Deloris doesn't have that kind of ambition. All she's ever been was a wife and mother," Simon grumbled. "Who the hell are you to tell me about my wife?"

"Don't belittle what she did in your absences," Matthew said, getting to his feet. "Your wife isn't a cocky green recruit that needs to be broken down before he can be trained as a good soldier. If I've learned anything over the past six years, it's that respect has to be earned, and that goes both ways. Good day, sir."

Since Matthew was in the area, he stopped at the Warner house. Neither Harry nor Sharon were there. Lily, Harry's mother, was watching the children. Harry was working. He was driving a delivery truck for the furniture store he'd inherited from his father. His only days off were Sundays and Wednesdays. He was told Sharon was visiting Deloris and wouldn't return for several hours.

Matthew took his time going home. Kara wouldn't be there for a while, and he went Christmas shopping. His problem was that his wife didn't need anything and hadn't mentioned wanting anything. Of the two of them, she was wealthier. She had inheritances from her parents and Selina. She had a massive amount of jewelry inherited from her mother and her aunt, but rarely wore it. He was carrying a gold watch that had been her father's. A salesman must have been watching him wander around because he was asked if he needed help.

"I don't know what I will get my wife for Christmas," Matthew said.

"A new dress?" the salesman suggested.

"She designs women's clothing," Matthew said.

"Jewelry usually works," was another suggestion.

"She's inherited a ton of it, and unless we're going out to impress, she rarely wears anything but her wedding ring and small earrings."

"Perfume? A fur coat?"

Matthew shook his head. "Thanks for trying to help." He left the store and stood on the sidewalk, watching men and women coming in and out of the stores with wrapped packages. He walked down the street where he'd parked and suddenly smiled. Returning to the hotel, Matthew went inside to talk to Mr. Daniels, the concierge. Twenty minutes later, he left again, this time heading north. He knew exactly what he was going to give Kara for Christmas.

Kara & Alaïs Couture Designs was so busy that Kara and Alice decided to delay closing for an hour. Kara made the announcement, and Elizabeth stayed busy at the cash register. The seamstresses working upstairs left at their usual time.

Kara and Alice assisted customers and carried down merchandise to refill the racks. After filling two racks and almost starting a stampede, Kara told Alice to not bring anything out. They would leave the stock in the backroom and fill the racks after they closed the doors. Kara announced a ten-minute warning: The shop was closing at six. If the customers were not checked out before six, they would have to return when the shop was open. The announcement triggered a frenzy, and Alice helped Elizabeth check out the customers while Kara knocked on the dressing room doors, calling out... 'We are closing in ten minutes. If you aren't checked out, you will have to come back tomorrow."

"Good grief! Have you ever seen anything like that?" Alice exclaimed, turning the sign over to Closed and pulling down the blinds on the front door. Kara pulled the curtains on the display window.

"No," Kara exclaimed. "But, I'm glad I ordered triple our normal inventory. If we are lucky, we might make it through to Christmas Eve."

Alice blew a piece of hair out of her eyes. "Let's get busy. Something tells me tomorrow isn't going to be any easier."

While Alice closed the register, Elizabeth and Kara refilled the racks and straightened the shelves. There was a knock on the door, and Kara answered it. She pushed the blinds out of the way and shouted. "We're closed!"

Then she unlocked and opened the door. "Sorry, I didn't know it was you!" Kara exclaimed, taking a stack of paintings from Sharon's arms.

Deloris followed Kara into the shop while Sharon returned to the car for another load.

"Goodness!" Alice exclaimed when Sharon finally closed the door behind her. There was a total of forty paintings.

"Do you have room to store them?" Sharon asked. "And, more if we bring them?"

"We'll make room," Kara said. "Why?"

Deloris only shook her head.

"You can't keep this a secret if they are willing to help," Sharon scolded. "Simon came home several days ago drunk, and destroyed the painting she was working on and several others. We've moved all of Deloris' paintings to Lily's house temporarily, but she has a small house and doesn't have the room for them."

"Let's take them upstairs," Kara suggested. "We can hang quite a few here in the shop, as the others have been sold. Our clientele are buying them for Christmas gifts."

They hung as many paintings as there was room for and carried the rest upstairs to the third floor that wasn't being used.

Kara asked Sharon in a whispered voice if it was safe for Deloris to return to her home.

"I honestly don't know. If I try to bring up the subject, she changes it," Sharon said.

"Walking away from thirty-plus years of marriage won't be easy," Kara said.

"If it was me, I'd knock some sense into him with a cast-iron skillet," Sharon said. "I'm shocked by Simon's behavior, but she has to be the one to make the decision."

Chapter 16

KARA WAS LATE COMING HOME. "Sorry, I'm late," she said as she collapsed on the couch and propped her feet on the coffee table."

"Rough day?" Matthew asked, stretching out beside her. He pulled her legs into his lap and removed her high heels to massage her feet.

"Humm," Kara mumbled, closing her eyes. "We kept the shop open an extra hour, and then Sharon and Deloris showed up with a carload of paintings we had to store upstairs. Deloris has lost a lot of weight and looks... tired and distressed. I managed to get her alone and reminded her of your empty apartment. She just thanked me for protecting her paintings. Apparently, her husband has started destroying them."

"I met with Simon today," Matthew said.

"And?"

"Whatever weight Deloris has lost, the Colonel found it. He looks... unhealthy," Matthew said. "He's got belly hanging over his belt, and he didn't deny spending most of his days in the tavern drinking and playing games with a rowdy bunch of unemployed men. He hasn't taken well to retirement."

"Then why did he retire?" Kara asked.

"He wasn't given a choice," Matthew said. "He had a stellar record, and although the U.S. entered the Great War late, his skills were needed to train civilian men to become soldiers. When the armistice was signed, the Army needed to disband, and they did it quickly. Older officers were phased out for younger men who wanted to stay in the services. After the war was over, the Army didn't need him.

"Harry and I knew the Colonel was on the shortlist to be retired early. We had jobs to fall back on. Simon had nothing but the Army, and suddenly it was gone.

"He has a retirement income, but from what I understand, it was scaled back because he didn't make the thirty-year requirement. I'm going to look into that because it doesn't sound right. He wouldn't discuss it with me. All I know is that golf and poker aren't enough to keep a man like him active. I don't know what to do to help him.

"The Colonel was three years from a full thirty-year retirement, and his next promotion would have made him a General. He worked toward that star for decades, the Army shafted him."

"Is that legal?" Kara asked.

"I don't know," Matthew said, frowning. "But, I am going to look into it. Military law is different from civilian law."

They sat comfortably in each other's company for a while, and then Matthew stood up and pulled Kara to her feet. "I'm hungry," he said.

"I'll call down for dinner," Kara offered.

"Not for food," Matthew said. "Since my wife wasn't here, and I had nothing else to do, I took your advice. I was reading one of Aunt Selina's illegal books."

Kara opened her mouth to question him but was guided

toward the bedroom. The bedspread had already been folded neatly at the bottom of the bed. Matthew turned her around, unbuttoned her blouse, and removed her clothing piece by piece. His eyes devoured her body, and Kara was beginning to tingle because she suspected this would be one of those evenings that was purely sexual.

She was right as Matthew led her to the bed. He stripped quickly and sat down beside her. Kara turned to climb into the bed, but she was stopped and pulled over his knee. The first spank was breathtaking, but it also sent a vibration through her sex. This wasn't a spanking because she'd done something wrong. This was a spanking to prep her for having sex while Matthew was displaying that he was in charge. This was a different kind of spanking, mixing discipline with sex. They had finally agreed that maintenance spankings were not necessary. But that didn't squelch Matthew's need to feel like an alpha male.

Kara allowed her husband to take the lead. He didn't know that she'd found and read several books he had under lock and key.

Matthew spanked, fondled, and played with her bottom and her sex. It was stimulating, and Kara was caught in mixed feelings. Her bottom was stinging, but his dominant hand knew her body and what to touch. This treatment went on until her buttocks felt like they were on fire. Then her husband turned her over and entered her womanhood.

He wasn't gentle, but she didn't try to stop him, as he gave her one of the best sexual experiences since they had reunited, and that was saying something, considering they had sex nearly every day.

They stopped for dinner, although Matthew called downstairs to the kitchens and only allowed Kara to escape the bed for the bathroom, and he joined her there. Sex in the bed, the shower, the tub... Nearly every waist-high surface in the apartment had become a platform for him to bend her over and have his way with her body.

She didn't object to anything he was doing.

When Matthew opened his eyes, they traversed over his wife's naked body. He touched himself, but that particular organ was flaccid, and he didn't think there was any chance of using it again until it had time to recuperate.

Kara turned over to cast her eyes at his naked body with a look that could only be described as lustful.

"Sweetheart, last night was amazing, but I'm wiped out! I may be walking bowlegged today."

Kara giggled. "I feel the same. I won't be sitting comfortably today, and I may have to take floor duty because my bottom is sore!"

"Probably not," Matthew disagreed. "That's the beauty of spanking. The results don't linger very long. It's supposed to be stimulating."

"It was," Kara admitted, and then she smiled. "You have been studying Aunt Selina's books! But..."

"But what?" Matthew demanded with a frown.

"Why is it okay for you to read them but not me?"

Matthew smiled and kissed her. "You are a delicate flower and the love of my life. If you don't mind, I'd rather you learn from me."

Sunday was supposed to be a day of rest. When Kara retreated to her studio in the apartment to draw designs, Matthew went to his law office to retrieve several law books. His company had a law library that he used judiciously. This time, he was searching for Military subsets. Each military branch had rules and regulations that only pertained to a particular branch of service.

The Uniform Code of Military Justice was the foundation of the military justice system for all the United States armed forces. He found several law books that might help him in his quest.

When Matthew had joined the Army, he'd expected to be assigned to the legal forces, but that hadn't happened. He'd been sent to decoding school and had found a secondary use for his unique mental skills. He had a lot of research to do before involving the military. Before returning to the hotel, Matthew stopped and bought two Christmas trees. One for their suite and a smaller one that would fit on the counter at the boutique. All the stores were closed on Sundays, but he went to a storage unit, where he'd stored their belongings when he joined the Army and emptied their tiny apartment. At that time, he hadn't known if he'd ever see his wife again.

Matthew unlocked the storage unit and stepped inside. Looking around, it was a journey back in time. He knew there were Christmas tree ornaments in a box somewhere. The entire storage unit was full of memories of their first years together. They had been so young and innocent then. He had been gullible and inexperienced. Matthew didn't blame Kara for running away. After losing his father, mother, and wife, it was a miracle he hadn't gone gray or dived into a bottle himself. He'd been a lost soul for a while.

Returning to New York City, he'd spent months searching for Kara. Living alone in their apartment had crushed him, and he finally packed everything they owned, stored it, and left. He'd taken lodging in a furnished apartment.

It wasn't until he joined the Army that Matthew found his footing again, with the help of his two commanding officers. Now, one of those officers needed his help, and he would do his best to offer assistance.

As usual, Kara let time get away from her when sketching new designs. Several hours passed before she realized that Matthew hadn't returned yet. Stretching to relieve stiff muscles, she returned to her sketches.

After a while, she heard a commotion in the living room and went to investigate. The door was open, and a large Christmas tree was carried through the entry with Mr. Groban behind it. Matthew followed with a much smaller tree, and a younger man followed with buckets.

Matthew set his tree down, and he and Mr. Groban moved a table out of the way of a large window. They set the big tree in a bucket and anchored it with bricks. The smaller tree was left leaning against the wall in a bucket of water.

"What's all this?" Kara exclaimed.

"It's almost Christmas," Matthew said. "I was told if we keep water in the buckets, the trees should last through the season. The smaller one is for the shop."

"Thank you," Kara said, giving him a hug. She had tears in her eyes. "I haven't celebrated Christmas in years. Observing the holidays in crowds was too dangerous, especially in the cathedrals. We'll have to buy or make ornaments."

There was a knock on the door, and Matthew opened it to the young man carrying three large boxes. Matthew tipped him and pulled a small knife from his pocket to cut through the tape. "Our old ornaments are in these boxes."

"You kept them?" Kara exclaimed, diving into the box and unwrapping a delicate angel ornament.

"I kept everything," Matthew admitted. "When I joined the Army, I put all our belongings into storage. I was in a position that required lockdown conditions. I wasn't allowed to leave our station."

"Everything?" Kara whispered. "Why didn't you tell me?"

Matthew shrugged. "We split up in the worst way, in a terrible time. I realized too late that my mother was making your life miserable. I don't blame you for leaving. I did at first, but as I matured, I understood. I was gutted by your leaving, but I had to face reality. I stopped blaming you and understood that I was being manipulated by my mentally ill mother."

"Will you take me to the storage place?" Kara asked.

Matthew shrugged and looked around at the opulent suite. "What we could afford in those days doesn't compare to this place."

"Price doesn't always equate to value," Kara said, holding another ornament in her hands as if it was precious. "These mean the world to me because we picked them out together. They hold memories of our first and only Christmas back then."

Matthew nodded and pulled her into him closer. "It's too late to go there now, but I will take you. We should probably go through the things and donate what we don't want to keep. I've probably spent ten times more in paying the storage fees than the stuff is worth."

"It's worth a lot to me that you didn't throw it away," Kara said, genuinely touched that he hadn't disposed of their shared belongings.

Monday morning, Kara ran over to Alice's car and asked her to park for a few minutes. She escorted her friends to her suite and showed them the fully decorated Christmas Tree.

"It's beautiful," Elizabeth said.

"Matthew bought a smaller tree for the boutique, and the ornaments we didn't use are in that box. There should be enough to trim the little tree."

"Let's go," Alice said, picking up the small tree. "Oops, we need a towel to wrap around the trunk where it's wet from being in the bucket.

"I'll dump the water down the sink," Elizabeth volunteered.

Carrying the small tree and the boxes was no problem. When they came upon one of Mr. Groban's men, he loaded the items in the car trunk for them. Once they arrived at the shop, Alice tried to get a close spot to park, but the shoppers were out early, and the sidewalks were lined with vehicles. She stopped for a few minutes and ignored the honking horns and shouts behind her while Kara and Elizabeth unloaded the tree and the boxes. Alice circled the block three times before finding an empty spot to park. Someone had illegally parked in the boutique's single space. When she entered the shop, the tree was in place in the front window, and Kara was hanging ornaments on the branches. Occasionally, she would turn to the manikins and hook a decoration on their hats or somewhere on their outfits.

"You know," Alice said, looking around the shop. "One of the larger paintings Deloris brought in was a snow scene. It would be perfect in the window."

"There were several smaller pictures of winter, too," Elizabeth said. "Should I get them?"

"No, prep the register," Alice said, looking at the clock. "If Saturday was any indication, we're going to be busy. I'll run upstairs and look for the paintings."

When Alice returned with a large painting, two customers were already in the shop. She made a second trip and brought four smaller canvases with her. Kara set the large landscape in the window, adding a price tag.

The shop was so busy they had to take shifts to eat lunch. Three of Deloris's smaller paintings had sold quickly, and there was no haggling, even though Kara had raised the prices.

When five o'clock finally arrived, the three women closed the shop and collapsed onto chairs in the storage room.

"I'd suggest a glass of wine, but I'm driving," Alice exclaimed, turning to Kara. "I must admit I was wrong about the number of dresses you ordered. I underestimated our selling capacity."

"I remembered how many new outfits my Aunt bought during the holidays," Kara said with a smile. "Believe me, it will settle down after the New Year, and we'll be lucky to sell a dozen garments in a week. That's why designers use the winter and spring months to design. That reminds me. We need to take turns next week to go shopping. I bought Matthew a Louis Cartier wristwatch and had it engraved, but I haven't had time to pick it up!"

"I have the same problem," Alice said. "The shop is so busy, I haven't had time to shop. In addition to having no idea what to get Thomas. I'm going to call his father for some ideas."

"It was in the newspaper that Macy's is staying open until eight p.m.," Elizabeth said. "As soon as they made the announcement, the Henri Bendel and Bergdorf Goodman stores announced they would do the same. The sales and floor people at Macy's were told their hours would be rearranged to accommodate the extra hours. Emma couldn't take the extra hours because she watches over her younger brother and sister until her mother comes home from work. She tried to explain but was fired because she couldn't do the extra hours."

"That's not fair," Kara said.

Elizabeth shrugged. "I help them as much as I can."

"Did Emma work on the floor?" Kara asked.

Elizabeth nodded. "I think she's had every job at Macy's, from cleaning, floor duty, and register. When she first went to work there, she was unloading boxes.

"Tell her to come in tomorrow," Kara said.

"Really?" Elizabeth exclaimed.

"She'll be here for a trial run," Alice agreed. "We need to see if she fits in well before deciding on additional hiring."

"She was working the early morning shift to be off work by three o'clock. She watches over her little brother and sister after school. The kids are only seven and eight years old. Her mother works the late shift at the shoe factory."

"We can work around those hours," Alice said. "Although she'll have to ride the bus to return home in the afternoons."

"Where is her father?" Kara asked.

"Who knows?" Elizabeth said. "He didn't come home one evening, and they haven't seen him since. That was two years ago. Her mother only lives two blocks from our room. I try to help out as much as possible. The rent I pay Emma goes straight to her mother."

"No promises, but we'll see how she fits in," Kara said.

"Can I tell her?" Elizabeth asked.

"Use the telephone in the office," Alice said.

A few minutes later, Elizabeth returned. "Thank you. Thank you. Thank you! Emma is so relieved that she's crying. I'll loan her some of my clothing. We're about the same size, so she'll be dressed properly."

Kara clapped her hands together. "Okay, the break is over. We have to get this place ready for tomorrow!"

Emma Finch was standing on the sidewalk with Elizabeth when Alice pulled over to pick them up the following day.

"I'm so grateful for this job," Emma exclaimed. "My supervisor told me that maybe after the holidays, they would give me back my job."

"Her supervisor also told her that she would take a cut in pay if she returned!" Elizabeth said angrily.

Hiring Emma was a godsend. The temporary floor help didn't show up to work, and when Kara called the given telephone number, she was told the number was out of service. Still, as the last couture dresses deadlined for Christmas were picked up, Kara and Alice had more time to help on the floor. During the last week before Christmas, the women took turns taking several hours to do their own shopping.

Kara picked up Matthew's wristwatch and a new hat and overcoat. Alice bought Thomas a drafting table for his home office and several tools suggested by her father-in-law. She didn't know what the expensive instruments were used for but had been assured they could be returned if necessary.

Elizabeth bought a reasonably priced man's wristwatch and blushed when teased about having a boyfriend. She wasn't ready to label Marcio as her boyfriend, although they had gone out a few times when he was given weekend leave from his training. Knowing her friend's problems, Elizabeth purchased Emma a new winter coat and boots. Kara and Alice had been generous with Emma as they had been to her. Damaged merchandise was given to them as long as it could be repaired.

Elizabeth also purchased a few toys for Emma's siblings. She knew Christmas would be sparse for her best friend's family.

On the Thursday before a Saturday Christmas date, Kara locked the front door at midday and turned over the closed sign. The boutique would be closed on Christmas Eve, Christmas Day, and the Sunday after. It was the first time since the shop's opening that it would be closed for three days straight. Even so, they deserved the break. It took both Alice and Kara to wrap the small Christmas Tree in muslin and stuff it in the back seat of Alice's car.

When Alice stopped next to Elizabeth's building, she turned from the front seat and asked Emma where her mother lived.

"Two buildings down," Emma said.

"That's good," Alice said with a smile. She drove down the street and parked in the alley.

"The tree is for your mother and the children," Kara

said, jumping out of the car. "What floor does your family live on?"

"Third floor, 304," Emma said, looking like she was about to start crying. "Thank you!"

"You two go on ahead with the tree," Alice said, and when the building door closed behind them, she opened the trunk. She handed a heavy sack to Kara and took another for herself. Carrying the bags up the stairs was challenging, but the door to 304 was open. They set the bags down inside and went back downstairs. On the second trip, they carried in boxed groceries.

"I can't believe you're doing this," Emma cried. "My family are strangers to you."

"You were there when Elizabeth needed help, and we appreciate it," Alice said.

"Have a good Christmas, and we'll see both of you Monday morning," Kara said, giving both young women an envelope. "Emma, you are now a full-time employee of Kara & Alaïs Couture Designs if you want to accept a permanent position with us. Elizabeth, you need to start studying if you aren't already. Night school classes begin January 4th and are three nights a week. The tuition has been paid. Alice and I can help with most of the subjects. If you need help with math, our husbands will have to tutor you."

"She flunked math," Alice said with a grin.

"I didn't flunk," Kara protested. "I passed. Barely, but I passed. Merry Christmas, girls, and we hope you have a good holiday!"

Chapter 17

KARA WAS OFF CHRISTMAS EVE, although Matthew was working a half-day. She had wrapped several gifts, and they were under the tree, although it didn't look like much. Kara told herself it wasn't the size of the packages that counted, although she did remember the massive piles of gifts she'd received from her aunt on Christmas morning.

Christmas was one of the few days Aunt Selina had focused on her niece each year. Christmas and Easter were celebrated, although not in a religious manner. Her birthday had been acknowledged with a card and a sum of money tucked into the envelope. There had never been phone calls or visitations when she returned to the boarding school, only fifteen miles away.

Time was slipping away, and watching the clock wasn't helping. Earlier, she'd received a phone call from Emma and her mother, thanking her for making Christmas possible for her family.

"You're very welcome," Kara expressed to a woman she hadn't met. "Christmas is a time to make childhood memories. I still regard my own memories as a wonderful time."

Kara entered the bedroom and laid out a dress she'd designed the year before but hadn't had an opportunity to wear. She laid out Matthew's best suit. They had been invited to a dinner party at the home of Mr. Cahill, one of the law firm's owners. Semi-formal was the statement on the invitation.

When the phone rang, she expected it to be her husband, but it was Sharon.

"What's wrong?" Kara asked.

"I'm sorry to bother you, especially today, but..." Sharon apologized.

"What's wrong?" Kara demanded.

There was a long silence before Sharon spoke, and she was crying. "I have Deloris, and she needs a safe place to stay. I'd love to have her at my house, but this is the first place Simon will look for her. I can't stay with her. I want to, but I have my children to think about. Harry is delivering last-minute furniture today, and I can't reach him. Lily will be here any minute to watch the kids."

"Bring Deloris to the Wolcott Hotel," Kara said. "I'll call down to the main desk to expect her."

"She can't afford a hotel like that," Sharon exclaimed.

"We live in a penthouse at the Wolcott," Kara explained.

"Oh," Sharon whispered. "She won't show her face to strangers, and she won't let me call the police or take her to the hospital."

Kara flinched. "Is it that bad?"

"Yes," Sharon said, sounding like she was crying.

"Drive around to the back of the hotel to the employee's entrance. It's clearly marked. I'll meet her there and bring her in the back way."

"Okay," Sharon said. "Lily is here, so I'm on my way."

As soon as the call was disconnected, Kara called Matthew's office.

"I'm coming," Matthew said.

"Hurry," Kara said. "Sharon is bringing Deloris here. Simon has hurt her. I didn't get the details, but I think she's been beaten. She won't call the police or go to the hospital."

Matthew locked his office and ran to his car, brushing off the snow before he could drive. Traffic was lighter than usual, even with last-minute shoppers. He parked and met Kara at the back entrance they used to exit the hotel because it was closer to the garages.

"Should we call a doctor?" he asked.

"Let's see what the damage is first," Kara said. "Don't forget that I was trained as a first aid attendant."

Matthew backed away as Kara and Sharon assisted Deloris inside the apartment. Kara took her into the small kitchen and sat her in a chair before removing the dark veil over her face.

Kara glanced at her husband as purple and blackish bruises and a split lip were uncovered. She gave a shooing motion with her hand and reached for a towel and the first-aid kit. Most of the bruising and swelling was on Deloris's face, neck, and hands. There were minor cuts with broken skin but not deep enough to scar. Her hands and forearms were also bruised, and Kara thought a finger might be broken.

"A doctor should see this," Kara told her friend. Deloris hadn't uttered a word since she sat down.

"Does she need to go to the hospital?" Matthew asked.

"No!" Deloris whispered, shaking her head furiously.

"Call downstairs and have them send the Wolcott doctor up," Kara said.

"The hotel has a doctor in residence?" he questioned.

"At any given time, the Wolcott has as many as five to six hundred residents," Kara said. "The hotel is independent, very much like a cruise ship."

"I didn't know that," Matthew mumbled. "I'll take care of it."

"Sharon," Deloris whispered.

"What do you need, honey?"

"Go home," Deloris said clearly. "Go home to your family. It's Christmas Eve, and you must get back there before it gets too dangerous to drive. When he realizes I'm gone, Simon will probably go to your place first."

"I won't tell him anything," Sharon said firmly. "But he's has gone too far this time!"

Deloris nodded and took her friend's hand. "Thank you. Go home to your babies. I'll be okay."

Sharon turned to Kara. "Does the apartment have a telephone?"

"No," Matthew answered. "I had it disconnected because we weren't using it. Deloris, you can stay with us until it's reinstalled."

"Go," Deloris said to her friend.

Sharon was reluctant to leave, but Kara promised that Deloris was safe. As Sharon left, the hotel doctor knocked on the open door.

"What's the problem?" Dr. Myers asked. "How can I be of assistance?"

Matthew pointed him to the kitchen. "Our friend has been assaulted, and my wife thinks one of her fingers is broken."

"Goodness," was the doctor's response when he saw the damage. "Ma'am, you should have gone to the hospital emergency intake."

"She won't, and that's why we called you," Kara said firmly. "I've treated the other wounds."

"And, what qualifies you, young lady?" Dr. Myers demanded.

"Four years in war-torn London, three as a Red Cross

medic," Kara snapped. "The finger is broken, not crushed! It needs a simple splint."

Dr. Myers looked surprised, but he opened his bag and began an exam of the fingers. Determining that the finger was indeed broken, he splinted and wrapped it. "Keep the finger on an icepack for forty-eight hours. When the swelling recedes, splint and wrap it firmly, or come to my office, and I'll do it. There shouldn't be any complications."

"Thank you," Deloris said.

After the doctor left, there was another knock on the door. Deloris reacted fearfully. Kara stood before her friend with her arms crossed. She couldn't hear what Matthew said but heard the door close, and her husband pushed a folded bed on wheels into the suite.

"I thought this would be more comfortable than the couch," Matthew said. "Your study or mine?"

"Mine," Kara said.

"No, I'll go to the apartment," Deloris said. "If the offer is still good."

"Of course it is," Matthew said. "But you should stay here a few days. Give us time to get the phone turned on. Now is a bad time to ask, but what do you intend to do about Simon?"

"What can I do?" Deloris asked.

"You can have him arrested for assault," Matthew said.

Deloris shook her head. "I don't want my boys to know how he has changed."

"You only have one boy. From what I know of him, he wouldn't approve of what his father has become," Matthew said gently. "The rest of your sons are grown men. The Colonel shouldn't be given a pass on this."

Deloris continued to shake her head.

Matthew studied Deloris. "Kara has a camera, and I want her to take pictures of your bruises. No, don't shake your head. You need photographs as evidence that can't be refuted. You may change your mind when you stew on what he's done to you. There won't be any proof if we don't take photographs."

Deloris turned to Kara, who was nodding her head.

"I'll go set up your bed," Matthew said.

Deloris was tucked into the study an hour later after taking several aspirins.

"What are we going to do about Mr. Cahill's dinner?" Kara whispered.

"I called him when the doctor was here," Matthew said. "I apologized and told him there was a family emergency. He invited us to their New Year's celebration, and I told him we'd try to make it."

"What are we going to do?" Kara asked.

"That's up to her. Not us," Matthew said. "We'll keep her here until the phone is reconnected, but that might not be until after the holidays."

The phone rang, and they both jumped. Matthew answered, listened, and then covered the receiver with his palm. "It's the Colonel," he whispered. "Go stand in front of your study door in case Deloris wakes up."

Kara peeked into the study, and it looked like Deloris was asleep. She didn't desert her post until Matthew waved to her.

"That was Simon. He was obviously drunk and carrying on about Deloris not being home, and he couldn't find her."

"What can she do if stupid judges are handing down verdicts that women should be beaten by their husbands."

"Not beaten, spanked," Matthew said. "That was only in a few cases. I've read the transcripts. Those women were spoiled rotten and deserved a sore sit-down! No judge would condone what Deloris has been through."

The phone rang again, and he answered and turned the

phone over to Kara. It was Sharon, and she was assured that Deloris was safe and she'd been seen by a doctor. Wishing her friend a Merry Christmas, she returned the phone to Matthew as Harry Warner wanted to speak to him. Kara went to the refrigerator, but it was slim pickings. They had planned to have dinner at the Cahills.

When Matthew was through, she called the kitchen and was surprised it wasn't closed. She apologized for the late call and was reminded that Wolcott Hotel services never closed.

"What did Harry say?" Kara asked.

"He's as shocked by the Colonel's behavior as I am. Harry will borrow a truck from the furniture store and keep a watch on the Colonel's house. When Simon leaves, they will swoop in to remove Deloris' belongings. Her clothes, paintings, paints, antiques, whatever. Sharon will know what to take. Harry will call me, and I'll meet him at my office building."

"That sounds like a good plan," Kara said.

"I'm sorry this has ruined our holiday plans," Matthew said.

"I'm not," Kara whispered. "I know this might sound strange, but I miss helping people. That's all I did during the war, and it felt good. Hiring Elizabeth and now Emma... helping Emma's family have a good Christmas feels good. Helping Deloris get away from an abusive husband is the right thing to do!

"I know growing up with all of Aunt Selina's wealth spoiled me. You spoiled me at the beginning of our marriage too. When it all fell apart, I thanked God daily for Alice's down-to-earth help. Through her eyes, I saw how real people lived. It was a much poorer world than I knew existed. But, we survived, and then we had a war to contend with... and we survived that too."

Dinner was eaten quietly, with the radio playing

Christmas music. Kara took a tray to Deloris, but she barely touched the food. Sharon called again later in the evening and was told Deloris was sleeping or pretending to sleep.

Either way, Christmas Eve wasn't being celebrated as Kara and Matthew had planned. They moved the radio into the bedroom, but neither felt like having *adventurous* sex with a guest in the next room. Both of them knew they weren't quiet while making love.

Matthew rolled over and gave a sigh. "This isn't working."

"No, it isn't," Kara said, but she sat up in bed. "But, I know where we can go for privacy."

"Where?"

"The suite next door," Kara said. "It belongs to Benny Silo."

"The gangster? I thought he was sent to jail," Matthew asked.

"That's him," Kara said. "He is in jail. He has served five years of a ten-year sentence. When Alice and I moved in, Mr. Daniels, the concierge, told me Benny Silo still owns the suite next door. He's in jail, and no one is using the suite. He also told me the cleaning staff cleans monthly to ensure everything is in good shape. They did the same to this suite when Selina went on long trips."

"You're suggesting that we break into the next-door suite?" Matthew said.

"We won't be breaking in," Kara said with a mischievous smile. "Benny was a friend of Selina's, and I know where my aunt kept the key."

Matthew smiled. "Do we dress or go over as-is?"

"Robes should be sufficient," Kara teased. "We're the only ones occupying the top floor." She found the key and wrote a note for Deloris in case she woke up.

They tiptoed down the hallway, and Kara used the key.

The suite was dark, and they turned on a few lights as they made their way to the bedroom, and then Matthew turned them back off as they closed the bedroom door. The apartment was masculine, with leather furniture and no female touches of nicknacks or fabric patterns. It was laid out exactly like their suite.

The bed was stripped of sheets and blankets, but Kara went to a linen closet, and they put a clean sheet on it.

Kara opened her robe to display her nakedness. She stretched out on the bed, and Matthew couldn't take his eyes off her.

He climbed onto the bed and kissed her deeply. Then he stroked her beautiful body, stopping at her center and entering her with his fingers.

Kara shivered with a flush of heat as she responded to his fondling. She copied his strokes eagerly, stroking his chest, and her hands went to his manhood.

"How do you want it?" Matthew whispered.

"Every way possible," Kara answered. "Take me, use me, and make this a Christmas Eve I will remember forever."

Matthew lowered his head and took a nipple into his mouth. His hands stroked over her skin, touching and needing to feel her sex. He wanted to feel every inch of her. "I'll try, but if I get too aggressive, just say stop!"

"I won't. I'm giving myself to you. Merry Christmas!" Kara groaned as his hand went between her legs, and he thrust fingers deep inside her.

Matthew was already stiff, and she stroked his length and played her fingers gently over the tip of his manhood. When he couldn't hold back any longer, he pushed her back against the mattress and then was inside, drilling himself into her deeper.

He rode her back and forth, and Kara closed her eyes as waves of pleasure and need swept over her. Matthew kept driving into her harder and deeper. His breath was coming in gasps, and suddenly he withdrew.

"No," Kara groaned.

"Yes," Matthew crooned, rolling over and positioning her on her knees. He laid his hand across her naked bottom, caressing it, and gave it a stinging smack. Her only response was to suck in her breath in anticipation.

Sexual spanking had become normal when they made love. Kara knew what was coming. She wanted the anticipation of the next smack and sting. She knew it would hurt, but the result was her having multiple orgasms. Kara might have stopped those horrible maintenance spankings, but sexual spankings were different. She wanted... needed those multiple orgasms. She wanted Matthew to spank her. He wasn't the only one learning from Aunt Selina's library of sex books.

The spanking finally stopped, but the pulsating yearning inside her was at its peak. Kara rolled over and pulled Matthew on top of her. She locked her legs around his waist and he filled her, thrusting harder and deeper. Kara lost track of how many times they changed positions before she cried out from a deep orgasm that she felt from her toes to the top of her head.

"What do you feel during an orgasm?" Matthew asked as he waited for his body to return to normal.

"It's euphoric," Kara gasped. "It starts slow, and then it's a wave of pleasure that slowly takes over my whole body. It's wonderful to feel but hard to describe. What does it feel like to you?"

"Like I've conquered the world, and all self-control has vanished," Matthew said.

Kara tucked herself against her husband. "How we spent our Christmas Eve was better than a boring old dinner."

"I can't disagree," Matthew laughed. "But we should try to make the New Year's party."

They fell asleep, awakened, and made love again before sneaking back to their suite in the wee hours of the morning. They shared a shower together before returning to bed.

Curling into each other, they didn't need words. It felt true to share their bodies. In the first bloom of their young marriage, neither had known much about sex.

When they opened their eyes again to daylight, they kissed and held each other.

"Merry Christmas," Matthew whispered, pulling the blanket down to view her body. Kara amazed him that she was so willing to follow his lead.

"What?" she asked.

"We've been on a sexual marathon all night, and I still need you again."

"Then have me," she whispered. "Only quietly."

Later they had a few minutes of privacy together to exchange well-thought-out Christmas gifts. Matthew loved his new watch, along with the other gifts. Kara received an engagement ring, something he couldn't afford when he first asked her to marry him.

"I know you have a lot of jewelry handed down from your family, but I always felt bad that I couldn't afford an engagement ring."

"It never mattered to me," Kara said as he slid the ring onto her finger. "We were happy, and I'm trying very hard to lock the bad memories away. We can't undo what happened, but we can grow past it."

While Matthew was fixing breakfast, Kara checked on Deloris. She was awake, dressed in the clothes she'd arrived in. Sitting at Kara's work table, she was sketching with her left hand. The bruises on her face and neck were darker and more awful to witness.

"Matthew is making breakfast," Kara said. "We don't cook very often, but we're pretty good at scrambled eggs and toast."

"I'm not hungry," Deloris said. "Thank you for helping me yesterday. I need to call Sharon, but I don't want to disturb her Christmas."

"She won't mind," Kara said. "She was worried and scared yesterday. We all were."

"I don't know what to do," Deloris said quietly. "The things Simon said were so awful. The alcohol has ruined him."

"Don't worry about it right now," Matthew said, standing in the doorway with a tray. "We'll take care of everything for a while. All you have to do is give yourself time to heal."

Deloris hid part of her face with her hand.

Matthew walked over and set the tray down. "Give yourself time, Deloris. Personally, I'd have his ass arrested, but as a lawyer, I tend to see things in black and white, right or wrong. Harry and I have already decided that once we get your things out of the house and you are safe, we will attack the problem." He rubbed his hand over his face. "I didn't mean that literally. The Colonel needs a wake-up call, the least of it being sent to an alcoholic aid facility."

"In another week, there won't be anywhere for him to go drinking," Deloris said.

"Don't believe it," Matthew said with a snort. "Drinkers will find a way."

Chapter 18

MATTHEW, Thomas, and Harry were treating the evacuation of Deloris like a military operation. They had neighbors watching the Rathforth house for any signs of activity. Simon had staggered into the Warner house late Christmas evening. He was drunk and complaining about Deloris not being home.

Not wanting his children's Christmas spoiled, Harry had taken his friend home, and Sharon followed him, driving Simon's car. Two days later, Sharon learned that Simon had left his house from a neighbor she knew and trusted.

She called her husband, and Operation Deloris commenced. Harry drove a delivery truck home, picking up his mother on the way to watch the kids while he and Sharon were at the Rathforth house removing Deloris' belongings.

Sharon called Matthew, who rushed away from the law firm to pick up Kara and Alice, leaving Elizabeth and Emma in charge of the boutique. Trusted neighbors were showing up to help. Alice called Thomas, and he was on his way in his truck.

When Thomas arrived, most of Deloris' beloved

antiques, passed down through her family, were already in the delivery truck. Her clothing had been bagged, boxed, and put in vehicles. Thomas' truck bed was filled with paintings carefully wrapped in towels and sheets from the linen closet. The load was tied down with ropes.

Within a few hours, Sharon walked through her friend's home and, using her best judgment, decided they had everything that meant anything to her best friend.

"All right," Harry instructed. "Everyone follow me. I'm taking a different route, and when I get to the bridge, I'll pull over. Matthew will take the lead to his building. You all have written instructions if we get separated."

"Not all this furniture will fit into the apartment," Kara said. "Matthew has already secured a storage room in the basement."

"We'll figure out what goes where when we get there," Harry said.

The convoy made it into the city together, but it became more complicated on the busy streets. Matthew had to pull over several times and wait for Harry's large truck to catch up. Pulling into the back parking lot behind the building, Matthew went inside and talked to the security men on duty. With the additional help of three guards and the janitor, the unloading didn't take long. Sharon directed what items would go upstairs to the apartment or downstairs to the storage cage in the basement. She knew Deloris the best.

Alice left with Thomas to deliver the finished paintings to the boutique, where they were stored in the third-floor area they weren't using.

Returning to the Cahill building, all the vehicles were emptied.

Harry shook hands with Matthew and Thomas. "I'm going to try to talk to Simon again. I don't know what we can do if that doesn't work. Deloris doesn't want her boys told, but except for Daniel, they're grown men. They should be told, but it's her call."

"I'm looking into the validity of how the Army handled his retirement," Matthew said. "There's something shady going on there."

"Thank you," Sharon exclaimed, hugging Alice and Kara.

"We'll take care of her," Kara promised as they waved off their friends.

Matthew and Kara went their separate ways. Matthew said he needed to make a few phone calls in his office. Kara went to the apartment to organize Deloris' things. Matthew went looking for his wife when he was through with his phone calls.

"I called the phone company," Matthew said. "They said the phone won't be connected until after the New Year."

"Deloris can stay with us until then. She won't want to go out in public until the bruises can be covered with makeup. You haven't told Simon where we live, have you?" Kara asked.

"No. It never came up," Matthew said. "Telling people you live in a penthouse in one of the wealthiest hotels in New York City is a little hard to explain. We should be getting back."

Matthew parked his car in the garage and took his wife's hand. As they were walking, he gave her a tug.

"What?" Kara asked, looking around to see why he was changing their direction.

"I have something I want to show you," Matthew said. "He turned her so her back was to a garage door. "Close your eyes. No peeking."

Kara rolled her eyes, but she did close them. She heard the metal door open and then his footsteps. He covered her eyes with his hands and turned her around.

"Merry Christmas," Matthew said, removing his hands.

Kara was looking at a bright yellow and brown automobile.

"This was my Christmas present, but with everything happening with Deloris, I didn't think it was the right time to give it to you," Matthew said.

"You bought me a car?" Kara exclaimed.

"Yes, it's a Studebaker, but it comes with restrictions. I want to take you out driving to make sure you can handle it, and you have to promise to be careful," Matthew said.

"I will!" Kara cried, and with a leap, her arms were wrapped around his neck. "I can't believe you bought me a car!"

"Well, there are times when I'm unavailable, and you need to get around," Matthew said.

"I can't believe it!" Kara exclaimed. "Can I drive it?"

"Tomorrow," Matthew said with a smile. "I think we need to go inside and see if Deloris is okay. We'll take the car out tomorrow for a trial run."

The days between Christmas and the New Year went by quickly. The boutique wasn't open to the public, but the time was used to restock the shelves and racks with merchandise. Emma was getting additional training to work the front of the store.

Night school started in the first week of the new year. Elizabeth had signed up for evening classes, three nights a week. Some of her workday hours would be spent learning to be a seamstress. The skills were necessary with the ultimate goal of becoming a designer.

Deloris was recovering. Over the Christmas holidays, she'd considered it a miracle that Daniel had already made plans to stay at school. His best friend was in the infirmary, and since his widowed father was on an overseas assignment,

Daniel didn't want his friend to be left alone during the holidays.

Once the holidays were over, Deloris went to work with Matthew in the mornings. She organized the apartment while he worked in his office, although he wasn't putting in a full day.

The Warners were keeping Kara and Matthew informed daily. A phone call came a week after the New Year celebrations. Simon was sober and furious that his wife had left him.

Obeying Deloris' wishes, Harry hadn't contacted the adult sons. He had spoken with the pastor of Rathforth's church. The pastor suggested counseling and a meeting with only Simon and Deloris.

Deloris refused.

"I don't blame her," Kara said, sitting in the Warner living room.

"Not facing the problem won't help," Harry said. "They've been married for over thirty years."

"And, how many of those years has she been denying how badly he's mistreated her, and she's been covering for him?" Kara asked. "How many times has she been told by their minister that she must submit to her husband's will? From what little she's told me, that's the same line of bull he gives all his counseled couples. That's a load of crap. How many times has he beaten her?"

Harry and Sharon exchanged looks. "We don't know. We've known the Rathforths for over a decade, and we never suspected," Harry said. "As far as I know, this is the first time he's crossed the line into abuse."

Sharon shook her head. "I'm pretty sure it's not the first time. She's been hiding and lying about bruises for a long time. She didn't want anyone to know."

"Why didn't you say something?" Harry demanded.

"Because it wasn't my business to tell, and you've told me

for years not to stick my nose into other people's problems," Sharon said. "I've tried to get her to talk to a lawyer. She has refused."

Harry turned to Matthew. "Has she spoken to you?"

"Yes," Matthew said. "She has asked questions, and I've advised her. I'm not a divorce lawyer, but I know the laws. With the photographs of her injuries, I don't know any judge who would refuse her a divorce. The decision has to be made by her. For now, she's safe. She has a place to stay, and I gave security a photograph of Simon, with the instructions that he is not allowed in the building, and to call me if he shows up. Deloris knows I'm only a phone call away."

"She needs to decide what she wants to do," Kara said. "She has a way of supporting herself now. Her paintings are selling well."

"I've tried talking to Simon, but he's not listening. The last time I saw him, he told me to mind my own business," Harry said.

"Then we do it," Sharon said. "We keep our mouths shut about what we do know. Deloris is safe, and that's all that matters. Does everyone agree?"

Heads nodded, except for Matthew. "I'm going to try again to get Simon into a facility. I don't think he will listen, but I'll try. With prohibition in effect, alcohol of any kind will be difficult to find."

"Where there is a will, there is a way," Harry disagreed. "I served under Simon for twenty years. I'm still having a problem believing he's changed so much. He always had a bottle of whiskey in his desk, but I rarely saw him drinking."

"This decision belongs to Deloris," Matthew said. "The worst thing we can do is interfere. She has a place to stay, and the lease is good until the end of May. We'll keep an eye on her."

Deloris began living in the apartment, and the friends she

could trust visited. With the assistance of Thomas's parents, she was introduced to the owner of an upscale gallery, and her paintings were selling well there in addition to the boutique.

Kara and Matthew were glad to have their privacy back. After the winter holidays, the boutique went through a slow period. The weather was miserable, and New York City saw more than its fair share of snow and freezing rain. The slower winter months were also a respite and allowed Kara and Alice more time to design for the spring collections. Traditionally, designers were six months to a year ahead of the seasons.

Emma was settling into her new job. Her previous manager had called and offered her a job back with a reduced salary. He'd been surprised when she refused and tried to guilt her into returning. She politely told him she didn't want to work for a company that didn't value their employees.

With Emma's help, Elizabeth had more time to learn from her employers and spent most of her breaks and lunch periods studying for her classes. Marcio Giordano was escorting her to and from school on the evenings of her classes.

Marcio had finished training at the top of his class and was rewarded with an assignment in the midtown north precinct. As the 'new' recruit, his shifts alternated two weeks of day and two weeks of night shifts. He took his night shift meal breaks when Elizabeth's classes ended and escorted her to the boarding house. They didn't mind the long walks, even though it was cold outside, and their walks usually ended with a kiss.

One evening, Marcio seemed preoccupied and didn't have much to say.

"Is something wrong?" Elizabeth asked.

"No... well, yes, there is," Marcio said. "Let's go into that café and get something hot to drink."

Sitting in a booth and sipping coffee, Elizabeth cocked an eyebrow. "What's the problem?"

"It's my folks," Marcio said. "My parents have been tossing out hints that it's time for me to settle down."

"And?" Elizabeth asked.

"My mother made a list of available girls in the neighborhood! I keep telling her I'm not interested, but she throws her hands in the air and tells me she wants grandchildren in Italian!"

Elizabeth laughed, and Marcio blushed. "You know how the folks are?"

"Tell them back off or that you've got your eye on a pretty nun," Elizabeth teased.

"Oh, geez, you know I can't do that. Every time Mom talks about me finding a *'good'* girl, your name comes up. Then they start talking about how horrible a daughter you've been for running away from your father."

"I left my father's house because he was dictating my life!" Elizabeth exclaimed. "I was a straight-A student, but he decided I didn't need further education. Father made me work for the newspaper, and I hated it. Then he took my paychecks and refused to allow me to spend any of it when it was my money! He and your parents decided I would make you the perfect docile housewife, and nothing I said mattered to him!"

"It wasn't my idea," Marcio said, taking her hand and giving it a squeeze. "All I wanted was to join the Army. The problem, Elizabeth, is that I have fallen in love with you. Now that I'm through training, settling down sounds like a good idea."

Elizabeth closed her eyes and then faced her friend. "I'm not ready to settle down. I lost a lot of years under my father's heavy foot. These past months have been the only time I've ever felt free. I'm going to finish high school, and I might even take some college courses. I am training to be a designer under the tutorship of Kara and Alice. Designing under my own label may take me years, but it's my dream."

"And, you think marriage would wreck your plans?" Marcio asked.

"I'm not willing to take that chance," Elizabeth said, shaking her head. "I do have feelings for you, but you're Italian to the bottom of your soul. I know your parents, your uncles, your siblings, and I also know their wives. I don't need someone bossing me around all the time and telling me how to live my life."

Marcio nodded. "I'm not like my father or my brothers. I'm also not like your father. If you give me a chance, I won't make demands. I'm beginning my new career, and telling the family that I wouldn't join the family business and be a plumber wasn't easy. My father was furious when I signed up to take the police training. I don't want to lose you, Elizabeth."

Elizabeth smiled. "I will give you a chance, but we must keep our feelings private. I won't tolerate any interference in my career, and I'm not ready to face my father yet! Deal?"

"Deal," Marcio agreed.

When they faced the snow outside, Marcio wrapped his arm around her shoulders. "I'm not in a hurry to marry, and I understand the pressure you were under. When I signed up to be a policeman, my family thought I was brain-damaged from the war!"

Matthew spent the rest of the winter fighting an entire team of attorneys trying to postpone the DeLuca trial. He was responsible for one of the delays, which created a ton of paperwork.

The boutique was doing well. There was always a slight decline between the end-of-the-year holidays and fashion week in late spring. Kara & Alaïs Couture Designs had been invited to show their fashions in New York's fashion week exhibit. Their fashions would be the last to walk the runway, but that was fine. They were thrilled to be asked. Having been involved with the Paris runways, they considered being asked an honor.

Kara didn't think American women were ready to be exhibitionists. The hemlines might be higher in post-war cities, but ministers and the older generations were fighting the changes in the name of decency. Alice and Kara's designs dealt with the shorter hems with beads, fringe, and ruffle extensions. It was the client's choice of how much leg they wanted to expose.

Matthew and Harry had been trying to convince Simon Rathforth that he needed help to cure his overuse of alcohol. The Colonel was a bitter man and denied that he had a problem. Deloris had finally contacted her two grown sons and explained why she'd left their father but was still refusing to confront her husband.

"If she won't face him, what will she do?" Kara asked.

"She's already talked to the manager of the Cahill building about taking over the lease to the apartment," Matthew said. "He called me to ask if I would co-sign for her, and I told him I would. Deloris said she has enough money in the bank to support herself for a while. That's thanks to her selling her paintings.

"New York laws on divorce haven't been changed since the mid-eighteen hundreds, and the only valid reason in the courts is adultery. Some people lie, and the attorneys allow it. People who can afford it go to a state with six-month citizen requirements. Reno, Nevada was built on quick divorces."

"Isn't there a law against brutality?"

"There's an exception for everything in the law, but it still has to go before a judge. It's up to him to interpret the law. Deloris would have to file suit against him, and she's unwilling to do that."

"So, we are right where we started," Kara exclaimed.

"No, Deloris is where she started," Matthew said. "All we can do is offer suggestions. If she wants help, we're willing. It's up to her to make the decisions."

Deloris was denied those decisions.

Matthew was awakened early in the morning by the ringing telephone. The previous evening he and Kara had gone dancing at a club. Even without alcohol, the music had been good, and they'd had a good time. They celebrated with a good wine after they'd returned home and continued to dance to music from the radio.

Whoever was calling interrupted his plans to sleep late, and they were persistent. He staggered out of bed to answer.

"Hello?"

"Matt, it's Harry," Harry Warner said.

"What's wrong?"

"I hate to tell you on the phone..."

"What?" Matthew demanded.

"I'm at Long Beach Memorial Hospital," Harry said. "I stopped by Simon's house early this morning on the way to work. His car was there, but he didn't answer, so I used my key to get in the house. He was there. I found him collapsed on the floor. I called for an ambulance."

"Is he okay?"

"No," Harry said. "There's no easy way to say this. The Colonel died on the way to the hospital."

"Dear God!"

"From what little the doctors told me, they believe he died of a heart attack. I haven't called Deloris yet, and I still have to go back home and tell Sharon," Harry said.

"We'll tell Deloris," Matthew said. "And, bring her to the hospital."

Deloris knew something was wrong when she opened the door. Upon hearing the news, she was initially inconsolable but finally pulled herself together. "Was it the liquor?" she asked.

Matthew shook his head. "The Hospital Director wouldn't give me the details over the phone. He did tell me that Harry told him to release the body to the Gardners Funeral Home."

Deloris took a deep breath. "I have to call the boys. I told them I was separated from their father but didn't explain why. This is going to be hard on them, especially Daniel."

"If you don't want to tell them, that's your business," Matthew advised.

"Let me get dressed," Deloris said, disappearing into the bedroom. A few minutes later, she returned to the living room, picked up the phone, and turned to her friends. "Would you please wait for me downstairs?"

Twenty minutes later, Deloris joined them. Her eyes were red from crying.

"We'll take you home and help with whatever you need help with," Matthew promised.

"David and John are coming home," Deloris said. "John said he'd pick up Daniel on the way."

The funeral for Colonel Simon Rathforth was a large affair. The Rathforth family had lived in the same neighborhood for sixteen years. Her oldest son David knew his father's wishes, as they had discussed many things during the war years. Simon was well-versed in dealing with deceased soldiers and their benefits and had informed his eldest son on what to do. David knew who to contact for veteran widow's benefits and life insurance policies. He had already contacted the agents.

The funeral was at St. Monica's Church, and the Colonel would be interned in the cemetery. Every pew was filled. The Ladies' Group held a reception in the basement of the church. Deloris finally went to her partially empty house, surrounded by family and friends.

"Call us if you need anything," Matthew said as they hugged her goodbye. "I do mean anything."

"I need some family time to talk with my boys," Deloris said.

Chapter 19

"IT WAS AWFUL, but she had her older sons there to help support her," Kara told Elizabeth and Emma. "Thank you for filling in this past week. Has anything happened that we should know about?"

"There are a lot of notes on your desk. We're out of stock on a few items. We've been careful to keep the records straight. Mrs. Cromwell's dress is completed, and so is Miss Hallaway's. You need to call them for the final fittings," Elizabeth said.

"Oh, and that horrible little man from the art store came by twice. He wanted to purchase several of Mrs. Rathforth's paintings, but we refused to sell them to him," Emma added.

"He tried to tell us that you had already agreed to sell them at a discounted rate. I suspected that wasn't true. I very politely told him I wasn't authorized to sell the paintings. He would have to speak to you in person," Elizabeth added.

"Good girl," Kara said. "How is night school going?"

"It's going very well," Emma teased.

"What's that supposed to mean?" Alice asked.

"Pay no mind to her," Elizabeth said. "A friend of mine,

who happens to be a policeman, doesn't want me walking home alone after classes. He's been showing up and walking me home."

"How good a friend?" Alice asked.

"Good enough that he's keeping my secrets," Elizabeth said. "And I told him I'm not interested in getting serious until I graduate and accomplish my goals."

"Nice guy," Kara said with a smile. "A side benefit of knowing you girls can handle the store is that it will give Alice and me more time to focus on new designs. Matthew has an important trial coming up, and I'd like to attend. I want to show him my support and watch him take down the bad guys. I've never been in a courtroom before."

The spring months seemed to be flying by. Sundays were the only days that were relatively free from work. On those days, they visited Deloris to see how she was faring.

With help from Harry Warner, Matthew tracked down the department head responsible for widow pensions. Once Deloris had completed all the necessary paperwork, she would receive pensions for herself and Daniel until he reached the age of eighteen. Daniel was given the choice of returning to his military boarding school or staying home and transferring to public school. The final decision was that he would finish the year at his school and then make a decision before enrollment for the following year. Her older sons returned to their homes and jobs when they were convinced their mother could handle everything. She'd told her adult sons what had transpired over the previous six months, although she didn't want her younger son to know.

The most significant decision Deloris made was that she decided to sell the house. Although it held good memories, it also held bad ones, and Deloris didn't want to live with those reminders. The house was too large for only her and Daniel. As the news traveled through her friends, a family in the neighborhood came knocking on her door. The four-bedroom was exactly what the growing family needed. By coincidence, the Warners had decided to move Harry's elderly mother, Lily, into their home. Lily's smaller house was exactly what Deloris wanted, and she banked the profits from selling her home and buying Lily's. She set aside money so Daniel could go to college if he was inclined to do so. His two older brothers hadn't attended. Both had joined the military, served overseas, and were lucky to come back unharmed.

Matthew was so busy preparing for his upcoming trial that the tables were turned. He was working sixteen-hour days, and coming home exhausted, only to stagger out early the next morning. One evening Matthew fell asleep at his desk and called Kara at five in the morning, apologizing. Driving home, there was only time for a shower and a change of clothes, and he headed back to the law firm. Now he regretted not renewing the contract on the apartment after Deloris moved into her new home.

The Spring Show of new fashions was also approaching quickly. The invitation to walk the runway with designs acknowledged the boutique's growing business. The cost of the models was outrageous, but Kara and Alice knew how to play the game. The boutique was asked to present eight new 'looks,' but Kara, Alice, Elizabeth, and Emma would also be wearing one-of-a-kind designs.

Kara had invited Matthew to the show and given him two tickets, but he'd been honest with her. He was buried with case evidence but would try to be there. Thomas had given a similar excuse and no promises.

The boutique was closed for the day of the show, and Elizabeth and Emma were brought along as assistants. The top designers displayed their designs in an order that had been decided months earlier. As a last-minute invitation by

Mrs. Leah Benton, the show's sponsor, their designs would be last. Thomas, Matthew, and an older woman slipped into empty seats halfway through the show.

"There they are," Elizabeth whispered to Kara. She was peeking through the runway curtains.

"Who?"

"Thomas, Matthew, and an older woman!" Elizabeth hissed.

Kara had to look for herself, and then she beamed a smile. Her husband was sitting in his assigned chair at the end of the runway. Mrs. Cahill was his companion.

"That's his boss's wife," she explained.

Matthew lowered his head and whispered to Thomas. "We're outnumbered in here by about fifty to one."

Thomas looked around at the auditorium filled with hundreds of well-dressed women. "I figured it was in my best interest to attend."

"Mine too," Matthew agreed with a smile.

"Shhh," Mrs. Cahill whispered, as nearly every woman was clapping while a tuxedoed man walked the runway waving a sequined top hat occasionally and bowing.

"We have to sit through the rest of this because our wives are last," Thomas whispered behind his hand. "Just pretend you know why they're clapping, and clap when the women clap."

Looking around the auditorium, filled with women, Matthew thought that was a good idea. The next designer was obviously pushing fur wraps and feathers. Mrs. Cahill clapped, and the husbands followed her lead.

The next designer was a bit of a throwback to the fashions of the late 1890s. Most of the models were wearing floor-length dresses and ballgowns. The audience wasn't enthused. The next batch was closer to what Matthew had seen in his wife's sketchbook. The applause was loud.

The next designer walk before their wives was somewhat shocking. The garments pushed the limits of what Matthew knew were the decency laws on record. He exchanged looks with Thomas, who looked equally shocked. Necklines were cut to the waist, and far too much of the model's breasts were exposed. In addition, there were slits in the skirts, revealing a lot of thigh. When the models turned at the end of the runway, the dress backs simply weren't there, and there was an audible hiss of disapproval.

The applause was scattered but with very little enthusiasm. When the designer walked around the stage, she looked like she was wearing a man's bathing suit, with stockings rolled above the knee and high heels. When she turned her back to them, her back was exposed well past her waistline. She would have been arrested for obscenity if she appeared publicly wearing the obscene outfit. She was more concerned about showing off. The audience was shocked and nearly silent.

"I apologize, ma'am," Matthew whispered to his boss's wife.

Mrs. Cahill only smiled. "I've been to many of these events, Matthew. I like the new changes in dress designs, but..." She looked down at the invitation card in her hand. "Miss Wanda Beardley's collection is quite vulgar."

"Kara and Alice are next," Matthew said proudly and mentally crossed his fingers. He'd seen the sketches of what Kara had told him were the designs she would be showing, but he also knew she wanted hemlines shorter than he approved.

Mrs. Leah Benton, the organizer, and lady in charge, walked to the podium and announced that the last designers were Kara Douglas and Alice Markham, owners of the New York based Kara & Alaïs Couture Designs Boutique.

As the models walked the runway, each dress was

received with loud clapping and enthusiastic murmurs from the women in the audience.

Matthew and Thomas grinned at each other and added their applause to support their wives. When Kara and Alice walked the runway, acknowledging the audience, it was obvious that the women in the audience were interested in the newcomers.

"My goodness," Mrs. Cahill exclaimed as they stood up. "I'm going to have to visit your wives' boutique."

"Let's see if they'll let us backstage?" Thomas said, looking at his watch. "Then I have to get back on the site!"

"I need to get back to work, too," Matthew agreed.

The trio was stopped by a security guard, but he promised to find the wives amidst the chaos of models and women backstage. Alice had already spotted them and excused themselves from their conversation with other designers.

"Congratulations!" Mrs. Cahill said. "I loved everything in your collection."

"Thank you!" Kara and Alice said together.

"I just wanted you to know we made it," Thomas said to Alice with a smile. "I may not want to buy a dress, but I'm proud of your talent."

Matthew was about to add something, but there was a loud scream of outrage on the other side of the room.

"I was supposed to be the last on the runway! The only one those rich idiots would remember!" It was the woman who was barely dressed in bodysuit swimwear.

"Wanda, I warned you not to switch or deviate from the approved outfits," Mrs. Benton, the woman in charge, exclaimed. "I've already received complaints that your designs are inappropriate! We've had this discussion before. Now, take your things and leave. I'm severing our working relationship. We will not show your designs at the Knicker-bocker Showroom next month or at any venue I sponsor!"

"You can't do that! I have a contract!" the woman named Wanda screamed.

"Which we will not honor because of your behavior," Mrs. Benton said sternly and turned to two young men wearing security uniforms. "Gentlemen, please escort Miss Beardley from the facility. She and her assistants will not be allowed back in the building."

The backstage area had gone silent during this discourse. Two young men picked up several large boxes and walked past the woman to the back door.

Wanda turned with narrowed eyes. "You will regret this!" She stormed across the room but stopped in front of Kara and Alice. "You took my spot, and you bitches will pay!" She raised her hand to slap Alice, but Thomas was faster.

He grabbed her wrist and, with a twist, held her arm behind her back.

"Let go of me!"

"Move!" Thomas growled, and he forced her to walk in front of him to the backdoor. Matthew ran ahead and opened the door, and Thomas pushed her outside. Two guards followed her outside the building.

When Thomas and Matthew returned to their wives, quite a few people clapped.

"Thank you, and I apologize," Mrs. Barton said, joining their small group. "Wanda Beardley has been a problem before, but she's never been this unruly or disrespectful. I can assure you this is not normal behavior at my events. She will not be invited to participate again!"

"Mrs. Barton, these gentlemen are our husbands. This is my husband, Thomas Markham, and this is Matthew Douglas, Kara's husband," Alice said, making the introductions."

"Thank you again, gentlemen," Mrs. Barton said.

Thomas looked a bit out of place. "I wasn't going to allow her to strike my wife. We just came backstage to tell our wives we are proud of them."

"You should be," the woman said with a smile. "Mrs. Cahill, it's nice to see you again. It's been a while."

"It has, and I enjoyed the show, with one exception. I think I'll be stopping into these two young ladies' boutique very soon," Mrs. Cahill said, smiling.

While Elizabeth and Emma were packing the dresses in boxes and carrying them to Alice's car, their employers were schmoozing with the elite of New York's designers. The venue was clearing out within an hour, and they returned to the shop.

"We're going to redress the front window," Kara said when they arrived.

"With the dresses from the runway?" Elizabeth asked.

"Sort of," Kara answered. "We'll use the samples we made before they were remade with expensive materials and silk. If we can sell the runway dresses, that will be fine, but we'll most likely get orders for new designs in specific sizes."

"I love working here," Emma exclaimed. "I wish I could draw or even think up new ideas."

"Most people are good at something," Kara said. "If your strengths aren't in dressmaking, maybe they are in something else. It could be writing, cooking, or even being a great clerk and salesperson. I can do the register, but as you have noticed, I have to write down everything and check the arithmetic two or three times to make sure I'm right."

"Don't sell yourself short," Alice added, smiling. "We appreciate what you do here. You are very good at dressing the window displays, so if you don't mind, you and Elizabeth can change it."

The girls changed out of the show dresses and went to

work while Kara and Alice handled the customers. Some women who had attended the show were excited about the boutique and the new clothing line. Even though the shop was only open for a half-day, the sales were above average. Closing was a little late because of the heavy foot traffic, but it was a good day for the shop.

Kara entered the apartment and immediately called for dinner to be sent up. She was tired, and she knew Matthew was going to be late. The DeLuca trial was approaching and would begin on Monday morning. Every moment he spent in the office with his team was crucial. Four lawyers were on the case, but Matthew was the lead.

Matthew entered the suite to find Kara asleep on the couch. There was a dinner tray, but when he uncovered the dishes, they didn't look like she'd eaten anything.

"Kara?" he nudged her gently.

"Ummm?"

"Wake up, sweetheart," Matthew said softly.

Her eyes flew open. "What time is it?"

"After midnight. I'm sorry, but we must know every fact by heart."

"I know what this trial means to you," she responded. "I was surprised to see you today."

"Thomas and I agreed that we had to support our wives. Besides, when I explained to Mr. Cahill why I needed a few hours off, his wife pulled a ticket from her purse. She said she'd bought the ticket but didn't want to go alone. After she said that Mr. Cahill didn't have a problem with me leaving for a few hours. We were late but arrived in time to see your part of the show. It was a hit!"

"It was. We were invited by Mrs. Barton to the Knicker-bocker Garment Show. It's about ten times bigger than the show today. She's replacing the woman she fired with our designs and wants us to add more to our collection. It means we've got to develop more new designs in a little over a month!"

"Is that going to be a problem?" Matthew asked as he tried to stifle a yawn.

"We'll manage. You need to eat something before going to bed," Kara said.

"So do you," Matthew said, pulling her to her feet. He took the covers off the meal plates, but the cold food didn't look appetizing.

"Peanut butter sandwiches?" Kara suggested.

"Sounds good to me!" Matthew said. "I need to jump into a cold shower, or I'm going to fall asleep standing up!"

"Go, I'll make us some sandwiches," she said, yawning. "I'll see if I can save any of the dinner on the cart. After so many years of doing without and rationing, it seems sinful to waste it."

"We had rationing here, but it was voluntary. President Wilson appealed to the public's patriotism. I'm not sure how much it affected most people, but it meant more potatoes and gruel for breakfast, lunch, and dinner in the military mess halls. We got so sick of it that it wasn't uncommon to find a jar of peanut butter in a soldier's locker."

"Go," Kara said with a smile. "I'll treat you and mix it with grape jelly."

When Matthew finished his shower, he returned to the living room, but Kara wasn't there. Neither was the dinner cart, and he suspected it was probably out in the hallway waiting for a hotel staff member to return it to the kitchen.

He returned to the bedroom to discover his wife stretched out on the bed nude. He smiled and couldn't take his eyes off her as a specific part of his anatomy went rigid. She was beautiful and had a mischievous look on her face.

Matthew dropped his robe to the floor and joined her on the bed.

Cupping her face in his hands, he kissed her.

"Are you too tired?" Kara whispered.

"Never," he answered. Lowering his head to kiss her again, his lips trailed down to her breasts.

Kara shivered as she responded to her husband's advances. Making love with Matthew was the best way of celebrating a day that had been nearly perfect. His lips felt like a powder puff caressing her skin. She enthusiastically returned his ardor, pushing him onto his back and straddling him. She rubbed her sex against his manhood.

"Dear God, I need you," Matthew warned.

"Then have me," she whispered. "I want you just as much!"

Rolling her onto her back, her husband supported his weight on his arms and held his weight from crushing her as he traveled over her skin, touching and needing to taste and feel.

Kara arched her back and opened herself for his pleasure.

Matthew entered her body with a deep, hard thrust and began to ride her.

Kara closed her eyes as waves of delight swept over her. As he thrust upward into her body, her hips rose to meet his body and take him in further.

Locking her legs around his waist, moving together with practiced ease. Each knew what the other wanted. When she shivered with an orgasm, Matthew kept driving into her until he satisfied his need. With racing hearts, they knew moments like this were special, but they were both exhausted. With limbs entangled, they closed their eyes and fell asleep in each other's arms.

When they heard the alarm clock, Kara and Matthew finally opened their eyes and untangled their legs and arms. Stiff from not moving, they stretched and yawned.

Matthew sat up and let his eyes take in his wife's beauty. She still amazed him, although she had dark circles under her eyes."

"What?" she asked through half-opened eyes.

"Now that the show is over, I want you to get more rest. When the trial is over, we need to take a vacation," Matthew said.

"Is that going to be possible?" Kara queried. "We lead busy lives."

"We'll make it happen," Matthew said. "Nothing is more important than our relationship, nothing." He turned her over onto her belly and stroked her bottom. "Just looking at you makes me want you." He gave a light smack to her bottom. "We need to take the time to be together." Kara's only response was to take a deep breath and push herself up on her knees. It was a position she liked, and she knew what he wanted. She might be sitting on a cushion in her car later, but she looked forward to the spanking and his deep penetration. The spanking might have started because Matthew had been getting cues from his former officers, but now it was a kinky sexual ritual they both enjoyed. It usually resulted in her body reacting with multiple orgasms, and what woman wouldn't like that?

Chapter 20

FOR THE NEXT SEVERAL DAYS, finding time for each other, although a high priority, was bumped down as Kara and Alice tried to envision different designs for the show. It took weeks to produce a couture garment, but they had to come up with six new and different looks for the runway in a month! The shop was busy with new customers, and Elizabeth and Emma took on more responsibility for helping the new clients.

The jurors for the DeLuca trial had been chosen. The trial would start the following Monday. Matthew and his team of lawyers were presenting the case. He was the lead, and this case could make or break him as an attorney.

The third day of the trial was interrupted, as three of the juror's family members had received thinly veiled death threats. The DeLuca family was suspected of gangster affiliations, but there was scarce proof to prove it. Judge Richard Seinfield was known for his hard stance against gangster violence and jury tampering. He ordered the jury members to be sequestered in a hotel with a police presence twenty-four hours a day to protect them and their families. He made it clear that he would not tolerate interference.

Matthew decided he didn't want Kara to be in the courtroom. He didn't want the DeLuca men he was prosecuting to know anything about his personal life, including that he was married.

Kara couldn't complain because the reality was that she and Alice needed the time to work on her designs. Two new sewing machines were purchased to put in the homes of women who had worked upstairs. It freed the machines upstairs over the shop for her and Alice's use.

Although Kara had a brand new car, she wasn't driving herself to work. Parking spaces were difficult to find, and only one space was designated for the shop's use. Alice continued to stop by each morning to pick up Kara and the girls.

On the fourth day of the trial, Alice's car was egged. Mr. Shores, the custodian for a store several buildings down the block, witnessed what he called hoodlums doing the deed. He yelled, chased them away, and apologized for being unable to stop them, although it wasn't his responsibility. He was kind enough to wash her car on his lunch hour.

Alice appreciated his efforts and paid for his lunch at the deli down the street for a week. The shop owners on their block were friendly and protective of each other. They didn't want crime on their block and looked out for one another.

Every evening Kara was given a detailed briefing of what was happening during the trial. The DeLuca attorneys were doing their best to challenge and undermine the evidence being brought forward in the case, claiming that the collapse of the building wasn't their fault. Even after the written complaints were shown as evidence, they denied all culpability. Then it was time to present the victims and families of those who had died in the collapse of the building.

Several days after Alice's car was egged, the phone rang in the middle of the night. The call was from Sam Purney, who owned the tobacco store. He had already called the police.

Matthew and Thomas arrived within minutes of each other, but the police would only allow Kara and Alice inside the shop to assess the damages. Paint cans without lids had been thrown through the glass window. The dresses on display were destroyed, drenched in blood-red paint. The tall folding screen behind the manikins had prevented the paint from splashing onto the clothing racks.

"I'm sorry I couldn't stop them," Sam exclaimed. "I saw them out the window 'cause I live upstairs, over my shop. I yelled at them, but I wasn't wearing my glasses. All I saw was three hoodlums dressed in black. When I shouted at them, they ran down the alley, jumped in a truck, and took off. Then I called the police!"

"Did you see anything that could help identify them?" a policeman asked.

"No, except the truck was strange looking, and one of those fellows had long hair. Hung down his back like a girl. Like I said, I can't see that good without my glasses. It might not have been hair, it could have been a scarf."

"What was strange about the truck?" Thomas asked, standing beside a policeman.

"It was painted weird, like that *Vincent Van Something* fellow that the newspapers and magazines write about. I can't remember his last name. He paints some weird stuff, and it don't make sense to me. I'm more of a Norman Rockwell guy, myself. I like his pictures. They make sense," Sam said.

"The truck was painted to look like a *Van Gogh* painting?" Thomas asked.

"Yeah, that's his last name. The poor man is probably

colorblind. Everything is blue and yellow. Swirls and strange-looking people," Sam said.

"We can put out a bulletin on the truck," the policeman said. "A paint job like that should be easy to identify."

As the police were about to leave, Thomas cornered Kara and Alice. "I'm going to one of my company's warehouses. I'll bring back some lumber to cover that window until you can replace the glass."

"Do you need help?" Matthew asked, following Thomas outside.

"I've seen you use a hammer," Thomas teased. "Stay with the wives, and don't let them out of your sight until I return. Is this the kind of crap the DeLuca family would pull to intimidate you into backing off the case?"

"Yeah, it is. Maybe the girls should close down for a while?" Matthew asked.

Thomas shook his head. "Don't play that card," he warned. "Kara is as stubborn as Alice, and neither will give up their dreams when they're so close to being recognized. I'll be back as soon as possible."

The police waited around until Thomas returned before leaving. After thanking Sam, Kara insisted he return to his apartment to get some sleep. Thomas went to work covering the broken window display with boards. Matthew mopped the paint-splattered floors, and Alice washed the paint off the antique screen they had used as a backdrop. It had stopped the paint from ruining thousands of dollars worth of merchandise.

Alice and Kara pulled the racks away from the area where Thomas was working. They inspected every garment for damage. Alice dragged a trash can inside, filling it with paint-smeared manikins and anything with paint on it. They were also examining Deloris' paintings. Luckily they were hung on the inside walls and high enough that they hadn't been damaged.

"Right now, I'm just glad we weren't displaying the runway couture items," Kara said to Alice, and she began to cry.

"Don't do that, honey. If you cry, I'm going to start, too! We have insurance to cover vandalism. At least they didn't get inside," Alice said, hugging her friend and trying to hold back her crumbling despair. She waved to Matthew, and he swapped places with her, holding and rocking Kara in his arms.

"Why?" Kara cried.

"I'm sorry," Matthew said. "This was probably the DeLucas' way of warning me off. I'll talk to the Judge and hire twenty-four-hour security so this doesn't happen again. You may have to close for a few days."

"No!" Kara exclaimed sharply. She dredged up some anger and resilience she hadn't used for a while. Taking a deep breath, she wiped her face and raised her chin. "I will not let them use me to scare you off! You will go home, change into your *court* suit, go after those bastards, and send their asses to jail!"

Matthew swallowed his inclination to rebuke his wife's swear words. Instead, he smiled and kissed her on the forehead. "Right!"

It was four o'clock in the morning when they arrived home. Trying to sleep was a lost effort, as they were both upset.

"I don't want you or anyone else working alone in the shop," Matthew warned. "Expect a policeman or a hired security guard sometime this morning."

"I have to contact the insurance company and hire someone to fix the window," Kara said. "Or should I wait until the trial is over?"

"Judge Seinfield won't allow this kind of harassment. The DeLuca brothers will be warned, although they'll deny it," Matthew said.

"Be careful," Kara said when Matthew left for work. She would be picked up by Alice, as usual.

A phone call to the boarding house had warned the girls that the boutique wouldn't be open and to wear trousers or something old because they would be checking every inch of the shop for red paint splatter.

It was a long day, and the shop was thoroughly cleaned. Kara spoke to the insurance people, who would send an agent to validate the claim. She ordered new manikins because the ones in the window had been destroyed. Matthew had taken photographs with a camera he carried in the trunk of his car.

Matthew's first stop was his office, where he called Judge Seinfield's office and asked to speak to the Judge before the trial started for the day. He explained to the Judge that his wife's shop was being targeted.

"The problem is that you have no proof that the DeLuca brothers are responsible for the harassment. I can only offer limited protection," the Judge said. "It's not the same as the jurors, who are already sequestered in a hotel. I'll notify the city Police Captain to take extra caution in that area. That's the best I can do."

Matthew left the office frustrated. He called a security company and hired guards to watch over the shop from four o'clock in the afternoon to seven in the morning. Then he called Kara and told her what to expect.

A policeman from the local precinct came by the shop and said that he would be making hourly rounds of the block during the day.

"I suppose that's going to have to do!" Alice complained.

"We'll put a sign on the door stating we are open," Kara

said, shrugging. "It's the best we can do until it is replaced. The girls can care for the shop while we finish our new designs upstairs. We've only got nine days until the Knickerbocker Show, and I have several thousand beads to sew on an evening gown!" The days leading up to the show were flying by quickly.

As the prosecuting attorney, Matthew gave the closing arguments in the case. He left the courthouse, knowing he'd done his best. It was in the hands of the jury to decide on the verdict. He would have loved to take Kara away and treat her to a vacation, but she was still involved with the last-minute details of getting ready for another fashion show. There was also the fact that he had to stay local for when the jury decided to announce the verdicts. It could be hours or weeks.

Elizabeth and Emma were surprised when Kara pulled into a loading zone beside the sidewalk. They slid into the backseat.

"Alice called. She came out to four flat tires this morning. She'll be in later," Kara explained.

"Why are they doing this?" Elizabeth asked. "The jury is deciding the verdict. It's too late for the DeLuca brothers to scare off Matthew's team."

"That's what he said," Kara answered as she pulled to the curb and let the girls out. "Open the shop. I'll be there in a minute. Someone has parked in *our* designated space again. Call the police to get them ticketed." Kara drove around the block three times before she found a space in an alley that wasn't tagged to belong to a business. She didn't notice a truck following her. Although Matthew had purchased a rearview mirror as an accessory to her new car, she wasn't used to using it. The truck stopped behind her momentarily while she parked in the empty space and drove past her.

While exiting her car, Kara opened the door and reached

for her purse, still on the seat. A black bag was thrown over her head, and her arms jerked roughly behind her. Something was tied over the black hood, forcing her mouth open and tied tightly behind her head. The sounds of her screams were muffled. She was dragged to the back of a truck, tossed in, shoved down, and covered with something heavy.

Elizabeth and Emma opened the shop and thanked the guard Matthew had hired to watch over the shop at night. They helped a few early bird shoppers. When the women left with their purchases, Elizabeth looked around. "Did Kara go straight upstairs?"

"I didn't see her," Emma said. She turned, ran up the stairs, and returned downstairs in seconds. "She's not there."

"It's been forty-five minutes since we opened," Elizabeth said.

"Where would she have gone?" Emma asked.

"I don't know," Elizabeth said. "Let's give her a few more minutes, and then we'll call for help."

The minutes turned to another half hour as they ushered out several customers. Elizabeth called Alice's home number, even though she knew Alice wouldn't be there. Thomas hadn't said what garage he'd hired to tow her car.

She called Matthew's office, but a young woman answered and said he was in a conference, whatever that meant. She left a message for him to call the boutique immediately when he returned. Elizabeth's next call was to the police. The person on the phone said there was nothing to be done until an adult person was officially declared missing for twenty-four hours.

"What do we do now?" Emma asked.

"I don't know," Elizabeth worried. "Maybe we should

walk around a few blocks. Maybe she sprained an ankle or something."

Emma shook her head. "We know all shop owners within three or four blocks in every direction. If she was hurt, they'd call or tell us."

Elizabeth bit down on her lower lip, picked up the phone, and dialed.

"Mrs. Giordano, is Marcio there?"

"He's asleep," Mrs. Giordano said.

"I know he's on night shift," Elizabeth said. "I need you to wake him. This is important."

"My son needs his rest," the matriarch of the Giordano house exclaimed. "Who are you?"

Elizabeth closed her eyes. "Mrs. Giordano, this is Claudina Gallo."

"Where have you been?" the woman demanded. "Your father has been worried to death."

"This is an emergency," Elizabeth shouted over Marcio's mother's scolding. "Wake up, Marcio, or I'll send the police to your home!"

Elizabeth heard the receiver being dropped on the table. She'd been to the Giordano apartment many times, and could imagine Marcio's mother, plump, short, and constantly wringing her hands.

"Hello?" Marcio's voice was gruff. "What's wrong?"

"I didn't know who else to call," Elizabeth said. "I called the police, but they aren't going to be any help!"

"What's wrong?" Marcio demanded.

"Kara's missing!" Elizabeth said. "I don't know what to do, and I can't get a hold of the Markhams or Matthew. That's why I called you!"

"Tell me exactly what you do know," Marcio said firmly.

"Alice's tires were slashed this morning, and I can't contact her or Thomas. Kara drove us in this morning. She drove us to the store, but someone parked in the shop's parking space. She told us to open the shop and drove away to find an empty parking space. We haven't seen her since. That was almost two hours ago. She's missing!"

"Have you looked for her?" he asked.

"No, we can't leave the shop because the guard left, and I don't want someone breaking in again."

"Did you call Matthew?" Marcio asked.

"I had to leave a message with his secretary," Elizabeth said. "I don't know what to do!"

"Close the shop and lock the doors," Marcio ordered. "Don't open them to anyone you don't know. I'll be there as soon as I can get there!" Marcio slammed the receiver down and ran to his bedroom.

His mother opened his door. "Marcio! Where are you going? Have you known where Claudina has been all this time?"

"Ma! Unless you want to see parts of me you haven't seen since I came out of diapers, you'd better turn around!" Marcio said, opening his closet door and dressing in his police uniform.

"Answer me!" his mother demanded, although she turned her back to him.

"Not the whole time, no, but I've known for a while," he answered.

"Why didn't you tell us?" she demanded.

"Because she ran away for a reason," Marcio said. "Claudina ran away because she wanted more than marrying a man her father had chosen for her husband. She wanted more schooling and a career. She's doing what she wants now. I ran into her accidentally, but I understand why she left, and I'm lucky enough that she didn't turn her back on me. She needs help, and I will help her and her friends.

Stay out of this, Ma, and don't call Mr. Gallo. It's none of your business."

Matthew and his team of attorneys were getting restless. They'd been waiting for over three hours, and Judge Seinfield hadn't entered the courtroom yet. Only the prosecuting and defense teams and an antsy gallery of mostly family members who had lost someone or, victims who had been injured were present.

When the Judge finally entered the courtroom, everyone stood as was proper etiquette and sat when the bailiff gave the order, "You may sit."

The side door opened, and the jury entered the courtroom and took their seats. Judge Seinfeld asked if the jury had come to a consensus. The Foreman of the jury stood and answered, "Yes, sir." He handed several pieces of paper to the Bailiff, who gave them to the Judge to read. Judge Seinfeld handed them to the Bailiff and returned them to the Foreman. There was formality in the courtroom, and everyone abided by it. One by one, the charges were read out loud by Judge Seinfeld. One by one, the Foreman announced guilty verdicts. The most critical charges were Involuntary Manslaughter and Culpable Homicide. Most of the family members of the victims and Matthew's team of lawyers were holding their breath. Both verdicts came in guilty.

Looking over to the DeLuca side of the courtroom, it was clear they hadn't expected to lose. Judge Seinfield had already frozen all the DeLucas' bank accounts. It would take months for accountants and lawyers to divide the funds among the victims of the collapsed building. Matthew was sure the DeLucas' bank accounts were in the million-dollar range, but he wasn't privy to that information.

Judge Seinfield asked the police to return the DeLuca brothers to their holding cells and declared a date that he would deliver his judgments for the crimes.

Matthew shook hands with his team while the DeLuca brothers were handcuffed and turned over to New York Police officers to be delivered back to prison to await their sentencing.

He was leaving the courtroom when he recognized Marcio Giordano in the hall.

"Marcio, what are you doing here?"

"Trying to find you," Marcio said. "Kara is missing."

"What do you mean missing?" Matthew demanded.

"Just what the word means," Marcio said. "She dropped Elizabeth and Emma off in front of the shop, and no one has seen her since. I've already been to every shop within a three-block radius. Someone had parked in the shop's designated space, so she drove down the street and hasn't been seen since. Her car has been found two blocks away. Her purse was still on the seat."

"Those sons-of-bitches!" Matthew exclaimed. "I'll kill them!"

"Whoa," Marcio exclaimed, looking around to see who might have heard him. "There's no proof the DeLuca brothers were behind this."

"Who else would want to get to me through my wife?" Matthew demanded.

"Someone who hates Kara," Marcio guessed.

"That's ridiculous; no one hates Kara," Matthew exclaimed. "Everyone likes her!"

"Add me to the list," Marcio said. "But, the police aren't going to be much help for at least twenty-four to forty-eight hours unless I can convince them to listen. We need to find out who might have a grudge against her, and Emma came up with a likely suspect."

"Who?"

"Let's take this back to the shop," Marcio said. "Alice and Thomas should be there by now."

It didn't take long to return to the shop. Alice's car was parked in front, although Matthew had to circle the block three times to find a spot. They ran inside to find everyone waiting for them.

"I was praying that Kara would be with you," Alice said.

"I was in court with the DeLuca brothers," Matthew said. "Marcio says he doesn't think the DeLuca brothers are behind this."

"Emma has suggested someone else," Alice explained.

"At the last show, that woman Wanda Beardley was furious because she was fired. If Thomas hadn't stopped her, she would have physically attacked Alice. It wasn't Alice or Kara's fault that the audience didn't like her designs, but she blamed them. When Mrs. Barton fired her, Wanda turned on Alice and Kara. We'd never met her before, and you saw what she designed and the audience's reaction. Anyone who would behave like that in public is probably dangerous. I think that crazy woman is trying to ruin the boutique," Emma said. "First, there was the egging of Alice's car. Then it was breaking the showcase window and the paint mess."

"Then it was your car tires this morning and Kara disappearing," Elizabeth added. "We need to find out where Wanda Beardley lives and works."

"What do you think?" Thomas asked of Matthew.

"They have a point," Matthew said. "Who else would want to shut down the boutique? But, all we have is a name."

"We can start with Mrs. Barton," Alice said, going into the office and searching through a stack of business cards. She called the number and asked Mrs. Barton if she had an address for Wanda Beardley.

Mrs. Barton said to give her a few minutes. She had to go into her office, and she would call back with the information.

When the phone rang, it was all Matthew could do not to snatch the receiver.

Alice answered but handed the phone to Matthew because he kept motioning for her to relinquish it.

"Mrs. Barton, this is Matthew Douglas, Kara's husband. If you could answer a few questions, it might help. Yes, ma'am, I am very protective of Kara.

"Mrs. Barton, have you ever seen the vehicle, Miss. Beardley drives? Yes, ma'am, that does help," Matthew said. "Do you happen to have her address? Yes, it would be most helpful. Just a few more questions, and I apologize for taking your time, but I am a lawyer, and we tend to ask a lot of questions. Yes, ma'am. Have you ever seen anyone helping Wanda Beardley with her merchandise? Assistants, or... Oh, you keep records of everyone who is allowed backstage. That's a good idea. Yes, I'd like the names and addresses of the two assistants. I see. They must be related. Thank you for the information. "No, ma'am, Kara and Alice will be at the Knickerbocker Show with bells on! Thank you again."

Matthew handed the phone receiver to Alice. "Wanda Beardley drives a truck, and I quote: *painted to look like a terrible rendition of Vincent Van Gogh's Starry Night*."

"The strange truck Mr. Purney described," Elizabeth said.

"Wanda Beardley has two men that usually accompany her to the fashion shows to lift and carry. She has registered them as assistants, but they have the same last name, so they must be brothers or cousins. They all have the same address. Mrs. Barton is very good at keeping records of everyone allowed backstage.

"Wanda has been pestering and warning Mrs. Barton that the show would be a disaster if she wasn't reinstated."

"I need to speak to my Captain," Marcio said.

"You're not going anywhere without us," Thomas said bluntly.

The boutique phone rang, and Matthew answered it and grabbed a piece of paper and a pencil. "Thank you, Mrs. Barton. We needed that information." He turned to Marcio. "This is the address."

Chapter 21

THE BOUTIQUE WAS CLOSED and secured, and everyone squeezed into the two vehicles. They descended on Marcio's precinct in full force.

Marcio explained what they suspected, but his Captain wanted no part of it.

"It's out of our jurisdiction," Captain Hollis said firmly to Matthew. "There's no proof your wife has been kidnapped, Mr. Douglas. She could have just run off."

"The evidence leads us to believe..." Matthew started.

"There is no evidence," Captain Hollis said. "What you have is conjecture, and I'm not wasting my time and manpower on a silly woman disappearing for a couple of hours. She's probably having her hair done!"

"Fine," Matthew said, although his eyes had turned into daggers. "I've been fighting to take down the DeLuca brothers for the last six months, and now that I've done it, I'll be sure to tell the newspapers how much *help* you were in finding my wife. Don't bother getting off your ass! You can clean out your desk from where you're sitting."

"Officer Giordano, step out that door, and you're fired," Captain Hollis snapped.

"Don't worry about it, Marcio," Matthew countered. "I spent ten years sharing a room with Teddy Roosevelt, Jr., and I know his father, the New York Police Commissioner, better than I knew my own. We'll see what he thinks about the cooperation we've received, and if one hair on my wife's head is hurt, I'll hold you, Captain Hollis, personally responsible."

"Now, hold on, hold on, and don't get bent out of shape," Captain Hollis barked. "Sometimes there are reasons to break protocol. Giordano, you're in charge. Take Bishop and Harris with you and keep these civilians out of police business!"

"We'll wait outside," Matthew told Marcio, ignoring the Captain.

Marcio did take control. Opening a conference room, he asked everyone to wait there for him. Returning ten minutes later, he was accompanied by two uniformed officers. He spread out a map and pointed to a position on the map. "This is the area where the address is located, Secaucus. Has anyone been in this sector of the city?"

"I have," Thomas said. "It's a cookie-cutter urban area. The housing is decent. It's a forty-minute drive to downtown. The two-story houses looked similar, with a front porch, street parking, standalone garages, or a small backyard. It's not in New York. It's in New Jersey."

"They have a small police force there," one of the officers said. "We should stop there and find out if any problems have been reported at that address."

"Good idea," another officer spoke up. "Who has a vehicle?"

Thomas and Matthew raised their hands.

"We'll be doubling up. We're inner-city cops, and the

new Commissioner hasn't issued more police vehicles for this unit yet. This station is mostly foot patrols and keeping our eyes open. I would also suggest that these women not be involved. They look underage."

"I'm not!" Elizabeth protested.

"We'll drop you off at the shop," Matthew said firmly. He looked at Alice, but she narrowed her eyes, and he wisely decided not to go there.

Marcio had a whispered conversation with Elizabeth, and she stopped complaining. She and Emma were dropped off in front of the shop, with promises of a phone call if they found Kara.

The Secaucus local police were surprised when the small office was invaded by New York City police. After an explanation, Chief of Police Howard Crane was immediately helpful. He pulled a file folder from a cabinet and opened it.

"I've had problems with those people," Chief Crane said. "I've cited them for indecency multiple times and dragged their butts in front of our local Judge Ben Cartmon. They've been cited and fined for painting obscene pictures on their vehicles, garage, and even on the back of their house. We made them paint over those obscenities. Little kids shouldn't be seeing those kinds of pictures. The latest complaint is that they've painted the house in crayon colors. The neighbors don't like it, but it's not against the law. You don't want to know what they did at Halloween."

Matthew interrupted his complaints. "All I want is to find my wife; we believe they have kidnapped her."

"Kidnapped?" Chief Crane repeated. "I'll admit those folks are strange, but why would they do that?"

"It doesn't matter why," Marcio said. "We need to go to their property and search it for a missing woman!"

"Well, I reckon it wouldn't hurt," the Chief said, getting to his feet. "I have to drive out there every couple of weeks anyway, to make sure they're not painting dirty pictures where kids can see them. Follow me, and I'll take you out there."

It didn't take long to arrive at the Beardley property. Several neighbors appeared on their porches, watching the procession of vehicles pull off the road in front of the house, led by Chief Crane's police car. He pulled into the driveway. Among a sea of repetitious houses painted white with blue or black painted shutters, the Beardley house was a profusion of bright colors. The porch floor was painted orange, and the porch posts were purple. The front door was pink. The first story of the house was painted red, and the second was painted green.

"It's hideous," Alice whispered. "It's also the same red color that destroyed our display window."

Chief Crane got out and pointed at Alice. "You stay back, ma'am. This ain't a job for a woman. He stormed up the stairs and pounded on the front door.

Alice ignored the Chief, and while the policemen and her husband were standing on the porch, she walked to the side of the house.

"They're not in the house," Alice screamed. "They're in the garage and closing the doors!"

All the policemen ran toward the garage.

"They've locked us out!" Marcio said.

"Son, you've spent too much time in the city. A couple of you men go on around back and make sure they don't go out of any windows or backdoors," Chief Crane ordered. He ran to his vehicle, opened the trunk, and pulled out an ax, a megaphone, and a shotgun.

"Now you Beardleys better listen," Chief Crane yelled through the megaphone. "I've had enough of your nonsense. You either open these doors, or I'll take an ax to them, and then I'll show you how much damage a shotgun can do. I ain't playing with you. You've been in my jail before, so don't push me!"

There was no response, so the Chief set the megaphone on the ground and picked up the ax. "You all move off to the side in case they try something stupid!" With three whacks of the ax, he swung the doors open. Chief Crane stepped out of the way as a wildly painted truck drove out and tried to escape.

Chief Crane dropped the ax and picked up his rifle. Several handguns were pulled, and the Beardley tires were flattened. The truck swerved to avoid hitting the Chief's car. He stomped to the driver's side, opened the door, yanked a young woman out of the driver's seat, and forced her on her knees. On the truck's passenger side, Marcio's policemen dragged two men out, handcuffed, and searched them for weapons.

"This isn't my fault!" Wanda Beardley protested. "This is that bitch's fault! She stole my place in the show!"

Matthew, Marcio, and Thomas rushed into the garage.

"Stay outside," Thomas said, but Alice ignored him and rushed in. The garage looked like it had been a carriage house previously. There were horse stalls, although they were obviously used as storage rooms. The stalls were clean and resembled the upstairs storage above the shop, equipped with manikins and sewing machines. There were metal racks filled with garments.

Alice ran into a small stall and found it to be only half size, with a door to another compartment. She could hear the men calling Kara's name. She opened the door and found Kara lying on the floor.

"She's here!" Alice screamed, kneeling in front of her friend. Kara tried to sit up, but whatever she said couldn't be understood.

Matthew skidded to his knees. He tried to untie the rope about her head.

"Let me through," Marcio exclaimed. He pulled a pocket knife from his trousers. "Hold her still!" he said to Matthew and spoke loudly, "Ma'am, you need to stop moving. I'm a policeman and a friend of Elizabeth. I'm going to cut these ropes."

Kara stopped moving, and Marcio sliced through the ropes. Matthew pulled the black hood off her head.

With glassy eyes, Kara fell forward into her husband's arms as Marcio cut the ropes off her hands and then her ankles.

"Thank you," Kara said hoarsely, and then she struggled to get away from her husband. She pushed him aside and emptied her stomach.

Thomas offered his handkerchief.

"Sorry," Kara whispered.

"Is she all right?" Chief Crane demanded, coming into the garage.

"Yes, I'm okay," Kara said, although the words sounded hoarse.

"There's a hospital ambulance on its way," the Chief said.

"I don't need a hospital," Kara whispered.

"Take that up with your husband, ma'am," the Chief said. "Officer Giordano, there are forms that need to be filled out before I can release this bunch to you. I will keep them in my jail until your superior wants them moved to New York."

"Yes, sir," Marcio answered while the officers from his precinct gave him a pat on the back.

Kara was cleared by a doctor at the hospital. She had scratches, bruises, and a bump on her head. She was still visibly shaken by her ordeal. Matthew refused to leave the room when the doctor examined her and stood by as a nurse gently washed her of blood and grime. The doctor explained to Matthew that she was in shock and would need to be treated gently for a few days.

They had to stop at the police station to give their statements after leaving the hospital, but that didn't take long.

Thomas drove, and Kara curled into her husband's lap in the backseat.

There was a rearrangement of who would be in what vehicle for the trip back to New York. Marcio borrowed Thomas' truck to take his squad members back to their precinct.

The Beardleys had already been arrested for kidnapping. They denied the charges and were told that more charges would be levied when they were returned to New York City.

Wanda Beardley might have thought she was dealing with an *'uninspired nobody'* in the fashion world. She hadn't counted on her victim being married to an up-and-coming hotshot attorney with a reputation that couldn't be faulted. Wanda and her assistants already had minor offenses on their records. Kidnapping was another matter. It wasn't a federal felony law yet, although several states treated it on the same scale as attempted murder.

Kara closed her eyes during the return trip. Once they were back in their suite, Matthew filled the bathtub and gently tried to wash away any remnants of her ordeal.

He dressed her in comfortable pajamas with a loose robe, tucked her into the couch, and ordered a late lunch. Nudging her, he stroked her shoulders and tried to reassure Kara that she was safe.

"Where did Alice and Thomas go?" Kara questioned.

"They, along with Marcio and his men, had to stop by the precinct to give additional details," Matthew said.

Meanwhile, Marcio and his police helpers filled out

forms for Captain Hollis for the second time. Thomas and Alice were included in this group and were told that Matthew and Kara would have to do the same at their convenience.

There was a jurisdiction conflict. Chief Crane wasn't releasing the Beardleys to the New York Police until everything was done by the book.

"The trick to getting a conviction is in the details," Captain Crane said. "And if I can get that sorry lot out of Secaucus, it will make my life easier!"

Alice made a phone call to Matthew, and he reluctantly asked Kara if she wanted company.

Kara nodded when asked.

"If you want peace and quiet, it's okay," Matthew said.

Kara shook her head. "I had hours of that when they locked me in that room. I'm okay, Matthew. I just have to get my nerves settled."

Matthew agreed to their visiting, answered the door, and stood aside as the kitchen staff brought a cart inside.

"Hungry?"

Kara sat up on the couch. "Not at all, but I'm feeling better." She rubbed her fingers over her lower cheeks. "My mouth and cheeks hurt though."

"That's from where they tied a rope to keep you from screaming," Matthew explained.

"What's going to happen to them?"

"I don't know, but they will be extradited back to New York, and I'll make sure they are prosecuted."

"Oh, I forgot," Kara exclaimed. "What were the jury results?"

"We won," Matthew said. "Manslaughter and Homicide were the top convictions, but straight down the list of charges, the jury came in with guilty decisions. The DeLuca bank accounts have been locked down for months and will be emptied before this is over. I hope this conviction will give the families some satisfaction. The compensation money will make their lives easier."

Kara only nodded.

"You need to eat something," Matthew said.

"I'll start with something to drink," Kara said. Matthew handed her a glass of iced tea when the doorbell rang.

He opened the door to Thomas and Alice. Alice ran to her best friend, hugged her, and began asking questions about Kara's health.

"I wasn't held that long," Kara answered when everyone hugged her. "Their plans were to hold me until after the show on Saturday. Wanda was convinced that if we weren't available, Mrs. Barton would reinstate her in the show."

"All three of them together don't have the intelligence of an ant," Thomas snorted. "She kept screaming at the jail that they wouldn't have harmed you. Like that makes a difference!"

There was another knock on the door. Marcio, Elizabeth, and Emma came in. The girls ran to Kara.

"I have all of you to thank for my rescue, don't I?" Kara asked Marcio.

"No, you have these two," Marcio said, nodding toward the girls. "Elizabeth and Emma put two and two together and figured out the Beardleys had something to do with the vandalism and the kidnapping. And, your husband, for putting the fear of God in Captain Hollis if we didn't follow the leads." He turned to Matthew. "Captain Hollis will take full credit for her rescue. When we reported in, he was already on the phone with his superiors."

"I don't care if they give him a Medal of Honor," Matthew said. "I'm just glad he finally listened to reason. If he causes you any trouble, I will pull strings on your behalf. I wasn't joking about knowing the Roosevelts."

"I do want to thank all of you," Kara said. "I'm feeling much better, and I'll be back to work tomorrow."

"I don't think so," Matthew said.

"The doctor said there was nothing physically wrong with me!" Kara said. "We have a show to do in three days, and we are not canceling. That woman has done enough damage to us and the shop. I am not going to allow her to win! Tomorrow will be a normal day for us, and if we're lucky, the new display window will be installed."

"We'll let you argue this out," Thomas said, taking his wife's hand with a smile. "We'll drop everyone off where they belong. Have a good evening."

Thomas dropped off his passengers in front of the boarding house.

Emma turned to Elizabeth. "I'm staying the night at my mother's. She's working two shifts." She ran down the sidewalk toward the building where her mother rented two rooms. Marcio stood on the sidewalk with Elizabeth.

"The cat is out of the bag," Marcio said. "I'd bet a hundred dollars that my mother called your father as soon as I left. If Ma did, I'll be moving out."

"I don't care anymore," Elizabeth said. "I'm going to face him. He doesn't scare me anymore. I'm a totally different person than I was when I left."

"I'll go with you," Marcio said. "We're in this together."

Elizabeth smiled. "Come upstairs with me."

Marcio's head jerked in surprise. "I thought men weren't allowed."

"What they don't know won't hurt them," Elizabeth said. "You can slip in through the fire escape window. I've been dating you for months, too afraid to commit myself. Today taught me that we can't rely on having a tomorrow. We have to live each day as if it might be our last. I love you, Marcio, and I want to show you that I love you. I've seen the rubbers you carry in your wallet when you open it to pull out money. I want you to use one or more of them with me tonight."

"Elizabeth, you don't owe me anything," Marcio said huskily.

"I want you to teach me and make me a woman," Elizabeth said.

Marcio swallowed. "Are you sure?"

"Very," Elizabeth said, standing on her tiptoes to kiss him. "Do you have the time?"

"Oh, yeah," Marcio whispered, taking a deep breath. "I'm on the midnight shift."

"You're already wearing your uniform, so you don't have to go home to change," Elizabeth said.

"Are you sure?"

"Let's see who can get to my bedsitter first," Elizabeth teased.

Marcio turned, ran a few steps, stopped, and turned. "Are you sure?"

Elizabeth only smiled. Going inside, she checked the mailbox and climbed the stairs. What she was about to do was flaunting the morals she'd been raised with, but she didn't care. Entering the little bedsitter, she shared with Emma, she went straight to the window. Marcio was waiting. She unlocked the window, and he climbed through.

"Are you sure?"

Elizabeth unbuttoned her jacket and tossed it onto Emma's narrow bed. Her blouse followed, and she rolled down her stockings, carefully set them aside, and dropped her skirt. "I'm beginning to feel this is very one-sided."

"I can fix that," Marcio said. "You're just so damn beautiful! I can't take my eyes off of you." He unbuttoned the top two buttons on his shirt and pulled it over his head, and the undershirt followed. He then unbuttoned his trousers and kicked out of his shoes.

It took all of a minute for Marcio to strip. He touched Elizabeth lightly, kissed her, and she returned his kisses. He kissed his way over her body, enjoying the view.

"I'm not sure what I'm supposed to be doing," Elizabeth whispered.

"Don't worry about it," Marcio promised. "I'll show you everything you need to know." They fell onto the mattress together, and he feasted on her mouth. Then lowered his head and suckled on her breasts.

"Do you like that?" he demanded.

"Yes," she responded. When Marcio stroked her sex, Elizabeth felt herself rising from a strange tingling between her legs. She gasped and became impatient.

"Do it," Elizabeth whispered.

"Just a second," Marcio exclaimed. He reached for his wallet, found his stash of rubbers, and covered himself. "Wrap your legs around my waist," he said, knowing he wouldn't have much control over himself. He hadn't had sex since he started dating Elizabeth. Thrusting into her, he heard a sharp intake of breath from her but continued to stroke inside her. He plunged into her deeper and knew he was taking her virginity. Still, Elizabeth had asked for this, and he was too far gone to stop. He needed her, and she was responding. Suddenly, she thrashed and shook with what he hoped was her first orgasm, and he responded in kind.

Several hours later, Marcio was dressed in his uniform. Elizabeth had dressed and gone down the hall with a wash basin. There was only one shared bathroom on each floor. "When Ma woke me up this morning, I never expected the day to end like this."

"Was it worth it?" Elizabeth asked. "You still might be in trouble with Chief Hollis."

"I'm not worried, and I don't want to talk about him," Marcio said. "I love you, Elizabeth. You're my girl now, and there's no turning back. How are you feeling?"

"Loved," Elizabeth said. She glanced over to the used rubbers in the trash can. "You're going to have to get some more."

Marcio laughed. "That's not a problem. Hell, I haven't had any use for them since we started seeing each other. I carry these things around because it's a guy thing to do. Who knew that sweet Elizabeth was a tigress?"

"Only for you," Elizabeth said with a surprisingly shy smile.

"Yes, ma'am, that's how it's going to be," Marcio agreed.

Across town, in a much larger bed, Matthew wished he was making love to his wife. Prior to retiring for the night, they had been arguing. Matthew thought Kara should take a few days off to recover. Kara argued this suggestion reminding him that she and Alice only had a few days to complete their runway show pieces. Besides, beyond a few scratches and feeling tired, she was fine. The arguing continued, and Kara knew Matthew was upset with her. They finally reached a compromise. She could continue working on the Knickerbocker Show but would take time off after it as they hadn't had a vacation since they'd started living with each other again. She agreed by making Matthew promise that he would have to turn the DeLuca case over to someone else in his firm while they were on vacation. He had no idea when Judge Seinfield would recall his law team and announce his decisions on the sentencing.

Chapter 22

THERE NEVER SEEMED to be enough time. Alice and Kara were trying to make use of every minute. Elizabeth and Emma were given the responsibility of the boutique while they worked at a frantic pace to finish the runway dresses. Mrs. Barton stopped by to approve of the collection and was all smiles when she left.

Two days before the Knickerbocker Show, Kara answered a phone call from Mrs. Barton asking if she could have the contact number of the artist displaying her paintings in the boutique. Mrs. Barton wanted to know if she could exhibit the paintings as an additional display of female talent.

"I'll call and find out," Kara answered. "She's a very private person."

After the call, she turned to Alice. "There's nothing like throwing in a last-minute request!"

"Call her," Alice said. "We haven't seen Deloris in a couple of weeks, and if the paintings sell, I'm sure she can use the income."

Deloris was interested, and she called Mrs. Barton to

make the arrangements. They agreed on how many paintings she would display and where they were to meet. She immediately called Sharon for help, and a few minutes later, Sharon called and said Harry would use one of the furniture store trucks to deliver the paintings the day before the show.

"I feel like I'm on a roller coaster," Kara exclaimed while she packed their fashions in garment bags for transport to the Knickerbocker Hotel. Although she'd only been held captive for a few hours, she felt fatigued and a little sick to her stomach.

"Nerves?" Alice asked.

"Probably," Kara agreed. "This show is going to be different. Mrs. Barton has a guest list including most of New York's high society. The event includes the runway show, Deloris' paintings on display in the lobby and for sale, and a buffet luncheon."

"Speak of the devil," Elizabeth said, entering the storeroom. "Deloris is downstairs with Sharon. They want to buy dresses for the event."

"Deloris!" Kara exclaimed, giving the older woman a hug. "Look at you! We haven't seen you for a while, and you look terrific!"

"I feel fantastic," Deloris said happily. "You and Matthew need to come over for Sunday dinner."

"We've been too busy," Kara said. "We've barely had time to do anything fun for the last few weeks. "We've made a pact, though. When Matthew's big trial is over, and after this show, we are taking some time off."

"So you should," Deloris scolded. "When I saw that piece in the newspaper about the kidnapping, I almost had a heart attack."

"What newspaper?" Kara asked.

"The Island Periodical, this morning," Deloris said. "There was a picture of Chief Crane, and the article said his team helped to catch the kidnappers. He said the victim wasn't hurt and didn't want to be named. Still, he gave so many hints about the boutique, and the designer shows that I knew it was you. I tried to call, but something is wrong with the telephone lines in our neighborhood. So Sharon and I decided to see for ourselves."

"As you can see," Kara said with her arms out, as she turned in a circle, "I am fine. Now what can we do for you, fine ladies?"

"New dresses," the women said together.

Sharon giggled. "We're housewives. I haven't had a party dress in years, and I'm going to the show as Deloris' guest."

Deloris smiled. "I can beat that. I haven't had a dress-up dress in decades, and everything I own is now too big!"

Kara looked over to the clock and then spoke quietly to Elizabeth, "When our lone shopper leaves, hang up the closed sign." She clapped her hands together. "This way to the dressing room, ladies. Alice, you work with Deloris, and I'll work with Sharon. When we get through with you, every woman there will wonder why you weren't on the runway."

It took nearly an hour to dress their friends. After a whispered conversation with the girls, they removed the price tags before carrying them into dressing rooms. Sharon, still trim and curvy, looked terrific in a turquoise flapper dress with a matching hat.

Deloris was a little harder to fit. She wasn't as adventurous. She *tsked* at the fringes, and long strings of pearls, claiming she was too old. Emma showed her a magazine picture of an older woman wearing a similar outfit and praised her new thinner figure. Deloris preened at her reflection in the mirror when a feathered hat and high heels were added.

"I like it," Deloris said with a smile.

"You just need a touch of makeup," Alice added. "Not

too much, and there's nothing wrong with lipstick and a little powder."

Neither of the women would accept the dresses and accessories without payment. They left the boutique, and there were smiles all around. Elizabeth and Emma hadn't reacted when Kara quoted less than half the retail price for her friends.

Alice clapped her hands. "Let's get everything retagged here and go home. Get a full night's sleep because tomorrow will be both a fabulous and a beast of a day!"

The Knickerbocker Show was a success. Newspaper photographers were there, and photographs were taken. Every year the newspapers supported 'fashion month.'

Matthew was again escorting Mrs. Cahill to the show at the Knickerbocker. Mrs. Cahill was wearing a design by Alice. She'd been to the boutique several times. Even though she was the wife of one of Matthew's employers, she wasn't offered a discount. Her reasoning was that Mr. Cahill was most likely a millionaire.

Winning the DeLuca case had raised his boss's opinion of his skills in the courtroom. Matthew was moving up the ladder at the Cahill, Gordon, and Reindel Law Firm. Mr. Cahill also didn't mind that Matthew could escort his wife to the fashion shows. It meant he could spend the day at the golf course.

Thomas didn't attend the show, but Alice wasn't upset. She'd been warned ahead of time. He was meeting with city planners, and rescheduling a meeting would have caused insurmountable delays in the building project.

When the runway walks were completed, Kara and Alice joined the designers in a meet and greet with potential customers. There were several newspaper photographers taking pictures. When the guests were invited to the ballroom for the buffet, most of the designers went backstage to supervise the repacking of their creations.

Elizabeth was surprised when Marcio arrived. He looked uncomfortable in a suit but helped load a borrowed truck. He seemed to be keeping close eyes on everyone backstage.

Kara raised an eyebrow at Alice as they watched the interaction between Elizabeth and Marcio. "Someone has a boyfriend," Kara whispered.

"I think so too, but don't tease her about it," Alice whispered. "Emma and Elizabeth figured out who kidnapped you, and Marcio risked his job as a policeman to go after you."

"I'll never forget," Kara retorted. "And, when she needs a wedding dress, it will be a top-of-the-line couture gown designed by Kara & Alaïs Couture Designs."

"Who needs a wedding dress?" a female voice asked behind them.

Alice and Kara turned around to find Deloris and Sharon.

"How did you get backstage?" Alice asked.

"By following your husband and his date, Mrs. Cahill," Sharon said, looking across the backstage area. "They are over there talking with Mrs. Barton."

"I'm a contributor, and Mrs. Barton gave me backstage tickets. People are leaving," Deloris said. "The show's been over for a while, and the buffet is almost empty."

"Did you enjoy yourselves?" Kara asked.

"More than we ever imagined," Sharon said. "We don't get to live the high life very often. We saw you right after the show but couldn't get anywhere near you."

"I've given out about a hundred business cards," Kara said.

"So have I," Alice agreed. "How did the paintings sell?"

"All but four," Deloris said. "It's hard to believe, and Mr.

Howard, who handled the sales and deliveries, has offered to take me on as a client. I've been painting all these years, but it was just a hobby."

"You were underestimating your talent," Sharon scolded.

Kara was late getting home. At some point backstage, she'd lost track of her husband. She looked for him backstage, but he wasn't at the venue, and neither was Mrs. Cahill.

She and Alice had followed the hired truck back to the boutique, where they stored the couture runway dresses in locked cabinets. After checking and rechecking the locks, everyone headed home.

Kara took a long, luxurious bath and removed the makeup she'd used to cover scratches and bruises. Matthew finally came in, and he was empty-handed. He hadn't been seen without his briefcase for months.

He gave her a wide smile with happy eyes.

"What happened?" she asked. "You left in a hurry!"

"Judge Seinfield decided to render a ruling. Why today, without warning? Who knows? That's why I left with Mrs. Cahill. Mr. Cahill called the front desk and left a message for me. You were surrounded, and I couldn't get near you.

"The judge laid out the penalties for the DeLuca brothers' personal involvement in the collapse of the DeLuca building. He likened their misconduct to being a serial killer. He sentenced both of them to fifteen years for culpable homicide. He also gave them twenty years each for involuntary manslaughter. The sentences are to run consecutively, with no parole until both sentences are served. The two sentences together are life in prison. The DeLucas are both in their early fifties. That means they'll probably die in prison. A committee will decide on compensation to the victims' families. Not so surprising was that the Judge knew precisely how much money the DeLuca brothers had in their frozen bank accounts."

"Congratulations," Kara said.

"Do you know what that means?" Matthew asked.

"You'll get a promotion?" she guessed.

"No one has mentioned one yet," he said. "But, I did get a bonus. But, more important, I got a two-week vacation."

"You deserve it," Kara said.

"Yes, I do," he agreed. "And we are leaving tomorrow morning."

"I can't leave Alice with all the responsibility of the boutique with no warning!" Kara protested.

"Yes, you can because when we get back, Thomas and Alice will be going on their own vacation," Matthew held up a hand. "We all need a break, and no excuses are allowed."

Kara walked over to her husband and wrapped her arms around his neck. With a leap, she wrapped her legs around his waist. "You're getting awfully bossy, but sometimes I don't mind, but we're not leaving until I check in with Alice and the girls to make sure they are okay with it."

"A telephone call can take care of that," Matthew said.

"If we're lucky, we'll get follow-up clients from the show," Kara said. "If we sell one couture dress, it will cover our expenses."

Matthew frowned. "You are selling the show dresses?"

"Of course."

"Aren't they considered used?"

Kara laughed. "They are couture, one of a kind. If women can afford couture, they don't quibble if it is presented in a runway show. It's a matter of vanity, and their wealthy husbands don't complain."

"So, I'm supposed to be grateful that my wife designs couture," Matthew asked with a smile.

"You better be," Kara teased. "You got a free ticket."

"I did, didn't I? Matthew said. "How much do they go for?"

Kara quoted the price.

He sucked in a breath. "Are you kidding?"

"No. All the proceeds go to charity. Even Deloris agreed to donate ten percent of what she earned if her paintings sold."

"Did someone explain to Mrs. Barton about Deloris' circumstances?" Matthew asked, dropping Kara to her feet and giving her a nudge toward the bedroom.

"I did, and Mrs. Barton's response was to double the prices. Deloris said she sold all but four paintings. She earned enough money in one show to put Daniel through college."

"She's getting higher survivor's benefits now too, and the Major in charge who did the paperwork on Simon's retirement on a twenty-year, and not a nearly thirty-year-retirement has been demoted for his *'misunderstanding'* of the military regulations. She was issued backpay and is now getting more than enough benefits to live well."

"She looked great today," Kara said. "She didn't look stressed."

"You know what?" Matthew said, walking backward and drawing her closer to the bedroom door.

"What?"

"I don't want to talk about Deloris, the show, or the boutique."

"What do you want to want to talk about?" Kara teased.

"Nothing," Matthew said. "I don't want to talk about anything. I want all your attention and to make love to you until we both collapse in exhaustion."

"That sounds like a challenge," Kara said in a husky voice. She untied her bathrobe and dropped it to the floor, exhibiting her naked body. "What's taking you so long?"

Matthew accepted the challenge happily.

Kara gasped when his fingers thrust into her in a pumping motion. She knew what Matthew would do, and she wished he'd hurry. The strokes were building to an orgasm, and she wanted it badly.

She was almost there and groaned as he withdrew his hand.

"No..."

"Don't be in such a hurry," Matthew scolded, sitting up. He pulled her over his lap and stroked her bottom.

The first spank was always a stinger, and Kara knew what was coming. She had a love/hate relationship with his spanking her during sex. She knew it turned him on, and in ways she still found hard to believe, she wanted it. He rubbed out the sting and smacked her bottom again. The spanks stung, but while his right hand delivered a sting, the left stroked her sex, arousing her need for him.

When Kara reached the point of nearly coming again, Matthew stopped and drew her close. Kissing his way down her body, she was shivering from his touch. He positioned her on her knees, with her head and shoulders on the mattress and her hips and bottom up. He loved seeing her naked. It made him feel strong and in control.

Kara had given Matthew the right to use her body as he saw fit. Her willingness to allow his possession of her body might not have fit in with her feminist ideas. She'd read the sex books, though, as had he, and she was willing to try whatever her husband suggested. Not that she'd ever had another man to compare him against.

They hadn't had time lately for their long sessions of sex, and it had been sorely missed. A ten-minute quickie wasn't enough.

Matthew peppered her bottom with light but stinging spanks and then entered her from behind. With a deep thrust, he was in her, buried to the hilt. His hand went under her, finding and working her clitoris.

Kara gasped. She could feel the residual sting on her bottom as his genitals whacked against her buttocks.

Matthew rode her, thrusting, pounding, until he couldn't hold back any longer. He turned her over and thrust deep into her womanhood.

Kara felt like her body would explode at any second, and every stroke and thrust brought her closer, and suddenly the orgasm came in waves.

Matthew continued to ride her. He knew she had more to give, and he wouldn't settle for less. She arched her back, and Matthew lifted her legs to straddle his shoulders. Together they gave in to shared need, and while a second orgasm took her breath, he flooded her with his release.

When their bodies went still, they rolled and were wrapped in each other's arms. Neither spoke as Matthew gathered her into his arms and tucked her close to his body.

"God, that was so worth it," he gasped. "I may not let you out of bed for the next two weeks."

Kara nodded, feeling... satisfied. Had it only been two hours? There wasn't a single inch of her that hadn't responded to her husband. She felt... ravaged, and now she knew why the word was used in carefully written romance books. A writer would be arrested for describing in detail what she'd just experienced. Her bottom stung, her breasts were tender, and her sex was throbbing. She knew, though if her husband turned over and initiated sex again, she would give as good as she got.

On the first day of Kara's vacation, Marcio went with Elizabeth after work to confront her father. He stood by as her father yelled at her angrily for running away from home. Elizabeth had simply listened, and when her father stopped, she began to speak. When he interrupted her, she calmly told Claude Gallo he'd had his turn to speak and for once, to shut up and listen.

Shocked into silence, Claude had stood up and raised his hand, but Marcio stepped in front of Elizabeth and told her father to sit down and listen.

Elizabeth explained to her father that she would no longer allow him to interfere with her life. She had ambitions and was willing to work toward her goals. It was up to him to accept her as an adult because she would no longer tolerate his demands or interference. She had every right to make decisions about her life.

Claude backed down and asked where Elizabeth was living, but she shook her head. "Frankly, that's none of your business."

Walking together to the car, Elizabeth laid her head on Marcio's shoulder.

"That was tough," Marcio said as he pulled into traffic. He was driving a car that he was buying from a friend in installments. "I'm proud of you for standing up to him. I love you, Elizabeth. I admire you for pursuing your dreams. I respect your stubbornness and your loyalty. You have no idea how your courage has affected me. Although I signed up to attend the Police Academy, everyone in my family was against it. You gave me the courage to stand against my family."

Marcio took a route to a wooded area on Long Island. Marcio turned onto a side road and parked behind an empty house. Elizabeth reached for the door handle, but he stopped her. They'd been to this place for privacy several times.

"Wait," Marcio said. "There's something I want to say."

Elizabeth bit down on her lip, expecting the worst.

Marcio's family was much larger than hers but had the same Italian beliefs. Without him saying a word, she knew that his family had been giving him a hard time because he refused to give out any information about her.

"Elizabeth, I've been saving like crazy since I came home from the Army. My first goal was to buy a car, and I'm almost done with the payments. My next goal is to move out and have my own place. When you're ready, I'd like you to join me as my wife." Marcio dug a small box out of his pocket. "I'd like you to be my girl."

Elizabeth opened the box and looked at the engagement ring. It wasn't showy big. It was three small diamonds, and it was perfect. "I love you too, but I'm not ready for marriage. I have to finish school, and..."

"I know," Marcio interrupted. "You can achieve your dreams. I won't stand in your way. I'm not ready for marriage yet, but I'm getting there. I want you to know that when you are ready, I'll be waiting. I want you and me to become *us*. Me and you together."

Marcio blushed. "We've sorta jumped the gun on the together part, and I love that part of our relationship, but I also want you to know that if you get pregnant, I'll stand by you."

"You're using those..."

"Rubbers aren't foolproof," Marcio said. "When you're ready, I'll be here. I want a lifetime with you. I know I'm asking a lot, but this feels right!"

Elizabeth was drawn into a kiss, and when she was released, she wiggled the finger on her left hand.

Marcio removed the ring from the box, slid it on her finger, and kissed her. "You're my girl now. All mine."

Elizabeth took his hand, guided it to the hem of her dress, and slid it up her leg. "Let's go inside," she whispered.

Marcio grinned, drew her from the front seat, and

removed a blanket-covered basket from the trunk. They'd found this old abandoned house a while back and used it for privacy at every opportunity. This was their hideaway from the world, and someday they would live there. He had more news for Elizabeth but would wait to tell her when she was inside.

With help from Thomas, Marcio researched who owned the vacant house and property. The previous occupant had died of old age. Back taxes were owed, and it had been easy to pay the taxes and fines to claim ownership. It had taken most of what Marcio had saved over his years in the Army, but it was worth it. He had two goals beyond his desire to be a good cop. One was to marry Elizabeth when she was ready, and the other was to work on the house and make it a home for them. He wanted to become the first homeowner in his family. For three generations, his family had been renters.

Chapter 23

IT WAS CHALLENGING to pack a suitcase when you didn't know where you were going. Matthew's only advice was to be 'casual' and to bring a good dress in case they wanted to eat out.

When the suitcases were put in the trunk, a big box was already in there, taking up most of the space, alongside a massive basket with a lid.

"What's all this stuff?" Kara had asked.

"A surprise," Matthew said mysteriously.

The stop at the boutique had only confirmed that Alice and the girls were happy that Kara was going on vacation.

"Quit worrying," Matthew said as they drove away.

"I'm not exactly worried," Kara said. "I know they can handle the shop. It's just a strange feeling of emptiness."

"I feel the same after I've won a case," Matthew said. "Both of us throw ourselves into whatever project we're working on one-hundred-percent. When it's over, resolved, and completed, we need something to replace that feeling of focus. We need to focus on ourselves for the next two weeks."

Kara smiled. "I like that idea. You haven't told me where we're going?"

"It's a surprise," Matthew said.

Not for long, though, as they crossed the bridge to Long Island. These were the roads Kara had driven the year before, and not much had changed.

Matthew pulled into the motor park, gave her a smile, and went inside the office. He came out swinging a key in his hand. He drove to the same isolated cabin they'd used before and parked.

"This is your idea of a vacation spot?" Kara asked.

"It's not the Riviera, but it has some delightful memories for me," Matthew said. "It's only for two days. We resolved a lot of issues here in a very short time."

"I remember," Kara said, looking around the small cabin and sticking her head into the bathroom. "Joe has spruced up the place. There's a tub in there now, and it doesn't look so..."

"Horrible?" Matthew inserted.

"I was going to say nasty, but he has cleaned and upgraded the cabin," Kara said.

"What are your best memories of those days we spent here?" Matthew asked.

Kara walked around the room. "The first few days were awful, and we fought constantly. My poor bottom took on the worst of your anger. The best memories are of our making love here. Uninterrupted and continuous sex."

"Good, because that's my only plan for the next two days. We've both been too busy, and we need to reconnect with each other. I want you naked in that bed, and I want to make love to you without interruptions or stray thoughts of anything except how to please you."

"I'd like that," Kara agreed.

She'd barely finished the words when Matthew took her breath by kissing her passionately. Her hands began to unbutton his shirt, while he only unbuttoned two buttons of her shirt and pulled it over her head, tossing it aside. Then it was a race to see who could get naked first.

"Matthew," Kara gasped. "Did you lock the door?"

"Hell," he mumbled, striding to the door and turning the lock. When he turned, Kara was already on the bed and naked.

The word *ravished* entered Kara's mind again in the next hour, but she was too invested in making love to her husband to care. She quickly decided she liked her husband's idea when he spread her legs apart and lowered his mouth to her sex.

He was devouring her, and she was loving every second of it. Matthew suckled her and tortured her clit until she was begging him to take her. When she thought she was about to lose her mind, he entered her in one long hard thrust clear to his balls. She exploded in a few minutes of ecstasy, but he wasn't finished. His fingers stroked her womanhood while his tongue savored her breasts and mouth. He brought her to another orgasm.

She wanted Matthew to claim her, but he had a different idea. As he had done so many times before, he directed his attention to her bottom, first spanking her and then entering her from the rear. Every time his balls collided with her reddened bottom, it was equal to another spank.

She didn't understand why spanking could be so deliciously sensuous, but it was. When Matthew finally allowed himself to go, she was quivering with spent passion and the desire to keep him inside her forever.

When they finally separated, Kara looked at the clock, rose over her husband's body, and kissed him. "We've been at this for several hours!"

Matthew smacked her already reddened bottom with a grin. "We've only just started and have forty-four hours to go! Problem?"

"Not at all," she said. "Where are we going next?"

"Elkton, Maryland," he said.

"Why?"

Matthew propped himself up against the headboard. "Because we were married there. Your aunt didn't believe in marriage at all. My father thought we hadn't known each other long enough, and my mother had a screaming fit that I couldn't marry a girl she hadn't approved! Everyone had a reason why we shouldn't marry. But I loved you, and I wanted you to be my wife.

Kara smiled and tucked herself into his side. "So did I."

"We eloped to Elkton because it was a marriage mill town. We kept our secrets. You bought a wedding dress, I bought a tuxedo, and we eloped. It was the best day of my life. The second best day was when I found out you'd survived the war and had returned.

"Your wedding dress is in that big box in the trunk, and so is my tuxedo. Your original dress will still fit you. I've outgrown my first tuxedo, but I brought my new one. I want to renew our marriage vows and use the rest of our vacation as the honeymoon we couldn't afford back then. What do you think of the idea?"

"I didn't know you were a closet romantic," Kara said. "I'm also surprised you kept the dress."

"Will you marry me again?" Matthew asked. "Someday, this will make a good story for our children."

"Yes, Matthew Douglas, I will marry you again because, although I may have run away, I wasn't running from you. I fell in love with you at first sight. It was outside forces that ruined our marriage the first time," Kara said as he leaned over to kiss her. She smiled and secretly touched her belly. It was too soon to tell, but by her husband's birthday, she might have a wonderful surprise for him.

Mariella Starr

Hello, this is Mariella.

I've often wondered what makes a writer. I never claimed to be one, because I wrote for myself. Even now, very few people know that I write.

Of the many gifts I received from my parents, the most important one was the encouragement to try things they didn't do themselves. They didn't understand their strange child so different from themselves and her brothers. I had a need to create. My parent's home over the years became a gallery for my artwork. Most of it now resides in the homes of my children and siblings. There hasn't been an empty wall in my home in years.

What fills a child with lifelong inspiration? In my case, it was my parents and two specific teachers. The first, was a grade school teacher who gave me two compliments in one by praising my art on the cover of a written story and the A+ grade was a boost, too. That was in sixth grade.

The second was a seventh-grade teacher who had a reputation for being tough. I was a new student to the school, my family having moved again because of my father's military deployment. I'd heard horror stories from the other kids about this teacher.

I was shocked when the teacher returned my writing assignment with a red copy editing marks all over my pages —something I'd never seen before. I was so embarrassed. I turned it over on my desk so no one else could see it.

My wonderful teacher, though, was walking around the

classroom returning the assignments papers to the students, returned to my desk. He turned over my stapled pages. Without a word, he tapped the top of the page with his finger.

I had missed it. Written across the top of the lined notebook page, in red was:

A+++ Best story I've ever read from a student! Ever! Keep writing!

That single incident has never been forgotten. Mr. Gregory taught me so much that year, but most importantly, he gave me encouragement. I kept writing and I have never stopped.

Simmer Down, Red
The Amazing Maven
A Little Bit of Sass
Heller On Wheels
A Path Worth Taking
Keeping Sunny Safe
Maybe, With Conditions
Posey's Assets
Broken Vows
The Promise
In Search of a Noble Man
Lacy's Rules
Desiree, A Woman of Defiance
Full Circle
Caitlin's Conspiracies
The Awakening of Alexandria
Charlotte's Comeuppance
Teaching Miss Maisie Jane

The McKenna Brothers
The Forever Kind: Sully
Holding Tess

The Overton Saga
Isabel's Independence, Book 1
Britannia's Blaggard, Book 2
Sweet Sarah, Book 3

Anthologies
12 Naughty Days of Christmas 2021

Connect with Mariella Starr:
MariStarr@outlook.com

Blushing Books

Blushing Books is one of the oldest eBook publishers on the web. We've been running websites that publish spanking and BDSM related romance and erotica since 1999, and we have been selling eBooks since 2003. We hope you'll check out our hundreds of offerings at http://www.blushingbooks.com.

Blushing Books Newsletter

Please join the Blushing Books newsletter
to receive updates & special promotional offers.
You can also join by using your mobile phone:
Just text BLUSHING to 22828.

Made in United States
Troutdale, OR
10/09/2023

13544334R00193